Seeds for All Seasons

Alan B. Gazzaniga

VANTAGE PRESS
New York

This is a work of fiction. Any similarity between
the characters appearing herein and any real persons,
living or dead, is purely coincidental.

Cover design by Susan Thomas

FIRST EDITION

Copyright © 2001 by Alan B. Gazzaniga

Published by Vantage Press, Inc.
516 West 34th Street, New York, New York 10001

Manufactured in the United States of America
ISBN: 0-533-13597-4

Library of Congress Catalog Card No.: 00-91511

0 9 8 7 6 5 4 3 2

Seeds for All Seasons

Prologue

The automatic doors slid open and a wave of bodies crashed into the Emergency Room. "We've got a head injury," one of the paramedics yelled out over the crowd.

Moments later a black Mercedes screeched to a halt behind the ambulance. Three men dressed in open-collared silk shirts stepped out, two from the back seat and one from the passenger side. The car backed down the ramp and pulled into an emergency visitor spot. A woman remained in the back seat.

The imposing man with graying hair was obviously in charge, but the short man led the way through the door and signaled to a policeman standing in the trauma room. The policeman seemed to know who they were and motioned for the trio to come into the room.

"B.P. is 110," one of the nurses shouted. "Who is this guy?" a second nurse whispered. Everyone in the room could hear her.

"My son," said the older man. "I'm Tony Santori. He collapsed when he was hit by the ball." The Red Sox uniform told the rest of the story.

Dr. Slater arrived and began to examine Joey Santori, unaware he was tending to the Sox's ace pitcher. He had missed Lefty Santori's introduction. "This man needs surgery. Get Dr. Maitlan, stat, and clear out this room, we need some space in here."

"Wait a damn minute. I don't know who Dr. Maitlan is. Hell, I don't know who you are! Nobody touches my son until I have some answers."

Dr. Slater quickly introduced himself while the man's son was stripped of his uniform. "We'll need you to fill out some papers, sir, if you will go with the nurse. There's nothing you can do here now. Your son has a serious head injury and he needs surgery immediately. Dr. Maitlan is the neurosurgeon on call and perfectly qualified to perform the operation."

1

"You listen to me, doctor. Joey Santori is going to need a whole lot better than "perfectly qualified." You find me the best, and you find him now. My son is not going to die in your hospital. Do you understand me?"

For the first time, Dr. Slater noted the Red Sox uniform and realized that he was being challenged by the notorious, and downright scary, Tony "Lefty" Santori. His two companions were equally unsavory—and there was something especially unsettling about the short guy waiting by the door.

Perfect. I have the mob on my doorstep and our only available neurosurgeon hasn't been answering his page!

One

As Tim entered his dorm room he was greeted with a loud, friendly, "Hi! How are ya? J.C. Parker, at your service." J.C. bolted up off the bed where he had been reading a pamphlet about Harvard. When Tim had received his admission packet from the medical school he had requested a roommate. He didn't want to be alone in this new adventure, but at the same time he was leery. A quick assessment of J.C. told him that everything should be fine.

J.C. Parker was an inch shorter than Tim, a little heavier, but well built, and he appeared athletic. He told Tim that his given name was James Carter, but he had always been known as J.C. Tim could see that J.C. had already settled in. Photographs of his family, pictures from a hunting trip, and a group shot of baseball players standing under a plaque with the letter Y, were prominently displayed. Next to the photographs was a diploma from Yale. Tim set his bags down and introduced himself.

"Where ya from?" J.C. asked as he fell back onto his bed and laced his hands behind his head.

"Southern California. Glendale," Tim answered, shoving his bags across the room.

"Where'd ya go to college?"

Might as well get the questions and answers over with now, Tim figured. "USC."

"Oh, big-time school out there."

Tim smiled and glanced over at the wall. "And you went to Yale?"

"Lawrenceville Prep and then Yale. That's my mom, dad and sister," he added proudly.

Tim got the idea he was supposed to be impressed with the prep school part. Public school was all he had known. He took a closer look at the team photo, searching for something they had in common. "Did you play baseball in college?"

"University."

Tim looked puzzled.

"Yale's a University," J.C. laughed. "I know you West Coast people call us Ivy League colleges, but we're bigger than that."

"Sorry," Tim said sheepishly. But instead of being put off, he found he admired J.C.'s candor. No false modesty for J.C.

"Anyway, we won the Ivy League. There I go, using that term. I was a catcher, and a damn good one, if I say so myself." J.C. sized up Tim's physique. "Did you play sports at SC?"

"I played a little baseball." Tim didn't elaborate.

"You look like you could be a jock." J.C. smiled as he pinched his nose.

"I keep in shape, play a little tennis."

J.C. sat up, becoming more interested in his new roommate. "You know there's a court right here in Vanderbilt. We'll have to play sometime."

"Sure."

Long before he arrived at Vanderbilt dormitory Tim had heard about the famous doctors who had stayed here during medical school: world-famous surgeons, basic scientists, and Nobel Prize winners. He was awe-struck when he walked into the front lobby, but when he noticed the tennis court in the dormitory courtyard, he was gratified to realize that even the great ones enjoyed recreation time.

Tim opened his bags and began to unpack and put his things in order. He noticed that J.C.'s desk was surprisingly neat. His class schedule was tacked to a small bulletin board, which hung over his desk. A phone was already hooked up and placed next to a container of pens and freshly sharpened pencils. In the center of the desk an anatomy book was opened to the first chapter. Any reservations he might have had about his decision to request a roommate were fast disappearing; J.C. obviously took medical school as seriously as he did.

"It's nearly dinner time. Let's go down to the dining room."

"Great," Tim replied. It had been a long flight from Los Angeles and he was starving. "You lead the way. You seem to know your way around."

They walked down a flight of stairs. The dining hall was just off the lobby. Tim took in the high ceiling and the mural covering the far wall. It was a depiction of the Boston Tea Party. Surround-

4

ing it were portraits of famous doctors who had graduated from Harvard or taught there.

Tim paused before a painting of Harvey Cushing, the father of neurosurgery. Tim himself was the proud recipient of the Cushing clip. Dr. Anderson, who had performed the operation on Tim years ago, had called to tell him about Harvey Cushing when he learned that Tim had been accepted at Harvard. It was the Cushing clip that sealed Tim's decision to become a doctor. Otherwise, he might have been lured into professional baseball. *Otherwise, I would have been dead,* Tim thought to himself. Tim's whole childhood had been spent playing sports and studying. He loved both. Playing Junior American League the summer before high school, he discovered he was a pretty decent left-handed pitcher. His fastball was accurate, his control was excellent, and he had developed a formidable curveball. He began varsity football as a freshman and decided, when he was a sophomore, to try out for baseball as well.

His coaches assured him he would be scouted by the professional teams. But Tim's only desire was to become a doctor, possibly even a surgeon, like his dad. So high school football and baseball were for Tim merely a means to an end: excellent grades and athletic ability provided him with his choice of colleges, and now, the finest medical school.

That baseball season of his sophomore year saw Glendale rocket to the top of the league. With the best pitching and hitting they consistently scored ten or more runs every game. As the play-offs began, Steve Graves observed to his son, "I've only been to a few of your games, but each time I see you, you seem to get better."

Remembering those rare words of praise could still cause Tim to grin with pleasure. Steve Graves, too, had been a football player, as well as a catcher at USC. Living up to his dad's expectations meant everything to Tim. He was thrilled that his father had taken time off to attend the championship game with Jefferson High in Los Angeles. It was only later they'd all realize how vital Steve Graves' presence would be.

At the top of the eighth the score was 0-0. Tim was up at bat and hit a long single into right field. He was only the third Glendale runner to reach base and Coach Trainor signaled a hit-and-

5

run play. On the third pitch Tim took off for second base, but the catcher, suspecting the play, called a pitch out and threw down. While Tim was sliding into second, the ball hit him in the forehead and landed in right field. The Glendale bench immediately jumped up and yelled for Tim to go to third. He got up, staggered, and fell to the ground. Coach Trainor raced onto the field, waving time-out. Dr. Graves, watching from the stands, pushed through the crowd and rushed onto the field as the stunned players from both sides gathered around. Tim's eyes were rolled into the back of his head and he didn't appear to be breathing. Dr. Graves tried to revive Tim with the usual measures of slapping him on the cheek and shaking his chest. Nothing. He elevated the boy's chin, opening his airway, and stimulated the back of his mouth with his finger. Tim started to breathe. Dr. Graves detected a weak pulse in his wrist.

"Call an ambulance," he shouted. "Get an ambulance now!" Several of the Jefferson players ran off the field to the gym to call.

Dr. Graves, who was always cool and collected, was visibly anxious. He kept running his hands through his hair as he bent down on one knee to watch his son, glancing impatiently at the road for signs of help. Tim was still unconscious and had not been moved when the ambulance arrived. He was now carefully placed on a stretcher by the driver and his partner. Dr. Graves jumped in the back and ordered the driver to take them to Los Angeles Children's Hospital. This was not protocol, but no one dared argue.

Of course, his father never told him any of this. Tim had pieced the story together from his teammates much later. Neither of his parents ever wanted to relive that day afterwards. "All's well that ends well," his mother would say. "Why dwell on it? I'm just grateful your father was there." And it wasn't until Dr. Anderson phoned to congratulate Tim on being accepted to Harvard and mentioned the Cushing clip that he really heard any details of what had happened at the hospital. All Tim had known was that his father's friend Dr. John Anderson, a well-known neurosurgeon and expert in treating brain injuries, had performed the surgery—and saved his life. When he took Tim to surgery he said he'd suspected either an epidural or subdural hematoma and was prepared to do a serious, but routine opera-

6

tion. As it turned out, he had to call on all of his experience and expertise to repair an anterior cerebral artery aneurysm. It seems the bump on the head from the baseball was incidental to this life-threatening defect. Dr. Anderson used the Cushing clip to clip the aneurysm.

Tim was brought back to the present by a friendly thump on the back from J.C. Apparently his "wool gathering" standing before the Cushing portrait had not gone unnoticed.

As they stood in line with other students waiting for their food, introductions were made all around. They all exchanged basic information: Harvard, MIT, Dartmouth, University of California, and Columbia. Tim's competitive spirit on the athletic field was just as fierce academically. He eyed those from the University of North Dakota and Iowa State, knowing they, like him, had worked doubly hard to be accepted from "lesser known" institutions. He could already feel himself wondering which of these students he'd be competing with for a surgical residency in Boston. The ultimate prize.

Tim let J.C. do the talking for both of them. *Let him break the ice. I'll listen and learn.* After dinner they headed back to their room. J.C. spent the next several hours going over the first semester curriculum, telling Tim everything he had already learned about classes, what textbooks to buy, which professor was a pain in the ass, and so on and so on. He was a bottomless well of information and Tim soaked it up.

Finally, the long flight and the excitement of the day caught up with Tim. He had to get some sleep. J.C. clicked on a small reading light he had hooked to the back of his bed and proceeded to read his anatomy book until three in the morning.

*　　*　　*

The next morning, when Tim and J.C. entered the amphitheater for their orientation class, they were greeted by one hundred and twenty eager students.

J.C. stopped and stared. "Jeez, Graves, doesn't this scare the shit out of you? Look at all these brilliant assholes." Then he smiled. "By the way, 'Graves' is not a great name for a doctor."

Tim was surveying the crowd. He ignored the joke he'd

7

already heard at his father's expense all his life. "I only count seven women and I don't see any black students. Haven't you Ivy League types gotten over your biases, yet?"

"Same thing at Yale, but it's not bias. We still believe that the best students win."

"USC is nothing like this."

"USC is coed and has the best football teams in the country. Enough said."

"Bias, J.C., is alive and well right in my own dorm room."

J.C. laughed and said, "Wait 'til you know me better. You'll see I'm a fair guy. To know me is to love me."

After the orientation it was time for their first anatomy lab. They were divided into groups of four. The other two students with Tim and J.C. were Korean War veterans and were several years older. The first assignment was dissection of the arm and hand. The professor said it would take two weeks to complete. The two vets teamed up and got to work immediately on theirs. J.C. had already read all about the anatomy of the arm the night before. He dove in with his dissecting tools. Soon Tim and the others were watching, mouths agape. It was clear that it wasn't going to take J.C. and Tim two weeks to do their side. But rather than gloat when their partners struggled, J.C. demonstrated some of that fairness he'd been bragging about: he showed them how to dissect and was soon answering their questions.

Keeping up with J.C. was a feat in itself, but J.C.'s prediction proved correct: to know him was to love him. He shared everything and was always happy to help. Although Tim worked day and night, somehow J.C. worked harder. J.C. would go to bed at two A.M. and get up at five—and, most frustrating, he was always bright and cheerful. Tim took on J.C.'s study habits, since he couldn't sleep knowing J.C. was awake. At exam time they would pull "all nighters." The weekends were spent in the library, poring over their textbooks, and their only recreation was an occasional game of tennis or a movie. Tennis was the one area where J.C. couldn't beat Tim, nor could anyone else. Word got around the dormitory that if you weren't a class A player, don't play against Tim Graves.

As the weeks wore on, the long hours of studying, lack of daily recreation and the constant competition began to take its toll. During the regular morning meetings of the entire class, people began to show up late and there were few "excuse mes" or "thank-yous" as students climbed over classmates to get to their seats. The cheerful chatter that had marked the earlier gatherings of the class disappeared. Instead, everybody seemed to be complaining about the lack of sleep, the mystery meat in the dining hall, poor lecturers and tough exams.

"Twelve weeks into medical school and we're only just getting into the liver," J.C. complained as he kicked at some fall leaves on the way to class. "I saw that dork, Gutless Gutman, getting a head start on today's lab: he was dissecting his liver yesterday." J.C. was famous for his nicknames, which trumpeted his feelings for the individual. "I overheard him say that he wasn't going to let that brown-noser, Parker, beat him this time."

"What did you expect? You've been kicking his ass since school started. People get jealous. If it makes you feel better, I saw Gutman and Edelstein working on their liver in the lab til late last night."

"I thought when I came to Boston I'd get away from those aggressive New York Jews, but here they are, making my life miserable," he said as he opened the door to the amphitheater.

Tim winced at this statement. "Take it easy. Nobody's going to beat you, and besides, Gutman wants to be a psychiatrist."

"He needs a psychiatrist."

*   *   *

When the hour-long lecture was over, Tim saw Gutman go up to J.C. and say something. J.C. turned red, but didn't say anything back.

"What'd Gutman say to you?" Tim asked as they were preparing for their dissection.

"He said if we—you and me—had any problems with our dissection, to let him know."

"You guys still working?" Gutman asked as he sauntered over. He barely acknowledged their two partners who were busy dissecting. "I'm all done so if you need any help . . . I wouldn't want you to fall behind."

"Piss off, Gutless," J.C. said, in a rare moment of anger.

9

"Touchy. Well, let me know. We're over there getting started on the next assignment."

Tim was reminded of the bullies of his childhood, but this wasn't the park. No fists or hard tackles would bring down this arrogant bully. Brains or wit would have to win out in this contest. While Tim was still forming this thought, J.C. suddenly picked up a portion of the liver they had been working on and hurled it at Gutman, hitting him squarely on the back of the head. When he realized what had hit him he ran to his cadaver and grabbed a piece of his recent dissection and he hurled it at J.C., emitting a loud grunt. It landed harmlessly at J.C.'s feet, but the "Liver War of the Class of '60" had begun. Soon the entire class was throwing organs, with the explosive energy that came from the pent up tension of twelve grueling weeks. Professor Johnson ran to the door and froze in amazement. When he sprang into action, he grabbed the last person to throw something and ushered him out of the room. Tim had to laugh. It was just like football: Unsportsmanlike conduct penalties always went to the guy throwing the retaliation punch.

That night at dinner, J.C. renamed Gutless. "I've got to hand it to Gutman. He coulda fried my ass. But he didn't fink on me. He said the whole thing was a misunderstanding. Here's to Gutsy Gutman." He raised his milk in a toast. "Maybe this competition is out of hand."

"I don't know. Competition can be good—if it's fair. Gutman really started it by trying to show you up by dissecting in advance."

"You gotta admit, I lost it. That's what can happen when you let it get to you. They'll be talking about this for years." J.C. smiled proudly.

Tim waved him away. "Don't flatter yourself. The liver war's not the worst thing that's happened here. One of the seniors told me today that when he was a freshman two students put their cadaver's arm in a coat and drove down the turnpike. They put a quarter between the cadaver's fingers and when the guy at the tollbooth took the quarter, the arm fell out."

"That sounds like bullshit."

"He swore it was the truth. They got a one-year suspension."

Within a few days reality set in again and in the coming

weeks it became apparent to all the students that becoming a doctor came with a hefty price tag. Friendships suffered, complaints were bitter and constant, and everyone was critical and quick to judge. The first two years of medical school were pronounced a necessary evil before they could get to the "good stuff." There was nothing to do but work hard and get through them.

Two

For years afterward, Tim remembered his first encounter with John McConnell, the chief resident in urology at University Hospital. It was his third year and Tim was finally getting to do the fun stuff: clinical medicine. He'd aced the first two rotations: surgery and pediatrics at Mass General. In February his third rotation began. From the start, he knew that things weren't going to be like his first two rotations. He had made a concise, but complete presentation on bedside rounds his second day on the service.

"What's your name?" McConnell asked when Tim had finished.

"Tim Graves."

"Where did you attend college?" McConnell asked with a sarcastic tone to his voice.

Tim knew this wasn't heading in the right direction. "USC."

"University of Spoiled Children," he laughed. McConnell was Tim's height with short, sandy brown hair. He had blue eyes and a constant smirk on his lips. His body was compact and he appeared to be in excellent physical condition. "When you make a presentation on my rounds, you 'Hahvard' students tell me the pertinent negatives of your systems review. That was a presentation I'd expect from a surgeon. Short and misleading. Did you ask Mrs. Lathrum if she was having back or flank pain?"

"No, I didn't," Tim blushed. He had forgotten to ask her.

"Well, if you did, genius, you'd have found out that she has kidney stones, and this is what brought her to the hospital. Her hyperparathyroidism was picked up on her lab workup. People do present with diseases other than surgical problems."

Tim was mortified. The USC joke didn't bother him. It was the humiliation and criticism in front of the patient. How was he going to live through a whole month of this? What effect would it have on his grades and his chances for a residency in Boston?

McConnell was obviously suffering from "Chief Resident Syndrome," too much power and control over the little people. Tim had heard of it, but this was the first time since coming to Harvard that he had met such an arrogant prick.

"J.C., do you know McConnell, Chief Resident in urology at University?"

It was a rare night in their year rotations when both were off duty at the same time.

"Yeah, I know McConnell. Did he ask you if you went to Yale?" J.C. grinned. "He graduated the year before I got there. Thinks of himself as a great baseball player. Holds the home run record at Yale."

"How am I going to put up with that prick for a month?"

"He's why I changed my rotation to the General."

"Thanks for warning me," Tim lamented.

"Look at it this way. If you can survive McConnell you can survive anything."

The next four weeks were hell for Tim. McConnell had it in for him, and Tim couldn't figure out why. He bit his tongue and stayed out of the Chief Resident's way.

*   *   *

In early April Tim met J.C. for dinner in the dining hall. Their paths had crossed little in the past two months.

"How are you getting along with McConnell?" J.C. asked before they had even sat down.

"I'm finished with his service, but I still present cases to him. Other than that, I just stay out of his way." They dug into their dinner. "He reminds me of a guy my brothers and I used to play football with in Glendale: Matt Beamer. He was the biggest kid at the park and he always picked on my brothers. Even gave my brother Jim a black eye one day."

"McConnell's no bruiser."

"No, but he's a bully like Beamer was. Nobody liked him— but everyone was afraid of him, so he always got to play. On my twelfth birthday my mom finally decided I was old enough for football in the park. I had a brand new ball and I couldn't wait to

13

try it out. Beamer got one look at it and decided to have some fun. He talked me into letting him see it and he proceeded to drop kick my brand new leather football into the street. I think that's the first time I experienced genuine hatred."

"So, did you kick his butt?"

"I was a big kid for a twelve year old, but this guy was seventeen and he'd been around. I wasn't stupid enough to think I could take him on, but revenge was on my mind. Lucky for me, Beamer was all brawn and no talent. I kicked his ass on the football field." Tim smiled, savoring the memory. "After a few games we saw less and less of Beamer."

"Hey! That reminds me, are you interested in playing in the Honors Day baseball game? Faculty vs. students. I've got about twelve people signed up."

"It's been a long time since I've played."

"Come on. You get a chance to meet faculty from all the hospitals." J.C. lured him in. "It can't hurt your chances to get a residency. Besides," he raised an eyebrow, "McConnell is the captain of the faculty team."

Tim thought that sounded like a recipe for more humiliation, not the pay-back he knew J.C. was imagining. He knew McConnell had been recruiting all over the place and the faculty had been practicing.

J.C. pushed on, reading his friend's mind. "You could practice on your nights off."

Tim was tempted. "Put me down as a strong maybe. I'll at least be there to watch the magnificent McConnell."

"He *was* a great shortstop at Yale—and he could hit the ball a mile."

"You know, he's mentioned that on rounds on more than one occasion? He also says that he could have made it in the big leagues if he hadn't gone into medicine."

"I think he's blowing smoke out his ass," J.C. chuckled. "Not many Yale players make it into the big leagues, at least not in baseball."

As Tim thought more about it, the idea of playing against McConnell might be a good way to put this bully in his place. So what if he had played baseball at Yale? Playing baseball at USC was, literally, a whole different ballgame. What sweet revenge it

14

would be to strike out McConnell in front of everybody, faculty and students.

After dinner, Tim went down to the dormitory game room and checked out some baseballs. He found a left-hander's glove among the athletic equipment and checked it out, too. He walked next door to Boston Latin School and headed for the gymnasium. Tim pulled at the double doors and they opened. The gym was never locked. He felt for the light switch and turned on some large lamps strung high overhead. The wood floor was old and cracking, and Tim wondered how anyone could bounce a basketball on such an uneven surface. Then he thought about the sandlot football he and his brothers used to play in Glendale. *Talk about crude playing grounds. We were tough.* Telling J.C. about Beamer had brought back some bittersweet memories for Tim.

As Tim had grown up, the pieces of his dad's complicated medical life began to come together. Steven Graves had been depressed for many years. Not knowing how to deal with it, Tim had chosen to ignore it. One night they were sitting in the family room listening to the Angels' game when his dad suddenly got up and turned off the radio. He returned to his chair near the fireplace and started talking. He told Tim about "hospital politics." Not the kind that plays itself out in banter and verbal bullying, and not the kind that stays in the doctors' lounge. "No, Tim, it's the kind that follows me home and walks in the door with me. It sticks in my head and I can't shake it. No matter how hard I try to ignore it, to put it aside for just one minute, it comes into my house with me. People I would never invite into my home are sitting at my dinner table and I can't control it. They are nesting themselves in my brain and are trying to ruin me."

Tim sat dumbly, listening to his dad, wondering who the "people" were. He didn't understand what was going on at the hospital, but it sounded like it had plagued his dad for years. Everything that he had just accepted about his father started to have new meaning—all the times his father had sat watching television, mute and oblivious, or the times at the dinner table when he wouldn't say a word. He would sometimes offer a grin to his family, just to give the impression that he was still there, hearing everything, but he really wasn't there, at all. *He was probably plotting his fight.*

15

Tim imagined McConnell to be one of those doctors who'd occupied his father's thoughts during his childhood—aspiring to be part of the vicious hospital circles, plaguing honest, hard-working doctors. McConnell was a person who could not stand to see another succeed. He wanted Tim to screw up. He wanted to belittle him.

After mulling it over, Tim decided not to stoop to McConnell's level: a faculty vs. student baseball game would not be the right forum to air a personal vendetta. Whatever was between them would not be settled on the baseball field. But it couldn't hurt anything to practice his pitching—just in case they needed a reliever. With that thought, Tim started tossing the baseball straight up in the air and catching it. He then bounced the ball off the concrete walls of the gym. When his arm felt warm enough, he threw a couple of pitches overhand. They made a dull thud as they hit the wall. He imagined the fence at home with the white circle he had chalked in as a boy. He walked over to the wall and took out a pen. He estimated two and a half feet up and made a mark with the pen. The mark was too hard to see from any distance. Then he remembered the roll of adhesive tape he always seemed to have in his pocket. He tore off some pieces and formed a rough circle. He counted off nine paces and positioned himself to throw. He pulled back and threw the ball, dead center.

Three

Dr. Malcolm Taylor preferred rounding at the same hour every day. He knew that at this time most of the medical staff would be in their morning staff meetings, or attending student presentations, or, more likely, still in bed. He liked to walk through the hallways alone and hear nothing but the clicking of his own shoes, the sound echoing off the walls. On this morning he had taken a detour through the third floor ward, just for a change of scenery.

He heard a low, clear voice coming from down the hall. Instead of turning the corner, he followed the voice to what looked like a treatment room. The door was open and several people were clustered just inside the doorway. What he heard of the presentation was given with great detail and insight. He inched his way through the door so that he could peer inside. He saw a roomful of students and doctors, but what captured his interest was the man who belonged to the voice. The presenter was strikingly handsome, with sandy hair, broad shoulders, and an athletic build. He turned to one of the students standing closest to the door and tapped him on the shoulder. "Who is that presenting today?" The student whispered, "Tim Graves." The man nodded and turned back into the hallway. He thought about Tim Graves all morning.

His secretary had written down the number on a slip of paper, which was now sitting on his desk. He had decided to wait until early evening to make the phone call, it was cheaper. He picked up a pencil and used the eraser end to dial the number. The phone was answered on the first ring.

"Chancellor's office. May I help you?" asked the woman on the other end.

"Yes, this is Dr. Taylor. I believe the Chancellor is expecting my call."

"Yes, he is, Dr. Taylor. One minute, please, while I connect you."

After a few seconds he heard the high-pitched voice come on the line. The voice could easily be mistaken for that of a woman.

"Malcolm, how's it going out there?"

"Fine, fine. Listen, did you get that information I asked for?" Taylor had no time for the usual civilities.

"Right. I didn't need a file for this one. I remember everything about this guy."

"Then let's hear it."

When Taylor finally hung up, he swiveled his chair to face his window and the city lights of Boston. It had been a long day with a lot of bullshit to handle, but now he allowed himself a satisfied smile. *Things are looking up.* The information the chancellor had given him concerning Timothy Graves far exceeded Taylor's expectations.

Tim Graves had come to USC from Glendale with a stellar reputation as an athlete and a 4.0 grade point average. He had turned down a "full-ride" baseball scholarship, ostensibly to "leave his options open." If he felt that his grades were suffering, he did not want to be committed to a sports program for the duration of his college years. With a solid 4.0 behind him at the end of his first semester, Tim did, in fact, try out for the baseball team. His reputation at Glendale preceded him, and the coaches were delighted. By the third week of practice he had made the varsity team and was their top left-handed pitcher. The Trojans whizzed through the Pac Eight Conference in Tim's senior year. Tim was 12-0 with two no-hitters. His fastball was faster and his curveball had an incredible drop. Pro scouts were foaming at the mouth as USC went to the round robin finals in Omaha. USC won the final playoff game with Tim leading them to victory. At the end of the game Tim hung up his glove and cleats and announced he was headed to Harvard Medical School. He could have had a great future in the majors, but as he told his coach, "My goal is to be a neurosurgeon."

Malcolm Taylor couldn't believe his good fortune.

Tim spent the rest of the day working on rounds. After work he went back to his dormitory and signed out the baseballs again. He threw pitches in the gym for a full hour. With each throw, he imagined McConnell's face in the strike zone and he was amazed at how accurate his pitches were.

The morning of the Honors Day picnic began with ominous black clouds, but by the time of the barbecue, the clouds had blown away and the sun was shining brightly. The baseball game was scheduled to begin after all the food and beer had been consumed. With the beer came the banter, where students and faculty drew the proverbial line in the sand. Verbal battles raged, but this was expected and everyone knew it was all in fun. McConnell, who had guzzled more beers than anyone, was less composed than usual. He joked loudly about the student "girlies," the little Harvard "powder puffs" who didn't stand a chance against the faculty team. After each jibe, the laughter was more forced; everyone knew that McConnell meant every word that he said.

Some of the players on J.C.'s team met each other for the first time on that day. None of them had practiced together and J.C. was feeling ever more skeptical about their chances. They looked all right warming up, but J.C. wasn't sure how they would perform as a team. Meanwhile, he stole a glance at the faculty team warming up on another diamond and couldn't help being impressed. McConnell was hitting balls to one group, who fielded them, and another group was doing mock play drills. He noticed that the pitcher was already warming up with his catcher. J.C. decided to get his pitcher warmed up, too.

The two teams finally gathered on the playing diamond for a coin toss. J.C. called heads and made the decision to take the field first. *At least we can have the home field advantage.* As J.C. walked to the third baseline dugout, he saw Tim approaching from the street. When Tim reached the dugout, he smiled at J.C.'s worried expression.

"You guys ready to whip these turkeys, J.C.?"

J.C. leaned in closer to the fence, keeping his gaze on the field. "I have a bad feeling about this. I hope I didn't make a big mistake here."

Tim was surprised that J.C. sounded so pessimistic. He was usually so positive. What surprised him even more was how seriously J.C. was taking this game.

"Just have fun. It *is* just a game." J.C. didn't like hearing the cliché. He gave Tim a dubious look, then flashed a huge smile and said with all the irony he could muster, "We'll do our best."

"I'll be in the stands over there if you need me."

J.C. nodded. "Why don't you just sit in the dugout with us?"

"I'll watch from the stands. I need to catch up on the latest gossip," Tim replied with a grin.

Tim found a place to sit. He recognized a lot of the nurses from the hospital who were seated around him. Two of them waved to Tim and then turned to giggle together. Tim felt self-conscious and prayed that J.C. would not need him in the game. The pitcher was warming up. Tim didn't recognize the guy and decided he was probably a third or fourth year student. Tim frowned. *His pitches are fast, but not accurate.*

The umpire called "play ball" and the first batter for the faculty team stepped up to the plate. The first pitch was wild. It hit the batter in the thigh and the crowd roared with laughter as he melodramatically limped to first base. McConnell jeered from the on-deck circle. McConnell hit a home run. McConnell yelled out to the pitcher as he crossed home plate, "You're making this too easy, boy." The crowd was muttering in disappointment. They had come out to see a game and it was turning into a slaughter. People began looking at their watches. They weren't going to waste an entire afternoon watching a boring, one-sided baseball game.

J.C. looked over to where Tim was sitting in the stands. Tim shrugged his shoulders, looking skyward with his palms up. The next eight batters all hit the ball and the score was now 7-0 with no one out. J.C. threw off his mask, spit on home plate, and yelled, "Goddamnit!" Those who knew J.C. looked on in amazement. The never excitable J.C. was totally losing it. Tim heard McConnell laughing with his teammates and he shook with anger. J.C. motioned for Tim to get in the game. Tim had expected that if J.C. did need him, he would make the switch between innings, not in the middle of play, but J.C. had already excused the other pitcher. There was nothing for Tim to do but make his way to the mound.

Some of the doctors on the faculty team recognized him, and one of them called out, "Cowboy Graves comes to save the day." Others wondered what the tall guy in the USC cap was planning to do to end this miserable inning. When Tim finally stepped on the mound he heard McConnell say, "I hope you can pitch better than you give presentations, Graves." He sneered and continued, "This game's over as far as I'm concerned." Some of the faculty members in the stands laughed, but they were embarrassed by McConnell's obvious dislike of Graves. He was making this personal.

J.C. dropped the ball in Tim's hand and said, "I hope to God you still remember how to pitch." With those encouraging words he turned and headed for home plate.

After eight or nine conservative pitches, Tim was warmed up. Appropriately, the next batter was the man himself, McConnell. They had already been through the line-up, so this was his second time at bat. Tim saw that McConnell could swing well enough, but he knew he would have trouble with anything other than straight down the middle. Tim pulled back and pitched a sinker. McConnell swung and missed. The crowd clapped as their interest picked up. McConnell stepped out of the box, annoyed. He tapped the ground with his bat and stepped back in. The second pitch was a ninety-five mile per hour fastball, down the middle, and McConnell didn't even have time to get the bat off his shoulder. J.C. grinned, despite the pain in his palm from catching Tim's rocket pitch. The third pitch was a steep curve ball that dropped so far that McConnell missed it by a mile and struck out. He spat angrily on the ground and threw down his bat. J.C. was amused by McConnell's theatrics. When McConnell flipped Tim the bird on his way back to the dugout, Tim and J.C. burst out laughing. The next two batters struck out— the first inning of the game was finally over.

The rest of the game was a blowout. The faculty team sent up their men to bat, three up and three down for eight innings. It occurred to Tim that it might be unfair of him to continue to throw impossible pitches, but then he'd look over at McConnell in the dugout and throw another sinker. The students won: 9-7.

The rules of good sportsmanship dictated that the two sides shake hands at the end of the game, all except McConnell, of course. He ducked out immediately after the game ended, allegedly to take a piss. After all the predictable promises of retaliation next year, the Honors Day Picnic came to an end. J.C. ran up to Tim and put his forearm into Tim's side, as if he were about to tackle him.

"You son of a bitch! Ya never told me ya could pitch like that."

"You knew I played at USC."

"What were you, an all-star or something?"

"Four years, '55 through '58."

"You bastard! SC won the NCAA championship two of those years. Jeez. Why the hell didn't you tell me?" J.C. was truly surprised. He had no idea.

"It just didn't seem important anymore. Today, though, we kicked McConnell's ass. Now, that's important."

"He didn't even have the guts to congratulate us."

"Everyone knows Yalies are poor sports," Tim joked.

They started walking toward the dorm when J.C. remembered he had left his stuff in the dugout.

"I'll meet you back at the dorm." J.C. turned around and headed back to the field. As he was about to step into the dugout he felt a hand come down on his shoulder. A heavy hand. As he turned to see who was there, the man leaned close to J.C. and whispered in his ear. J.C. nodded his head, but the man had already turned his back on him. Not until he was halfway home did he ask himself, "What the hell does the great Dr. Malcolm Taylor want with me?"

Four

He licked his bony finger and flipped the page. Taylor knew this was gold, but he couldn't help going over the file again and again, in case he found some flaw or inconsistency that would dampen his enthusiasm. Yet here it was, plain as day, sitting open faced and waiting on Taylor's newly arrived antique mahogany desk. The file was that of a star pitcher at USC, a perfect student with a 4.0 grade point average who had gotten into Harvard Medical School with MCAT scores in the 90th percentile. Add to this a tall, incredibly handsome, blond, blue-eyed young man, and he couldn't lose. *This is worth thousands.*

What was most appealing about Tim Graves, however, was his unassuming air. Taylor had watched him carefully at the game and noted his quiet, humble demeanor. Taylor liked the shy, retiring type. He picked up his phone and buzzed his secretary.

"Yes, Dr. Taylor?"

"Meredith, I'm expecting someone in about twenty minutes. Just show him in as soon as he arrives."

"All right, but you have a meeting with Mr. Sanders this afternoon about grant applications."

"You'll have to reschedule it, okay?"

"No problem."

Taylor knew Sanders wouldn't be offended, nor would he even bring it up. Although Sanders was president of University Hospital, he knew that the success of the hospital depended on the players. As president of a hospital, Sanders had to keep the important players happy. Knowing what kept people like Taylor happy was not a high science. There were just two requirements—give him money and stay out of his way. Since Taylor had taken over the fertility department at the University Hospital, his practice had grown to be the largest in the country. He had become the leading expert in the field. Patients were referred to him from all over the world. Couples praying for miracles came to Taylor in hopes of having induced pregnancies, and they usually were not disappointed. Taylor had mastered a procedure which wedged out a piece of the ovary in order to stimulate it and allow it to function in a normal fashion. He did so many of these operations that he was called "The Wedge," although never to his face. The wedge is the simplest tool known to man. To reproduce should be the simplest of human functions, but because this was not so, Dr. Taylor's practice knew no bounds.

Taylor's work was constantly talked about or cited, but the man was an enigma in the eyes of his colleagues. His name was always on the surgical schedule, but he was rarely seen. This gave him more of a holy aura, as if Taylor were not a man, but a sacrament—the patron saint of fertility. Indeed, he was revered and feared among the hospital hierarchy. He brought a tremendous amount of money and prestige to the hospital, which gave him extraordinary power.

The elevator stopped at the fourth floor and J.C. Parker stepped out. He was still at a loss as to why Dr. Taylor would want to see him. The possibilities had been driving him crazy. The most far-fetched idea that J.C. had come up with was that Taylor did not like the way the baseball game had turned out and that somehow this was going to hurt his chances of getting a residency. The idea was ludicrous, really, but he had no other plausible ideas. His only other thought was that perhaps Dr. Taylor was looking for a sperm donor. He had heard through the grapevine that he was asking some of the residents for donations for his research. *Maybe he wants me to donate. Could I do that?* His initial reaction would be to decline, but if Dr. Taylor was asking for a personal favor, it might be hard to turn him down. *Oh, well. I'll find out soon enough.*

J.C. entered Dr. Taylor's office and the secretary immediately said, "He's expecting you. It's right through there." She pointed to the double doors at the end of the hallway. J.C. knocked and heard a low, firm voice call out, "It's open." As J.C. gingerly stepped inside he was impressed, and slightly intimidated, by the decor. Wide bookcases filled with medical books covered two entire walls. The remaining walls featured pictures elegantly displayed on the dark paneling. These were obviously photographs from trips Dr. Taylor had taken. The floor was covered in a thick, maroon rug. What left J.C. speechless, however, was the view from the huge window behind Dr. Taylor's desk. He'd love to come back here at night—the city lights must be fantastic.

Dr. Taylor stood and motioned for J.C. to sit down in one of the chairs in front of his heavy desk. Taylor came around and sat next to him, an obvious attempt to put J.C. at ease, for which he was grateful. *If he wanted to chew me out, he would have stayed behind his desk.*

"It's Mr. Parker, isn't it? Or is it J.C.?"

"Just call me J.C., sir, everybody does," J.C. said with a smile, as he continued to inspect the room and all its exotic objects.

"I'm sure you're wondering why I asked you here, so I'll get right to the point. I wanted to talk with you about your roommate." Dr. Taylor's eyes never left J.C.'s face as he spoke.

"Oh?" was all J.C. could think of to say.

"I talked with some of the other students after the game and learned that your roommate wants to become a neurosurgeon. He's interested in doing his training here at Harvard?"

"Yes, but you know, Dr. Taylor, I can't speak for Tim." J.C. felt uncomfortable discussing his friend. The question seemed harmless enough, but he couldn't help being suspicious. Why wouldn't Taylor just ask Tim?

"That's okay," Dr. Taylor said, sounding a bit too reassuring. "I just wanted to get a feeling for what his plans are. I checked his application at the Admissions Office and there was no mention of him being a college athlete. Do you have any idea what he did?"

J.C. couldn't help bragging in response to this question.

"I found out at the game: He played baseball for USC. They went to the NCAA championships four years in a row and won twice with him pitching."

"Yes, I called USC; so I knew about that."

J.C. tried to hide his surprise. Taylor was obviously investigating Tim for some reason, but why?

"Why would you do that?" J.C. blurted out before he could stop himself.

"I'm interested in attracting top-flight people, particularly those who have a great interest in athletics. I think athletics promote a healthy individual. And one needs to be healthy, to go through a residency."

"Oh?" *Credit J.C. Parker with another brilliant and pithy comeback.*

"Surely you've noticed at Harvard that all of our residents are very athletic and into other activities. We encourage that in our surgical and other training programs."

This was the first J.C. had heard that athletic prowess was mandatory for the residency program. He wondered where all this was going.

"I learned from the Chancellor at USC that Tim Graves was the most outstanding pitcher to ever go through that school. He threw fastballs at over ninety miles per hour. You didn't know anything about this?" Taylor leaned back in his chair and fastened his gaze on J.C.

The question sounded more like an accusation. This was getting way too personal.

"Look, Dr. Taylor, I don't mean to be disrespectful, but I don't know what you're getting at. Tim is a good roommate and a good friend. He doesn't talk much about his past, and even if he did, I don't feel comfortable talking to you about Tim this way."

"Of course. I was just trying to start a recruitment program for him and see what we could do to get him here. I appreciate any information on a candidate's personal endeavors, you know what I mean?" He smiled and patted J.C. on the knee.

J.C. didn't know what Dr. Taylor meant and he decided to get out of there. "If you'll excuse me, sir, I've got clinic this afternoon."

"Of course, of course," was the too-hearty reply. "Oh, and J.C., let me just say again that your input is very much appreciated."

J.C. nodded and headed out the door. He re-played the conversation in his head, trying to figure out Taylor's motive. *Was he threatening me? Was he using my friendship with Tim to coax something out of me? What? Tim's grades and reputation could get him into this residency program without any help from Taylor. What the hell does throwing a ninety-mile per hour fastball have to do with medicine?* J. C. looked down and saw that his hands were shaking. He decided not to tell Tim about his meeting with Dr. Taylor. There was no use in worrying him, too.

The students would often play "name that meat," but tonight the "mystery meat" being served in the dormitory dining hall was actually recognizable—beef stroganoff. Tim and J.C. were on their second helping.

"I'll need a gallon of coffee to keep me awake after this," Tim said, stuffing another forkful of potatoes into his mouth.

"Or a stomach pump," J. C. joked. He continued to eat, putting off the conversation he knew was inevitable. He knew if he didn't get this over with, he wouldn't be able to sleep. But he didn't want to make Tim suspicious.

"Fourth year's coming up," J.C. said between bites. "Have you thought about what internships you want?"

Tim looked over at J.C., his fork poised above his plate. "From stomach pumps to the future. Man, I don't know what's worse." Tim flashed a grin, but J.C. seemed unnaturally serious. "I've wanted to be a neurosurgeon, since I was 12. You know that. Why?"

J.C. tried to maintain interest in the stroganoff. "No reason. I'm still undecided and I wondered if maybe you changed your mind or something." To distract him, he decided to switch gears.

"You know, Tim, you have a good shot at getting a residency here at Harvard."

"You think?" Tim thought about a residency at Harvard almost daily. The program was one of the best in the country, he already knew most of the doctors, and he didn't like the idea of having to start over again in a different city. Until now, he'd never heard anyone say that he had a chance; his hopes had always been in his own mind.

He fished for what made J.C. say this. "I've heard that Harvard likes to take people from the outside. I'm really at a disadvantage, just being here."

"Come on. You're one of the best students, your reputation is excellent. The faculty loves you—with one exception, of course."

Tim gave J.C. a look of feigned ignorance.

"I hear he's still really pissed off at you for humiliating him at the baseball game."

"He'll get over it."

27

"My father always told me that your friends come and go, but enemies accumulate, and they stick. No sense in making an enemy of McConnell, you never know where he's going to end up. He's ambitious and political. I heard he's taking a junior faculty position at University Hospital."

Tim thought J.C. was joking around, pretending to be a wise old sage giving advice to a young fellow. When he looked closely, he discovered that his friend was serious, oddly serious. It was so out of character he didn't know how to respond.

"Thanks for your concern. I'll steer clear of McConnell."

J.C. bobbed his head approvingly, picked up his untouched glass of milk and downed it in one gulp. *And watch your back.* J.C. thought. *McConnell's not the only guy to worry about.*

Five

"Run by the places you're applying for residency, Tim."

Tim and J.C. were lying on their beds with their window open. It was a beautiful fall day, and their fourth year rotations were about to begin. Tim had completed his pediatrics and pathology rotations in the spring and spent the summer at home in California. Now he was back and raring to go.

He and J.C. knew each other's picks by heart—they happened to be identical—but he rattled off the list anyway: "University, Mass General, Columbia, New York Hospital, Johns Hopkins, Barnes in St. Louis; Duke; and the Mayo Clinic."

"I'm not too optimistic about Harvard. I didn't do well on my orthopedic rotation."

"I didn't do that well at my surgery rotation at Mass General." In truth, both of them were well positioned to get top residencies. But they could never admit that. Instead they went over and over everything that could go wrong, as if they were huddled around a campfire telling horror stories. Tim continued with the blow by blow: "The General and University Hospital have oral *and* written interviews. No other program in the country does that. It's almost always a one-on-one interview," he moaned.

"The worst part is that you can't study! They can cover any subject and in any depth. Harvard wants you to be a Renaissance man—know everything about everything."

Tim knew J.C. was right and figured the only way for him to get into Harvard would be at the University Hospital. There, he was a working stiff. He did everything possible, including any work that others didn't want to do. He started IVs for nurses and did extra work-ups for the interns to take some of the load off of them. He was not good at delegating. He felt it would get done sooner, and better, if he just did it himself. But because he worked so hard and always made himself available, he had become popular with the surgical residents. He hoped that rapport would

29

reach the ears of the attending doctors.

Tim turned to J.C. "Where do you think you'll end up?"

"Even though I'm trying for the programs here in Boston, and I know I could get in at Mass General . . . I think I'll go back to New York. Columbia has a great orthopedic program and I'll be close to home."

J.C.'s family lived in New Jersey, just across the river. His parents were older and would appreciate having him around.

Tim had chosen radiology, internal medicine and neuro-surgery for his elective rotations that fall. He'd wanted the neuro-surgeons at University Hospital to be familiar with him when it came time to interview.

Tim's first interview was in December at the Massachusetts General Hospital, the top surgical residency program in the country. The room he entered was filled with over 250 students. They were all applying for the same eight positions. They came from California, Washington, Illinois and Florida. Blue books were passed out and several essay questions were given. It took Tim a solid hour of writing to complete his answers.

Then came the oral interview. It turned out to be with not just one doctor, but four. He knew all of the surgeons by reputation. The interview was tough, and afterward he mentally kicked himself for missing a left pneumothorax, instead calling it a descending aortic aneurysm. *I knew that. I just blew it.* Tim wasn't surprised when his name wasn't on the final interview list for the afternoon.

But he had no time to lick his wounds. The following day was his interview at University Hospital. He did the blue book examination in the morning and felt that he had done well. Tim's oral interview was scheduled for 3:30 that afternoon, coincidentally, right after J.C. He waited restlessly outside of the interview room, which was next to the office of the Chief of Surgery. He had been on the surgery rotation with the Chief. They had gotten along well and Tim hoped that would be a plus.

He was leafing listlessly through a magazine when the door opened and J.C. walked out. His expression was grim and he did not look in Tim's direction.

"How'd it go?"

"Brutal. They asked me questions about endocrinology and

30

physiology that I couldn't answer . . . See you back at the dorm," he mumbled as he shuffled away, shoulders slumped. Tim had never seen his friend look so defeated.

"Graves!"

Tim jumped up and walked through the door. Around a table twelve Harvard professors of surgery sat at attention. They wore coats and ties. Tim didn't trust their smiles and nods. J.C. could charm anyone. If these doctors destroyed J.C., what would they do to him?

Dr. Peters, the Chief of Surgery, was the first to speak.

"If you have a patient with metastatic breast cancer and her urine calcium secretion is elevated, how are you going to treat that?"

Dr. Peters was an expert on breast cancer. Tim paused a moment to consider his answer.

"If her urine calcium is elevated and she has radiographic proof of metastasis to her bone, then bilateral adrenalectomy would be in order."

Dr. Peters merely said, "Bob, you're next."

Tim waited for the question from Dr. Gross, who was the Chief of Surgery at Boston Children's Hospital. He was the world's leading pediatric surgeon, but more important at this moment, he had a kind face.

"You have a six-week-old baby who's been vomiting. The mother brought him to the Emergency Department and he's dehydrated, with a low serum potassium. What's the diagnosis, and what do you do?"

Tim had done his pediatric surgery rotation through Boston Children's and had seen a number of babies with pyloric stenosis who came in dehydrated. He looked Dr. Gross in the eye and said, "I would feel for an olive, I mean a pyloric obstruction, rehydrate the baby and take him to the operating room for a pyloric myotomy."

Dr. Gross smiled. "Your turn, Malcolm." He gestured to Dr. Taylor.

Tim sat straighter in his chair. *Maybe this won't be as bad as J.C. made it sound.*

"How many no-hitters did you pitch at USC?"

Tim's face fell. Had he heard Dr. Taylor right? All eyes were

31

upon him and Tim didn't know how to respond. He didn't know how Dr. Taylor had come by that information to begin with.

When Tim didn't answer, Taylor continued. "I didn't intend to embarrass you. How about a question about a ruptured ectopic pregnancy, instead?"

The questions continued, and despite his ignorance in some areas, Tim was able to break down the questions and use logic with the knowledge he had to piece together acceptable answers. At the conclusion, Dr. Peters stood up and shook his hand.

"Thank you very much, Dr. Graves. Well done. Good luck."

Tim thanked everyone and left the room. He walked into the alley between the hospital and the library, through the library and the administration building, down through the Commons, across the street, and into Vanderbilt Hall. He climbed the stairs to his room with some trepidation, knowing that J.C. would be waiting in their room. He didn't want to show too much enthusiasm around his dejected friend.

When he opened the door, J.C. slapped him on the back and laughed like a lunatic.

"I really had ya going, didn't I? Of course, I aced it. It was a breeze, right?"

Tim gathered himself and turned a solemn face to his friend. "I decided if you weren't good enough for them, then they weren't good enough for me. I passed on most of the answers, we talked a little baseball, and I left." Unfortunately, Tim could not maintain his serious expression. J.C. wasn't fooled for a second. Tim was about to tell him about Dr. Taylor's strange question, but before he could, J.C. broke in, "Okay, no more practical jokes. I promise. Let's take the night off and grab some dinner and a movie."

The following month, Tim was notified that he was accepted at University Hospital; and J.C. was off to Columbia University in New York.

Six

Saturday morning was Tim's first day of internship. He didn't leave the hospital until Monday night. He slept for one hour early Monday morning, until a nurse nudged him awake to check on a patient. He was responsible for forty patients, covering three different ward services, and had spent the entire weekend running from ward to ward. In addition, each day he made rounds with the chief and senior residents. They managed to find more for Tim to do on top of his assigned duties—more diagnoses to run down with tests, more laboratory studies and more consultations.

Each morning he was up by four so that he could see each patient, write a note on the chart, and be ready to go around again with the same patients· at six A.M. Each chart had to be perfect, describing the patient's problem and progress, because it was later checked by the chief resident. After morning rounds, Tim would be in the operating room, holding retractors. He would then admit five or six more patients, which meant doing a complete work-up on each of them. This routine was repeated day after endless day. The world outside the hospital held no meaning for him. He worked, and when time allowed, he slept. On only $100 per month, he couldn't afford a social life. His meals consisted of vending machine food or cookies baked by one of the nurses and left in the doctors' lounge. He noticed that his once taut stomach was getting soft. Too much junk food, not enough sleep, and no exercise. In his effort to heal others, he was seriously compromising his own body.

In his third month, Tim rotated to the neurosurgical service. The first day of duty, he arrived at the hospital before the senior resident was even thinking about getting out of bed. Tim wanted to get his bearings and check up on the patients who were already admitted. It never hurt to have a thorough knowledge of each patient before rounding with the residents and attendings.

Tim ducked into a patient's room. He was scanning a chart when a commanding voice asked, "What do you think you're doing in here?"

Tim's head shot up and he saw a plump figure standing in the doorway with her hands placed firmly on her hips. He was taken aback by her tone and her no-nonsense demeanor.

"I . . . I'm just looking through this chart here," he stuttered, indicating the clipboard in his hand.

"And who are you?"

"I, I'm an intern. I'm starting my neurosurgical rotation today . . . I was just trying to get a headstart, you know, get to know the patients before I . . ." He stumbled over his words until he ran out of steam.

The woman eyed Tim appraisingly. Finally, she extended her right hand. "Nurse O'Reilly. Chief Nurse. You're on my ward, now. We'll get along just fine if you don't try to do my job and you don't expect me to do yours. It's nice to meet you, Dr. . . . ?"

"Graves. Timothy Graves. Tim." He shook her outstretched hand and tried not to wince at her painfully tight squeeze.

"Dr. Graves." With that, O'Reilly swung her wide hips around and was gone. *This is new, a nurse who wants to do her own job.* He was intimidated by her, but couldn't help hoping that he might have found an ally. He hung the chart back on the bed frame and stepped out into the hall. Two men in white coats were walking rapidly toward him. He stepped closer to the wall to allow them to get by. As they passed him, one of them called out, "Student or resident?" To answer, Tim had to walk with them.

"Intern."

Without missing a step the one who had first addressed him said, "Come on, then, we need your help."

They were entering the scrub room. *Surgery? On my first day?* Tim swallowed his urge to protest. This was no time to make excuses. The two doctors were scrubbing and shouting orders to begin prepping the patient. Tim scrubbed his hands and a masked nurse held out the rubber gloves for him and coaxed them on. The two doctors were about to enter the operating room and they motioned for Tim to join them.

"What's your name?"

"Graves. Tim Graves, sir."

"This is Dr. West and I'm Dr. Stern. Glad we found you. This is a sensitive operation and we need hands. You'll be holding the brain retractor and whatever else we ask you to handle. Except when you're told, don't touch anything and don't say anything. Any questions?"

He understood what his role was to be, but he had no idea what operation was to be performed.

"Just one, sir, what procedure will we, uh, you, be doing?"

Dr. West, who had been impatiently waiting for this exchange to end, spoke up.

"We're clipping a cerebral aneurysm. If you're unfamiliar with this procedure, then watch and learn. This woman was wheeled into the ER about an hour ago and we have no time to lose."

Dr. West pushed the doors open and took his position at the head of the table. Dr. Stern followed, with Tim close on his heels. *If only they knew just how familiar I am with this procedure*

Taylor removed the file from the top drawer and slapped it on the desk. He hated paperwork. If his secretary weren't such a klutz, he'd have her do the work, but she always seemed to write either too much or not enough. Of course, he had never taken the time to properly train her. He had no tolerance for teaching. And he couldn't just get another, more competent secretary. Meredith had been with him too long and she knew too much.

In addition to Meredith, there were only two other people on his payroll: Gretchen, the accountant, and Carlos, the lab tech. He had hired Carlos after one of his patients suggested that he needed a little more help around the office and recommended his nephew. Taylor took him up on the offer—he felt that it was time to move his lab operations out of the hospital and into his private office. He was able to buy the office next door to his own and to turn the space into a fully outfitted lab. This turned out to be less costly than renting lab space from the hospital, as he had done in the past, and it also ensured the security of the samples he used by limiting access to himself and his three employees. His employees worked hard and were very loyal. He didn't kid himself about the reason for their loyalty. Dr. Taylor knew he was a difficult taskmaster. There was no love lost between him and his staff. But loyalty can usually be purchased by the highest bidder. His employees received fat checks at the end of every month . . . Very fat checks.

The buzzer on his desk interrupted his musing. He reached over and pressed the button.

"Yes, Meredith."

"Dr. Taylor? I think you should take this call. It's Senator Fitzgerald's office. You know, Senator Fitzgerald of Massachusetts."

Taylor cringed at Meredith's naivete.

"Give me a minute and then put the call through." Taylor needed a minute to gather his thoughts. *Why would the senator be calling me? Solicitations for campaign contributions would just come through his office.* Then he had a frightening thought—*Are they investigating me?*

Taylor jumped when the phone rang. He took a deep breath and picked up the receiver.

"Hello, Dr. Taylor speaking."

A low voice with a quite pronounced Boston accent replied, "Dr. Taylor. I've heard so much about you. This is Bob Fitzgerald. How are you?'

"Fine Senator." Taylor couldn't imagine what this was about. "And you?"

"Fine. Just fine. I'm sorry to interrupt your day, I know you're a busy man."

"No, no. Not at all. What can I do for you?"

"I'd like to arrange to talk in person."

Here it comes.

"And the sooner the better. I have some questions. I'm very curious about your practice."

Taylor's brow was damp. He picked up a pencil and started tapping it on his desk.

"What would you like to discuss, Senator, I mean, specifically?"

"That's better left for when we meet face to face, don't you think?"

Taylor cursed silently. He wanted to know what the Irish lush wanted to discuss with him, and he didn't want to wait.

36

Bob Fitzgerald's voice came through the line again, but this time, something had changed. The friendly lilt was missing.

"I know that doctors are required by law to respect the privacy of their patients. So this meeting is between you and me."

"I understand." Tapping the pencil furiously, Taylor was struggling to figure out where all this was leading.

"Good. I'll have my secretary call. I look forward to our meeting." The line went dead.

What the hell was that about? Taylor stopped tapping the pencil and snapped it in half with one hand. *Snap. That's right. I'm going to snap.* He stood up and walked over to the bookcase. On the top shelf was a little wooden box. His wife had brought it back from Hawaii. He lifted the lid and pulled out a cigarette, lighting it with the lighter his wife had had sent from Paris. He fell into one of the leather chairs in front of the bookcase and inhaled deeply. It was going to be a long week.

Tim left the OR in a daze. The operation had taken six hours. He had been standing for six hours. The surgery was a success and he was trying to replay every step in his mind. Dr. West breezed past Tim and disappeared down the hall. Dr. Stern walked up and slapped Tim on the back. "Nice job," he said, and walked on. *Nice job? I didn't do anything.* All he could do during the operation was imagine his own head on that table. He had finally witnessed what had gone on in his brain ten years ago. It was incredible to learn how close he had been to death.

It wasn't until he started to make his way back to the ward that he remembered his rotation schedule. He had missed orientation and his first rounds on the neurosurgical rotation. He would be considered a flake. He should have left some kind of message on the board. He had to find the senior resident and explain that he literally had had no time. He picked up his pace and headed to the reception desk. The secretary was busy writing in a file and did not look up when Tim spoke.

"Did the senior resident come through here today? Dr. Levi?"

"Yep."

"Did he leave a message or anything, or ask about Dr. Graves?"

"Nope."

"Were there some new residents here today? Did they have their orientation?"

"Yep." She finally looked up and asked, "Do you need something?"

"I think I need to page Dr. Levi. See, I was supposed to start my rotation today, but I got asked to assist with surgery. Clip a cerebral aneurysm. I just got out. I'm afraid I missed everything."

"What's the name?"

"Dr. Levi."

Heavy sigh. "I mean *your* name."

"Dr. Graves." Tim spun around. Nurse O'Reilly supplied his name before Tim had a chance.

She said to Tim, "I spoke with Dr. Levi this morning. You report to this ward tomorrow at six A.M."

Tim stared blankly at Nurse O'Reilly. "Did he say anything about . . . anything?"

"I told him what happened. I wouldn't worry." She stepped closer to him and whispered, "That's one for me and none for you."

The receptionist spoke up, irritated. "Do you still want that page?"

Tim shook his head. "No, I guess not." He turned back to Nurse O'Reilly, but she was gone.

Meredith had scheduled the appointment for Friday afternoon in Taylor's office. It was now Thursday evening and Taylor needed a drink. He had done two wedges that day, three artificial inseminations, and seen a dozen patients, most of whom he rejected. He did accept one young woman, a buxom lady with irregular cycles. He liked her smile, but he had been afraid she would not have the funds necessary for her treatment. When he learned that her husband was a lawyer, he grinned with pleasure. *The bastard lawyer could pay.* Insurance had only started to be a problem for Taylor once he began practicing his artificial inseminations. They would cover any correctional surgery, the usual cut and paste, but they would never pay for sperm injections. The insurance companies held to the opinion that infertility was the problem of the individual, like they were born to be barren and it should be left at that. Fortunately, his wealthy patients did not share this opinion, and they were willing to pay just about anything to have a baby. This worked out very well for Taylor. He took cash up front and had no billing and collection problems, just pure profit. Until now.

What does Fitzgerald want with me? It has to be about money. All these politicians think about is money and power. Taylor wondered how anyone could devote himself to a profession that was only about money and power. *It's not like being a doctor. I give new life and people worship me for it.* He failed to recognize the irony of his thoughts, but he had made himself feel better. Nevertheless, a drink was still in order. He grabbed his coat and locked his office door behind him.

He thought about calling his wife, but decided not to bother. She would be out spending his money, anyway. They had slept in separate beds since their son had left for Emory University. He rarely came home for visits, choosing to spend holidays with his friends. He seemed to resent his privileged life, and got involved with social projects and volunteer work. He initially wrote home about his "do-good" projects, but stopped when he received no encouragement from his dad. After he graduated he had stayed in Atlanta. His mother sent him checks, though Blaine never asked his parents for money. They would hear from mutual friends that Blaine was marching for trash collectors in Georgia, or walking a picket line for laid-off factory workers. Taylor could only imagine his son's lifestyle, and wanted no details. His only comment to his wife was that he hoped Blaine was not doing anything illegal, otherwise, it was a closed subject. His work occupied all of his time and he did not want to dwell on what he considered the one failure in his life, marriage and family.

Taylor parked his white Mercedes on the street and entered Julianne's bar. The bar was in a quiet borough and the clientele were professional people looking for solitude and anonymity. Taylor slid onto a stool at the bar and nodded to Frank, the bartender. The place was busy for a Thursday evening. He scanned the room, noting young men dressed in business suits and a few ladies with crossed legs enticingly revealed by their short skirts.

"How are you this evening, Dr. Taylor?" Frank inquired, as he put a cardboard coaster in front of him.

"Not bad, but I could use a drink."

"Scotch and water?"

"Make it a double."

Frank set the drink down and Taylor took a healthy sip. He glanced to his left and noticed a woman who looked to be in her early twenties sitting on the end stool. She was wearing a fitted skirt and jacket that looked smoky gray in the dimness of the bar. Her long red hair was pulled back into an elegant ponytail. She was drinking beer from a bottle, a bold move for a lady. Taylor's eyes assessed the length of her body. He was stirred by her well-defined curves and long, slender legs. *Maybe she needs some company.*

He kept his eye on her as he finished his drink and ordered another. She was deep in thought and appeared to be unaware of her surroundings or his presence. He picked up his drink and walked to where she was sitting. Their eyes met in the mirror over the bar.

"May I sit here?"

"You can sit anywhere you want."

Taylor smiled and sat down. She continued to stare at the mirror.

"You look sad. Do you want to talk about it?" Women always responded when he appeared sensitive to their moods. He was proud of his smooth opening.

"I'm not sad and you should mind your own business."

"I'm trying to make you my business."

She finally turned her head away from the mirror and gave Taylor an appraising glance.

"I look sad," she asked rhetorically, "And you look married."

"Guilty as charged."

"Then why don't you go home and worry about your wife's business."

"Because my wife makes it her business to stay away from me."

"Poor man. Married and lonely."

"Aren't they the same thing?" Taylor flashed a smile. She cracked a smile, too, for the first time.

"I suppose."

"Do you speak from experience?"

She looked at Taylor, wondering how much she wanted to

tell this guy. She conceded that a middle-aged, married stranger drinking scotch in a bar seemed harmless enough. "My boyfriend didn't like me having my own life and I didn't like him sleeping with other women. A doomed relationship, wouldn't you say?"

"What do you mean 'having your own life'?"

"He wanted a traditional woman, someone to cook, clean and have his babies. That's not my style. I have other plans."

"And what plans might you have?"

"Right now I'm still a journalism student, but I plan to be an investigative reporter for a major newspaper."

Taylor nodded. He was finding the conversation, and the woman, intriguing. A woman reporter was rare. As if she had read his thoughts, she began a monologue on the difficulty of women in the newsroom. Most women reporters cover the home and food pages. She became more animated as she elaborated. This woman's emancipation was all well and good, but Taylor tuned her out as he wondered how he might get her into bed.

"I hope this conversation is off the record," he broke in.

"Why? We haven't talked about anything incriminating."

"Well, the night is young, who knows what we might want to keep just between us."

Here it comes. Will I ever have a conversation with a man that doesn't end in some kind of invitation for sex? She decided it was time for her to leave—alone.

"I don't think we'll have to worry about any scandals," she said, rising.

"It's early. Don't go. I'd like to hear more about your plans."

Taylor was sinking fast, and he knew it. She already had her coat on. He jumped up.

"Do you have a car? Let me take you home."

"I'm fine." She was glad she had not told him her name.

"If you see me around here again, you can buy me a drink, okay?"

That wasn't the response he wanted. She was already out the door.

Taylor slumped back onto the barstool and finished off his scotch. The thought of going home depressed him. He was on the verge of ordering another, but thought better of it. *Tomorrow is another wedge. Tomorrow is the appointment with Fitzgerald. Tomorrow is another goddamn day.*

*   *   *

He had tried to avoid any publicity by driving himself to the hospital, leaving the secret service agents behind. When the senator breezed through the lobby toward the elevator, he was still wearing his hat and dark glasses. Nobody seemed to notice him. He gave his name to Dr. Taylor's secretary and she told him to have a seat, the doctor wasn't in yet. He would have to wait. The senator was pissed. Senator Bob Fitzgerald did not expect to be kept waiting.

By the time Dr. Taylor burst through the door, a good twenty minutes later, Fitzgerald was fuming and there were other patients in the waiting room.

"I'm sorry you had to wait, Senator Fitzgerald, please come in."

Fitzgerald glanced furtively around the room when Taylor addressed him. *The fool. Using my name out here in the open. Didn't I tell him to keep this confidential?*

He joined Taylor in his office and took a seat in one of the leather chairs near the bookcase. He didn't want to stay any longer than necessary.

"I really didn't expect to be kept waiting. I don't have a lot of time, so I'll get right to the point."

"I was caught in a very sensitive surgery, Senator, and I apologize. I intend to cooperate fully with you." Taylor was obviously ill at ease, and this made Fitzgerald feel a little better.

"Let's get down to business, doctor. I assume you've already guessed why I'm here." He looked at Taylor with raised eyebrows.

Taylor decided to follow the senator's lead. He certainly wasn't going to put his own head in the noose.

"I'm afraid you'll have to tell me why you're here, sir. I'd rather not speculate."

"You are the expert in fertility, are you not?"

"Well I consider myself to be one of the best," Taylor said, attempting to sound humble.

"According to my research, you are the best. So why don't

42

you start giving me some options to consider."

"I'm afraid I'm not following you. You want me to give you some options about what?"

Fitzgerald spoke firmly, "About how my wife and I can have a baby."

Taylor relaxed in his chair and suppressed a smile. So the senator wasn't after his head, he wanted a baby.

"Well," Taylor spoke more easily now, "you've come to the right place."

Frustrated with Taylor's unresponsiveness, he spoke to him as if he were speaking to a child. "Yes, and now that I'm here, why don't you start giving me some answers."

Ignoring the condescension, Taylor said, "Relax, Senator. I can take care of everything."

Tim's stomach growled so loudly that the attending doctor who was rounding with the interns heard it.

"Skip breakfast today, Graves?" he jibed. The other interns smiled sympathetically. They were hungry, too. Tim couldn't remember the last time he had eaten breakfast. There was never time in the morning to take more than a swig or two of milk as he rushed through the interns' and residents' quarters to the hospital.

When the group of interns broke up, Tim headed for the phone. He had heard his name paged. The operator told him to hold for Dr. Taylor. He was taken aback. He didn't really know Taylor, though he remembered him as one of the faculty members who interviewed him for his internship. He had heard that Dr. Taylor had strongly supported his application, but he couldn't imagine why he would be calling.

A voice came on the line. "Dr. Graves, this is Malcolm Taylor."

"Hello, Dr. Taylor." Tim waited.

"If you have a moment, could you stop by my office? I have something I want to discuss with you."

Tim looked at his watch. "I have clinic in twenty minutes. Can I come by now?"

"Certainly. You know where I am . . . the fourth floor."

Tim hung up the phone. *This should be interesting.* He took the

43

stairs and headed down the hallway and around the first bend. Tim knew where the office was, even though he had never been there. Taylor's office was infamous around the hospital—when he walked through the door he understood why. The waiting area was elegantly decorated. Fine artwork was displayed. The feeling was that of a well appointed home, rather than a doctor's office.

Meredith led Tim through the massive double doors into the inner office. Tim took in stride the wood paneling, bookcases and artifacts. But he couldn't help being impressed with the view of the Boston skyline through the huge window behind Taylor's desk.

Taylor invited Tim to sit, and welcomed him with a smile.

"You know, last year at the faculty-student baseball game I saw you take care of the faculty single-handedly."

Tim shrugged and said nothing as Taylor continued.

"I know some people at USC and I've heard that you were quite a pitcher for the varsity team."

"I was lucky at SC. I'm out of baseball, though. Medicine takes all of my time now." Tim thought back to his interview, when Taylor had asked him how many no-hitters he had pitched at USC. *What is his problem? Is he some kind of baseball freak?*

"Of course, but what I'm interested in is your athletic ability. I'm doing some fertility research and I'm particularly interested in using the sperm from athletes who have significant talent. I feel I can study genetic patterns and the motility of their sperm, and other tests to see if they're suitable for donation."

"Donation?" Tim's eyes widened.

"I'm a fertility expert. I expect to study sperm to be sure they are motile, that they have a pH which is compatible with recipients, and other factors. I find that in the case of healthy young males, such as yourself, the sperm are easier to investigate and are more compatible with my patients."

Tim understood Dr. Taylor's theories, he had read several of his articles in medical journals, and he was impressed by his innovations. He still wasn't clear what this had to do with him.

"Are you asking me to donate my sperm?"

"I think you would offer me some excellent material for my research."

After some hesitation, Tim spoke haltingly, "I'd be willing to help you out with your research experiments, but I have a problem with donating for potential use with patients." Tim said this with a furrowed brow, looking straight into Taylor's eyes.

Taylor was prepared for some reluctance. "That's a separate issue. I am chiefly interested in the scientific experiments. If I were to find a compatible recipient, I wouldn't use your sperm without your permission."

Tim sat back, thinking about what he had just heard. He didn't want to get involved with anything like this. It made him uncomfortable, even if it were for the sake of science.

"I can assure you that I won't ever give you permission to donate my sperm to anybody," Tim said. He wanted to make that clear, even though he was still hesitant about donating sperm for any purpose.

Dr. Taylor decided to play his trump card.

"You know we'll pay you for this. Fifteen dollars per specimen."

That got Tim's attention. He could certainly use the additional income. He had donated blood twice since starting his internship, for the twenty dollars it brought in, but donating blood made him even more tired and he couldn't do it on a regular basis. He thought about his empty stomach and finally said, "I'll do it. As long as it's just for research."

"Great. Thank you, Tim. It will be a great help," Taylor rose. The two men shook hands and the meeting was over.

Thursday morning Dr. Taylor found Tim alone in the doctors' lounge. "I'd like that specimen today. My locker is over there. It's open. Just get the jar from inside and put it back when you're through."

Tim wanted to say he had changed his mind, this was so awkward. But then he thought about the fifteen dollars and nodded. He was glad nobody else was around. He went to the locker and found the specimen jar sitting on the shelf. He went to the bathroom and began to masturbate. *To think I used to make extra money delivering newspapers.* He finished and placed the jar back in Taylor's locker. In another month he'd do it again.

Seven

Tim slumped in a waiting room chair with his left hand holding his head up and one finger pressed against his closed eyeball. He had stolen a few minutes to glance through a *Time* magazine, but it had slipped to the floor near his feet. Jennifer recognized him as soon as she stepped off the elevator. *Poor guy. He works longer and harder than any other surgical resident.* She knew many doctors who let the long hours and lack of sleep get to them and then they vented their frustrations on those around them. Those were the doctors the nurses tried to avoid. Of course, the nurses talked about all the doctors. They would gather in the lounges, empty hallways, or even over unconscious patients, and gossip. Jennifer tried to stay away from the gossips. Most of the doctors she encountered treated her well enough, although there was the occasional egomaniac who had no respect for nurses. Dr. Graves, she observed fondly, was the sweetest. She knew of more than one nurse who had a crush on him.

Whenever Dr. Graves did a case, the nurses had to draw straws just to decide who would get to assist him. *He is so handsome.* Jennifer admired his honesty most of all. He could be brutally forthright, but was never condescending and he was quick to praise. When he had noticed a charting error she had made, he pointed it out to her and reminded her of the important responsibility she had in the patient's overall care. Rather than making her feel ashamed or defensive, he made her feel proud of her profession and she vowed to be even more careful in the future.

Alas, Dr. Graves never dated any of the nurses. In fact, they were pretty sure he had no social life. He was always at the hospital, working. The thought of ministering to Dr. Graves' loneliness made Jennifer's nerves jump. She walked over to where he was asleep in the chair. As she kneeled down to pick up the fallen magazine, her shoulder brushed against his knee. She had tried not to wake him, but he gave a start when she touched him and

46

bolted upright in his seat. She smiled and held up the magazine.

"Just picking this up." She was embarrassed that he had caught her in such a compulsive act. "I didn't mean to wake you. I'm a neatnik."

Tim was confused. Her head was blocking the ceiling light and he had to squint a little to make out the features of her face.

"Jennifer? I must have dozed off."

"I . . . I'm sorry, Dr. Graves. For disturbing you, I mean. I just thought, well, I don't know what I thought. I just wanted to pick up the magazine you dropped."

Jennifer liked the way Dr. Graves said her name. He didn't seem embarrassed or sorry to see her here. In fact, he seemed pleased.

Tim took a moment to get his bearings. He had been aware of Jennifer for some time, but had never found an opportunity to talk to her alone. He started to rise and Jennifer put out a hand to help him. She did this impulsively, before she could stop herself. Tim looked at her hand, so delicate. He noticed she wore no rings. He reached for it and felt a surge from her strong, confident grip. They were standing close together, face to face. She was nearly as tall as he was. Jennifer tipped her head to one side and gave him an inquiring look. The spell was broken.

"You're a tall woman," he said and quickly turned to walk down the hallway. As an afterthought, he paused and said "thanks" over his shoulder, flashing her a smile. Jennifer felt let down, although she didn't know what she had expected him to do. Sweep her into his arms and declare his undying love?

Tim could not get his encounter with Jennifer out of his mind. He interacted with nurses daily, and rarely even thought of them as women. They were fellow workers and he respected and admired them, but he always kept his distance. He had no time, no money, and no intention of getting involved in a potentially sticky situation. Now, suddenly, he was finding ways to cross paths with one particular female. He made what he hoped were discreet inquiries, and was able to put together some information about her. She came from a Polish background, her grandparents had immigrated to Boston when her father was three years old. She spoke Russian and Polish dialect. She was apparently something of an artist; some of the nurses had mentioned paintings she

47

gave as gifts, and some of them were hanging in the hospital. Tim had already tracked them down, beautiful watercolors of botanicals and flowers. He continued his silent pursuit of Jennifer until he began to feel foolish.

One morning, crossing the lobby to the elevator, he decided to change direction and take the stairs. With little time to exercise, he felt he could at least get his heart pumping a little bit. In the third floor stairwell, he ran into Jennifer. They both blushed.

Since their brief encounter in the patient waiting area, Jennifer had noticed Dr. Graves much more often. *Perhaps it's like when you learn a new word. Once you learn it you hear it everywhere.* She had continued to amuse herself with her fantasy of Dr. Graves falling head over heels in love with her, but she was not delusional enough to think of it as anything but that—a fantasy. That didn't stop her from taking extra care with her hair and make-up, and she had started using a little rose water on her neck and behind her knees. *Nothing wrong with a girl looking her best, even at work.*

Jennifer was on her way to the fourth floor, where the nurses were short-handed. She couldn't believe her luck when she saw Dr. Graves. She had been hoping for just such a meeting for weeks. After the usual banal exchange, he made no move to leave. Jennifer decided to take the plunge.

"I know how hard you work, but do you enjoy doing anything special when you're not on duty? Any hobbies or anything?"

"Well, if I ever have time, I enjoy reading and baseball, playing, that is."

"Oh, you play baseball?"

"I used to, in college. I haven't in a while. Just too busy." Tim didn't want the conversation to end. "What do you do in your spare time?"

"I like having fun. Music, dancing, laughing with friends."

Tim looked distant. "I haven't been dancing in so long, I wonder if I still remember how."

"You should get out and try it some time." Jennifer liked the way the conversation was progressing. She hoped that Tim would pick up on the invitation in her voice.

"Actually, I've never found anyone I wanted to dance with," he said, trying to be cool.

This game Jennifer could play.

"And why haven't you found anyone to dance with?"

"Because not many girls interest me."

"And why is that?"

"Because they're not interesting."

"And what *is* interesting to you?"

"People who don't let me sleep on the job."

"Oh?"

"Yes. I find that *very* interesting."

"Well, that is . . . *very* . . . interesting."

They couldn't go any further without erupting in laughter. Though they were laughing at the silliness of their game, they were also aware of the step they had taken toward . . . something. When their laughter died down and they were left looking at each other, Tim spoke up.

"So, I guess we'll have to try this dancing thing," he said.

"I guess we will."

"Soon."

"Yes." She couldn't stop smiling.

*　　*　　*

In March Tim was shocked to receive a letter from the Defense Department. He had not asked for a deferment as a physician, but he had not expected to be called to active duty. There were currently trouble spots throughout the world and the military was gearing up for potential problems. Now it was too late to obtain a deferment. Tim suddenly found himself a member of the United States Navy.

The timing could not have been worse. It was not that Tim was opposed to serving his country, but he was in the middle of his internship year. Plus, his relationship with Jennifer was blossoming. Tim had heard repeatedly that the Chief of Surgery did not like the interns or residents to date student nurses. It was an unwritten rule that student nurses were off limits. But Tim also knew that Jennifer was special. This was not going to be a casual fling. After their first date, Tim had decided that this was the girl for him. He may not have experienced the "fireworks" of some romantic novels, but there was a steadiness to Jennifer that Tim appreciated. With her he felt "grounded." Now, everything he had been working for would have to be put on hold. Jennifer was understanding and supportive, but he knew that she, too, was disappointed.

In late June he said goodbye to Jennifer and returned to California. He visited with his family and then reported for active duty in San Diego. During his induction, the medical officer who examined him had noted the scars on his scalp. Up to this point, Tim had not disclosed his brain surgery to anyone. Now, he knew he could receive a medical deferment if he told the Navy that he had been operated on for a cerebral aneurysm. He'd be back at his residency and back with Jennifer in no time. But Tim's pride got the better of him. He did not want this information on his military record. He especially didn't want Jennifer to know about the aneurysm. It was over and done. Why risk being diminished in any way in her eyes? If he were deferred for a medical reason, she would find out. He explained away the scars as an injury when he was a child. The officer appeared skeptical, but after making a note of the scalp scars on his record, he cleared him.

Before long, Tim was serving as General Medical Officer on a destroyer in the Far East. Duty was not particularly challenging, but the travel was interesting. He wrote to Jennifer weekly and called when he could. She had finished nursing school and had started working the night shift at Massachusetts General Hospital. Her letters were glowing reports of how much she enjoyed being a duty nurse and how busy she was. If she found time to miss Tim, she kept it to herself.

Most of his first year of duty was spent at sea, visiting various ports throughout Southeast Asia. When they stopped at Saigon he could tell that war was inevitable. The build-up of military presence was obvious. Fortunately, he had only six more months in the Navy and had requested his final duty station to be Boston.

When he returned to Boston he and Jennifer were able to pick up where they had left off. It was as if they had never been apart. Tim finally felt everything was falling into place. He'd found a partner, his tour of duty with the Navy was over, and his goal of being a neurosurgeon was within his grasp. Nothing would stop him now.

When Tim proposed, Jennifer accepted—on the condition

that they elope. She came from a poor, East Boston Polish family and she didn't want to burden her parents with an expensive wedding. So their life together began uneventfully and modestly. Tim called his family after he and Jennifer had their marriage license in hand to let them know the news. They were disappointed their son hadn't included them—let alone introduced them to his new bride. But they congratulated him and said they looked forward to meeting Jennifer.

Eight

1965

The dark-haired woman shifted in her chair. "You know who I am, don't you, Dr. Taylor?"

"Of course, I know who you are, Maria. Don't forget, I grew up in Newton."

Maria smiled. "I guess you're not Irish Catholic, are you?"

"I'm afraid not," he grimaced. "Protestant, and proud of it."

Maria crossed her legs, keeping her eyes focused on the man in front of her. *Attenzione*, she told herself. This one she didn't trust.

"My husband is getting frustrated with me, and it's hurting our marriage."

"What's the problem?" Taylor was feeling impatient. *Why can't these women just get to the point?*

"We have four children, all girls. We adore them, of course. But Tony's Sicilian and it's no good to have all girls. It looks bad for a man to have no sons. You know, no one to carry on his name. It makes him look weak to his friends."

And to his enemies. Dr. Taylor understood. He had dealt with many husbands who demanded that their wives produce a son. If they could not produce, they were often replaced. *The ignorant fools. They don't even know that it's the man who determines the sex of the child.*

Maria spoke again. "Tony says this is the last time I'm getting pregnant. *Finito.* I can't take any chances. I must give him a son or our marriage is over."

Dr. Taylor sat back in his chair with his hands clasped behind his head, looking up at the ceiling, dollar signs dancing in his head.

"Well, I think that can be arranged, Maria. I can almost guarantee that you can have a boy."

"Almost is not good enough."

"It's practically certain, but nothing is a hundred percent. This is a very delicate, and very expensive procedure."

Maria sat forward in her chair, her accent more pronounced with each word she spoke.

"The cost is of no concern to me. You must make sure I have a boy and you *must* make sure Tony never finds out about this. It is not something I do proudly, but I must be certain I give him a son, and soon."

"It's just between you and me. An office procedure." Taylor clasped his hands on his desk, quite pleased with himself.

Maria was surprised. "An office procedure?"

"Of course. You won't even have to enter the hospital, so there will be no hospital record. You'll pick out what you want, and we'll get it for you."

"Anything I want?" Maria sounded skeptical.

"We'll do our best. We have a wide selection of donors. I've got a hospital here, full of young male doctors who are handsome, intelligent, athletic, anything you want." Taylor chuckled at his own humor.

"Please, Dr. Taylor. This is no joke. I came to you because it is said you are the best, a serious doctor who does serious work. Perhaps I have made a mistake." Maria gave him a hard look.

Taylor back pedaled. "I'm sorry, I didn't mean to offend you. This is very serious business, you're right. I was only trying to lighten the moment. I apologize. Why don't I get a little history about you and Tony. I'd better not use your real name. We'll label your file Maria and Tony X."

Maria relaxed her grip on the arm of the chair and nodded in agreement.

"Describe Tony for me."

"He's about six feet, tall for a Sicilian. His father's Italian but his mother was an American girl. That's where he gets his sandy hair. He has dimples when he smiles, which is not often. He has wide shoulders and big hands. Oh, and he's left-handed."

Taylor stopped writing. "Left-handed?"

"Yes. You know, being left-handed is considered an affliction in Sicily. They force all the children in school to write with their right hands. But Tony, he refused. All the kids back home made fun of him, but they're not making fun of him now." She allowed herself a small smile, then added, "That's where he gets his nickname, La Sinestra—The Lefty."

Dr. Taylor put down his pen. He was intrigued with Maria's story, but he was more intrigued with the prospect of finding the perfect match for Tony X.

"I believe, Maria, I've got the answer to your prayers."

Maria clasped her hands together and shook them in front of her. "*Grazia al Dio*," she chanted.

Taylor hated the histrionics of these people. He said, "I want you to record your ovulation cycles and the next time you are mid-cycle, give me a call."

"I'm in the middle of my cycle right now."

Taylor smiled and pushed the button on his intercom. "Meredith, do we have time on Wednesday?"

"Time for what?" Meredith asked.

Taylor forced a smile. "Time, Meredith, just *time*. For an appointment."

"Yes, Dr. Taylor, there is time on Wednesday afternoon."

"Good. We'll take that."

"And the name?"

"Maria X." Taylor clicked off.

"We'll try for insemination on Wednesday, then."

"Do I get to meet the father?"

This was a common request and Taylor had a prepared answer that usually satisfied his patients. The one time a patient insisted on meeting the donor, the discussion turned ugly when he refused. She threatened to sue and the adverse publicity would have severely damaged his practice. So Taylor had solved the problem by having his attorney pose as the donor. The woman was satisfied and never uttered another peep. Of course, he had to pay off his attorney for the inconvenience and embarrassment, but chalked it up to the cost of doing business.

With Maria, Taylor did not foresee any problems. *These people understand secrets.* He responded to her question in a most conciliatory tone, "I don't think that would be a good idea, Maria. Most donors want to remain anonymous, and in your case, so do you. It would be dangerous for you to meet face to face. What if he were to recognize you? You can trust me to obtain the best possible donor, and to make sure all the necessary screening is done."

54

Trusting Taylor wasn't Maria's automatic response, but what he said was true . . . discretion was more important to her than meeting the donor. She nodded and rose. "Anything you say, Dr. Taylor. Anything you say."

Taylor rose and took her hand. "I'll see you here on Wednesday. See Meredith on your way out. She'll give you your instructions and you can take care of the financial arrangements."

"I'll be here Wednesday. With cash."

Taylor loved cash. As soon as Maria was gone, Taylor called up the hospital exchange.

"This is Dr. Taylor. Will you please page Dr. Graves? It's urgent."

Tim had been reviewing the chart of a young girl who had just been admitted, when his pager went off. He went to the nearest phone and dialed the operator.

"Please hold for Dr. Taylor."

Once again, Tim found himself waiting on the phone, wondering why Taylor would be calling. He hadn't spoken to him in four years, except for an occasional encounter in the hallways of the hospital. Taylor's infertility clinic had become world-famous and the hospital had benefited from all the positive publicity. Tim had to admit he was a little proud to know that he had contributed, however slightly, to Dr. Taylor's success. He had never told anyone about his sperm donation, not even Jennifer. He still felt embarrassed about it, even though he knew there was nothing wrong with donating sperm for use in scientific experiments. Ironically, the extra money he had received for his donations had enabled him to take Jennifer out to dinner. His first fifteen dollars was spent on their first date. *I guess I owe the guy.* Just then the line clicked and Taylor was speaking.

"Tim. How are you?"

"I'm keeping busy."

"Great. I hear good things about you. Listen, I wonder if you could stop by my office this afternoon. It's important that I talk with you."

"I'm pretty swamped. Can you tell me what it is?"

"I'd prefer to talk to you in person."

"Look, I'm through making any sperm donations. I don't

55

want to do it anymore, so if this is about . . . "

Taylor cut him off. "You don't have to worry about that. You've been a big help to me in the past, and I appreciate it. Let's just get together and talk."

Tim was still suspicious but Taylor was a big name around the hospital. "I can probably come in sometime after four."

"See you at five."

Taylor leaned back in his chair. He hadn't anticipated resistance from Tim. Now it seemed that he would have to get creative. Although he had developed a technique for storing sperm over a long period of time, he didn't want to trust one of Tim's old specimens. This one was too important to screw up. He looked over the Boston skyline. He smiled, sure of what he must do.

At ten past five Tim knocked on Taylor's office door.

"Come in," Taylor boomed from the other side.

Tim entered the office and shut the door behind him. Taylor's office was as impressive as it had been five years ago. The view was just as magnificent.

Taylor smiled, but made no attempt to rise from behind his desk and shake Tim's hand. He had to proceed with caution.

"Tim, how are you doing?"

"Fine."

"How long do you have left?"

"Two more years and then I'll be finished with the white suit." The white suit, white coat and white pants, were mandatory for residents. They had to dress in white all of the time and their clothes had to be impeccably clean.

"Like I said, I've heard good things about your work." Taylor could be truthful about this. He had heard good things about Tim. In fact, Tim had proved to be one of the most talented surgical residents to come through Harvard in a long time. There were rumors that the Chief of Neurosurgery wanted to keep Tim at Harvard in order to bolster his own department, although there would be young, qualified neurosurgeons from all over the country vying for that position. Taylor also knew that although Tim was a stellar candidate for a permanent faculty position, he lacked the schmoozing techniques needed to land the job. Tim never brown-nosed and this gave him the reputation of being aloof and arrogant. Tim recognized that he didn't connect well with many people on a social level, but he was satisfied that they respected his abilities as a surgeon. *The young Dr. Graves needs to learn that doing one's job doesn't always get you where you want to go.*

"You know, Tim, there has been some talk about you coming on staff here."

Tim never relied on rumors, though he had heard them. He hated the insecurity of the future and the prospect of looking for a different job. He and Jennifer had only been married a year, and he hated the idea of having to move. He wanted nothing more than a job at University Hospital.

Dr. Taylor continued, "I'm on the board of our private practice group and it would give me a great deal of pleasure to sponsor you here." He paused, letting the words sink in. He spoke slowly, "I could also strongly support a faculty appointment at Harvard."

Tim could not believe what he was hearing. Although Dr. Taylor was in an area of medicine that was still considered experimental, he was well respected. To have his backing would practically guarantee Tim a position.

Taylor noted Tim's smile. "Tim, I don't want you to think that this second item of business has anything to do with the first. You know me well enough to know that if you decline, I will still strongly support your position here," he paused. "But I have a dire need for one more sperm donation from you. Our experiments have come to a point where we have nearly perfected the ability to store sperm over a long period of time and to look at genetic material. You have remarkable genetic findings and certain alleles, which we want to study further. I need just one more specimen."

Tim barely heard Taylor's speech. His mind was busy envisioning a secured position at Harvard. Everything he had been working for these past years was within his reach. Tim's decision not to donate again now seemed petty. It would be unreasonable to refuse Dr. Taylor's request when he was offering Tim so much.

"Okay. I'll donate one more time, just for old time's sake," Tim quipped, "But you don't need to pay me—this one's on the house."

"Excellent. I'll need the specimen Wednesday morning so that we'll have fresh material for our final experiments. I can't tell you what this means to me."

Nine

1981

"Where are the rakes?" Tim called from the garage. He was home earlier than usual from Saturday rounds.

Jennifer, working in the kitchen, answered, "In the cabinet at the back of the garage, to the left. You can't miss them." She sighed as she thought for the hundredth time, *If you ever spent any time at home, you'd know where they were.*

Tim found the rake and went out to the front lawn to rake leaves. It was a beautiful afternoon. Ten years ago, after establishing his practice, he and Jennifer looked for an upper middle class community, in the suburbs, with a good school system. Needham appeared to fit the bill. The homes were well maintained, some of them quite expensive, with spacious grounds. There were plenty of open fields and parks where the children could play. The town had a small square and shops. It was a place where the professional people of Boston lived. The trip down Route 9 early in the morning could be made in twenty minutes. It was, Tim felt, an ideal setting.

The house they had bought was a classic New England colonial, white with green shutters. Jennifer had decorated the interior exquisitely, and expensively. She quickly adapted to this new community, leaving her lower class background behind. She had no trouble making friends with the neighbors, and was soon immersed in play dates, fundraisers, and potlucks.

Their son Jonathan was born two years after Tim finished his training. Jennifer experienced complications, her placenta was incorporated into her uterus and she had to undergo an emergency hysterectomy to control the severe bleeding. She barely survived the operation and would be unable to bear any more children. Tim had been tied up in the operating room while this was happening, and was not with her when she needed him most. For this, Jennifer had never forgiven him. She had always dreamed of having a big family, and she somehow blamed him for destroying that dream. Their perfect relationship and their ideal marriage had become strained. He loved her, and he believed that she loved him, but time and circumstances had changed them. She was a nurse and Tim thought she should have been able to understand the long nights, long weekends, endless hours in the operating room and all the other demands made of a surgeon. She coped by devoting her life to her home and to their son.

Jennifer came to the front door and called to Tim, "I'm going to pick up Jonathan. They're through playing football and he needs a ride home."

Tim waved back. "Okay, I'll be here."

As he watched Jennifer back out of the driveway he wondered where the time had gone. Jon was already twelve years old. He loved football and baseball. Each year he was on the Little League all-star team. When his team played, the opposing coach sometimes questioned if Jon was a ringer, because he was so big for his age. More than once Jennifer had to produce a birth certificate. Although he was an only child, Jon was not the least bit spoiled. He rarely gave them any problems. He was enthusiastic about his schoolwork and sports and he worked hard on and off the field.

Last spring had been Jon's last Little League game. He would be moving up to American Legion baseball. The coaches, who had followed his progress, were eager to have him play. *A chip off the old block.* Tim couldn't help being proud of him, even though he had not spent much time with him over the years. He was too busy with his neurosurgery practice in Boston. He had missed so many games that it was assumed that Jennifer was divorced. Now that his practice was firmly established and he had partners to share the burden, Tim vowed that he would spend more time with his family. He could see the years slipping away and often felt as if he were on the outside looking in. Jennifer and Jonathan had become a family of their own, out of necessity. *I'm going to change all that. My family is going to be my number one priority.*

Jennifer drove into the driveway and before she'd pulled to a stop, Jon was out the door and running to where Tim was raking leaves.

"Dad! I threw two touchdown passes!"

"Way to go!" As proud as he was of Jon's athletic ability, he secretly hoped Jon would opt for just baseball. He had tried to put the events of his own childhood behind him, but he couldn't be a father without worrying about the safety of his own son, and football was certainly the more dangerous sport. "Are you going to keep playing football and baseball when you get to high school?"

Jon paused before answering his father's question. "I love football, but I know Mom thinks it's too rough. She wants to be sure my grades don't slip, so she said I have to choose only one sport during the school year. I guess I really like baseball the best. Besides, I'm years away from getting my driver's license, and Mom's getting tired of taking me to all my practices and all my games."

Tim was at a loss for words. For Jon to have so much insight into the family dynamics amazed him. He was sensitive enough to leave out the part about his father *never* having time for practices or games, but the unspoken words hung in the air between them.

The front door opened and Jennifer called out, "Lunch is ready. Then the two of you can move on to the backyard and tackle those leaves."

Tim dragged the barrel and the rake around to the back of the house and went in through the kitchen door. He felt like a stranger in his own home. His wife and son shared a bond that he had not even recognized. His wife had established a life for herself and their son, while he remained on the periphery. That this had been his choice did not make it any easier to accept. He definitely needed to spend more time at home.

*   *   *

It had been four years since Tim had resolved to spend more time with his family. He signed out more often and allowed his junior associates to assume more responsibility for the practice. Initially, this had been very difficult. He was considered one of the leading neurosurgeons in the world. He was always being asked to speak at medical conferences and this required much traveling. He had worked long and hard to be the surgeon that he was. He could cut back, but never give up all that he had attained. He thrived on the respect and admiration of the medical community, and, of course, there was his first love, the surgery itself.

Jon's sophomore year in high school was devoted to studying and baseball. His pitching and batting made Needham one of the highest ranked high school teams in the state. During league play, Needham was undefeated. Tim, for his part, was making a real effort to spend more time with his son. On Saturdays, instead of making rounds, he would attend Jon's games. He tried his best to get to the weekday games, but his practice was demanding, so this was rarely possible. Tomorrow, however, was the first game of the play-offs, and his son was pitching. He had already told anyone who would listen that he was going to the game, no matter what, and he had arranged his schedule accordingly.

Friday evening Tim was home early enough to have dinner with Jennifer and Jon. Jon knew his dad was going to be at his game the next day, but he asked anyway, "Are you going to be able to make my game tomorrow, Dad?"

"I was thinking I'd play golf instead." He grinned. "Of course I'll be there. I wouldn't miss it for the world."

"The coach says I've been pitching 'consistent enough' to start tomorrow, which is high praise from him."

Jennifer smiled, looking relaxed and happy. It had been years since Tim had seen such contentment on her face. It seemed they were finally getting back to where they had been at the beginning of their relationship.

Tim and Jon helped Jennifer clear the table then she shooed them out of the kitchen so that she could do the dishes. In the living room, Tim sat down to read the newspaper. Jon hesitated before turning on the television.

"Dad . . . ?"

Tim waited for Jon to continue.

"I've had this headache for the past few days . . ." Jon was pointing to the right side of his head as he spoke and Tim's heart sank. *Don't over-react. How could that happen twice in one family? Besides, my dad never had a problem with an aneurysm, and neither did my brothers. The kid's been under a lot of pressure. The coaches work the players hard, it's hot, and the play-offs mean everything to them.*

61

"It's probably just nerves. Tomorrow's a big day. I'm not surprised that you have a little headache."

"The first time Needham High has been in the play-offs in ten years? Yeah, I'm nervous all right."

"Here's what you do. Take a couple of aspirin and go to bed early tonight. Get a good night's sleep and we'll see how you feel in the morning. I'm sure it's nothing to worry about." He gave Jon his most reassuring smile.

"Okay. I'm going to finish some homework." He went to kiss his mother good night.

Jennifer said good night to Jonathan and went looking for Tim. "Jonathan said something about a headache?" she asked with concern.

"I gave him my usual prescription, 'take two aspirin and call me in the morning'." He reached up and pulled her into his lap.

Jennifer laughed, but pulled herself up again. "It is unusual for Jonathan to complain about anything."

"I think we can let him go ahead and play tomorrow if he feels all right."

"Who am I to argue with the great Dr. Graves?" She kissed him playfully and then looked at him more seriously. "It means so much to him that you've been coming to his games. His whole attitude has changed. He's more confident . . . "

Tim brushed off the compliment. "You'd been telling me for years how much I was missing, and you were right. I'm just glad I didn't wait until it was too late."

The next morning when Jon came down for breakfast, Tim looked at him with concern.

"Do you feel all right?"

"I feel great. Headache's gone. Don't forget the game starts at one, but you might want to get to the school early to get a good seat. It's going to be crowded." Jon had to be at the field at eleven, but he was driving himself. Tim marvelled that his son was old enough to be driving himself to games.

Jennifer tried to keep the worry out of her voice. "We'll be there, front and center."

When Jonathan went upstairs, Jennifer turned to Tim, "Do you really think his headache is gone, or does he just want to play so badly that it doesn't matter?"

"I think he'd tell us if it hadn't gone away." He got up from the table and carried his dishes to the sink.

"I'm going to go in and make quick rounds. I'll be back by noon and we'll go to the game together." He kissed Jennifer and went out to his car.

It was hot and humid for early May. By the time they arrived at the field Tim's shirt was already damp. Walking to the stands, they watched Jon's team finish fielding practice. Tim pointed to a spot in the stands that was shaded by a large maple tree. He and Jennifer settled in their seats and waited anxiously for the game to begin.

By the sixth inning the score was 2-0 and Jonathan had allowed no hits and showed no signs of tiring. His fastball was in the 80-mile-per hour range and his curve ball had a life of its own. Tim smiled at Jennifer, whose eyes shone with pride. In the bottom of the sixth Jon called a time-out and waved the coach to the mound. He had pulled off his hat and was rubbing his forehead, squeezing down on his eyes with his thumb and forefinger.

"Coach, I don't know if I can keep pitching. It's either the hot weather or this headache. I've had it off and on all week, and now it's back. I don't think I can go on."

The coach immediately motioned for a pitcher to warm up. He turned back to Jon and said, "That's okay, son. Don't worry. You've done a fine job out here today. Let's give someone else a chance."

Jon sighed heavily, kicked the dust and walked toward the dugout. Suddenly his vision blurred and the grass came up to meet him. He fell to one side and collapsed on the ground. The coach, who had his back turned away from Jonathan, sensed him falling and yelled, "Jesus!" The players from the bench immediately ran to where Jon was lying.

Jennifer screamed and Tim tore from the stands and sprinted down the sidelines to his son. His trained eye immediately took in the situation. Jon's pupils were pointing backward and to the left. He began to have a generalized convulsion and lost control of his bladder. He arched his back and began to breathe hard. Tim tried to remain calm, but his voice quivered as he ordered, "Call an ambulance, now." The coach ran to the gym and made the call.

When Jon's seizure was over he went limp and Tim could barely feel his pulse. His breathing was easier, but his pupils were pinpoint and he was unconscious. Jennifer hovered in the background, too much in shock to make any sense of what was happening. Her nurse's training told her that her son was gravely ill, but she couldn't think of a thing to do to help him. She would have to trust that Tim would take care of Jonathan.

An ambulance arrived within minutes. Jon continued with a weak pulse and his color was pale. Tim shouted to the driver to take him to University Hospital, shivering at the sense of déjà vu. *Not again,* he thought. *What have I let happen?*

At the hospital Jon's trachea was rapidly intubated, an IV was started and a urinary catheter placed. He was given medication to shrink his brain because his pupils had dilated. He was taken immediately for a CAT scan. During the scan he had another seizure, resulting in cardiac arrest. CPR was used to restore his heart. On his return to the Emergency Room he suffered yet another cardiac arrest. The ER doctors worked to resuscitate him.

Tim had to stand by helplessly while the Emergency Room team worked on his son. He ran to Radiology and looked at the CAT scan. He could see the deviation of the brain from the right side to the left. The right side was swollen and he did not see a subdural hematoma. *He wasn't hit on the head. There is no blood outside the brain itself. He must have hemorrhaged, from...an aneurysm? What was going on?*

He ran back to the Emergency Room to alert the doctors about the CAT scan results. But after an hour of trying to get the boy's heart started again, the doctors had just abandoned their attempt at resuscitation. Approximately two hours after his collapse on the baseball field, Jonathan Graves was dead.

The ER doctor attempted to console Tim, but he pulled away and broke down and cried. Jennifer rushed in and became hysterical at the news. "What happened?" she screamed at Tim. "How could you let this happen to my son?"

Tim pulled himself together and tried to calm Jennifer. He looked down at the floor and shook his head. "I don't know. It looks like he must have bled from an aneurysm."

"An aneurysm? You said his headaches were 'nothing.' You

said he was just under 'stress' because of the game!" She was screaming. "He tried to tell you he was sick! But you're always too busy for us. And now you've let him die! You killed my son!"

Tim finally got Jennifer to lie down in a private room off the Emergency Room. He had asked a nurse to call J.C. Parker. His old roommate had joined the faculty back at University Hospital several years after he completed his training at Columbia. He and Tim had maintained the close relationship they had had during medical school.

An hour later, J.C. rushed in to find Jennifer lying on a couch in the quiet room, sedated, her face deathly white and streaked with tears. She did not acknowledge him. Tim was slumped in a corner, incapable of speech.

J.C. kneeled in front of him and grabbed his shoulder. "What happened?"

Tim barely looked up. "He collapsed during a game today. He had an intracerebral bleed. He died after the second cardiac arrest. It's my fault." He looked over at Jennifer.

"Take it easy, Tim. I'm going to talk to some people, make sure everything's taken care of. Then I'll be back."

J.C. made a move toward Jennifer, saw that she was beyond caring, and left the room to talk to the head nurse and track down the doctors who had treated Jon. When J.C. returned, there was no sign that either Tim or Jennifer had moved. They were too shell-shocked.

J.C. whispered to Tim, "I called your partner in to go over the CT scan with me. He thinks it was a ruptured aneurysm. The only way to confirm it is with an autopsy. We can have it done today. Dr. Speaks is willing to come in and do it as soon as he gets the word. He'll need your permission. We can limit it to just the head if that's what you want."

Tim looked to Jennifer for an answer, but she was clearly incapable of making any decision. He merely nodded to J.C. and then closed his eyes. Normally this is what doctors do, he reminded himself. *Look for the explanation.* Knowing what happened somehow made it bearable. Made it make sense. Now Tim was struck by the futility of this. He already knew what had happened. His son was dead. There would never be anything bearable about it. It would never make sense.

Several hours late, J.C. drove Jennifer and Tim home. He waited in the living room while Tim put Jennifer to bed. She was wailing uncontrollably, crying out for Jonathan and her mother. He gave her a sedative and waited until she drifted off. Tim came downstairs and sat with J.C.

"It's my fault, J.C.," Tim said, tears running down his face.

J.C. had never seen his friend show so much emotion. He leaned in, wondering if he should hug him. "Stop it, Tim. There's nothing you could have done to stop this. There's no way you could have known."

"He told me had a headache yesterday . . . "

J.C. interrupted him. "A kid with a headache? Come on. You couldn't have diagnosed it from that . . . "

"Stop!" Tim shouted. J.C. looked at his friend in surprise.

Tim took a breath. Without looking up, he whispered, "I never told anyone this, but I had a right sided cerebral aneurysm that ruptured while I was playing baseball. Almost identical to what happened to Jon. I was rushed to the hospital. Only the neurosurgeon there saved me. He clipped my aneurysm."

J.C. was stunned. "Why didn't you ever tell me?"

Tim made no response.

"How could a father and son have a cerebral aneurysm on the same side unless it was inherited?" J.C. asked with a frown. "Is there a family history?"

"No! No one in my family had ever had this problem. My brothers are healthy. My dad has high blood pressure, but otherwise he's in excellent health. My mother has no medical problems . . . there's no history on either side of the family. I figured I was just an isolated case. "

"It doesn't make any sense," J.C. said. "Does Jennifer know?"

Tim shook his head. "I couldn't tell her. I wanted to forget it ever happened. I almost had—I hardly remember it. But last night when Jon complained about a headache . . . it scared me. But I just pushed the thought away. I told him to take aspirin! I should have paid more attention. She'll never forgive me. And I don't blame her."

J.C. remained focused.

"She'll have to be told." J.C. knew that Jennifer and Tim had

had their problems and this certainly wasn't going to help their marriage. "Sometimes women handle these things better than men. I wouldn't wait too long to tell her. If she finds out from someone else, it would be even worse."

"How could I have known that my aneurysm might have been hereditary?"

"Do your parents know what happened? Do Jennifer's parents know?"

"Oh God. I haven't thought that far ahead."

"Do you want me to call your folks? I can give them the news and then you can talk to them later."

Tim thought for several seconds and decided that this was not his style. He always faced his problems. He wasn't about to shirk this responsibility. Jonathan had spent several weeks last summer with his grandparents in California. They were deeply fond of each other. He knew what he had to do. He went to the phone in the library and dialed his parents' home number. On the third ring his mother picked up.

"Hello. Graves residence."

"Mom, it's Tim."

"Tim . . . you sound terrible. What's wrong?"

"I've got bad news, Mom. It's Jonathan. He . . . he died today."

"Oh, my God!" she inhaled sharply. "What happened?"

"He was pitching in the first play-off game and had a seizure. We rushed him to the hospital, but he died before we could do anything. A CT scan showed he probably had a cerebral aneurysm." Tim's voice broke as he struggled to continue. "Why would he? No one in the family has ever had one, except for me."

There was silence on the other end of the line.

"Hello? Mom, are you still there?"

After a further pause, she came back with a weak voice, "I'm sorry, Tim. I have to go find your father. I have to tell him what happened. I'm sorry, Tim. I have to go now." She hung up. Tim replaced the phone—his mother's reaction jarred him. Before he could consider it further, the doorbell rang and Tim went to open the door. It was Helen, J.C.'s wife.

"Tim, what can I say?" Helen said as she hugged him. She planned to stay with Jennifer while Tim and J.C. went back to the hospital to pick up Tim's car. J.C. thought it would be a good idea to get Tim out of the house for a while.

When Tim and J.C. returned home, Helen told Tim that his mother had called. She wanted to know about funeral arrangements. Helen assumed they wanted to make travel plans, but his mother said that she and Dr. Graves would not be able to come for the funeral, but that they wanted to send flowers. This sounded so absurd that Tim immediately called home. His mother would only say that his father could not get away and that she could not leave him there alone. His father refused to talk to him, and Tim was baffled. They had just lost their grandson and they want to know where to send flowers? Had the whole world gone crazy? He slammed down the phone. At a time when he needed them the most, they could not bother to be there for him. *How much is a man supposed to take?* He vowed never to speak to them again.

Ten

Six weeks after Jon died, Tim could not put it off any longer. He chose a beautiful Sunday afternoon in late June. He packed a lunch and convinced Jennifer to take a drive over to the Wellesley College campus. She'd moved through the weeks since the funeral in a daze. Her mother had been staying with them, trying to help her daughter regain her grip on reality. Even church—she'd attended Catholic mass every Sunday since she was a child—was no comfort. It too, reminded her of Jonathan. He had been an altar boy.

Green grass rolled like a carpet down to the still lake that centered the campus. As Tim strolled beside the water with Jennifer, she seemed to perk up—or at least take an interest in her surroundings. There were few students around on a summer Sunday afternoon, and it felt as if they had the campus to themselves. Tim stopped at a bench along the path overlooking the lake and they sat. He offered her a sandwich, which she politely refused. He gazed out at the lake, mesmerized by the water rippling when a light breeze played across its surface. Suddenly he blurted, "I blame myself for Jon's death."

"His name is Jonathan. I always hated it when you called him Jon." She took a breath, as if this outburst had sapped all her energy. In a more controlled voice she stated, "You didn't give him the aneurysm." It was the closest she could get to not blaming him.

"I'm afraid I did."

She looked at him blankly.

He suddenly got cold feet. For just a moment she had seemed like the old Jennifer, until he had started talking. *There will never be a good time for this.*

"There is something I never told you, never told anyone. Few people outside my family know. When I was in high school, I had an accident similar to what happened to Jon...Jonathan. My

69

father was there when it happened and he rushed me to the hospital. They were able to operate . . . and clip the aneurysm." He said all this without looking at her, staring out at the lake.

She couldn't believe what she was hearing. "Why in the world would you keep something like this from me, your wife, the mother of your child?" she sputtered.

"I don't know. It happened and I recovered. I just wanted to put it behind me and never think about it again." He paused, searching for a better answer. "Nobody wants a doctor who's flawed."

"Didn't it ever occur to you that Jonathan might inherit this?" She was furious.

"No one in my family had ever had a problem. We thought it was a fluke. It never crossed my mind that it might be hereditary."

"My God!" She raised her eyes heavenward. What he was confessing was still sinking in. "If I'd known . . . I might have pushed for some explanation for the headaches he'd been having," she turned on him. "Jonathan could be alive today if you hadn't been so self-involved about your medical history. What right did you have to play God with my son's life?"

"The headaches he was having didn't sound serious, like the kind you'd expect with a cerebral aneurysm. I ought to know."

"Yes, you ought to know. Did you shine it on so that he could play that baseball game that meant so much to you? Did you even listen to him at all?"

That was the question that had been haunting Tim since Jonathan died. If Jonathan had been Tim's patient, he certainly would have pursued the headaches more aggressively, knowing his father had a history of a cerebral aneurysm.

"This is too much," she said, crying. "I don't see how I can live with you after this."

"I would give everything I have to change what happened."

"Take me home," was all Jennifer could manage.

Over the next month, they barely spoke. Jennifer was depressed and withdrawn. During the day she would drive to her mother's and spend the day. She would come home at night and go straight to bed. She refused all calls. Tim was left to fend for himself. When he tried to confront her, she told him as far as she was concerned, their marriage was as dead as Jonathan was. Tim begged her to try counseling. She only shook her head in disgust. There was nothing more to do. Three months after Jonathan's funeral, Tim moved out. It was time for both of them to get on with whatever they could salvage of their lives.

Jennifer was working with a real estate agent to sell their house. With the exception of his few personal possessions, Tim had given the house and everything in it to her. His guilt did not allow him to protest when she asked for a divorce. He still loved her, but she neither wanted nor needed him. She was right. He had been too wrapped up in his practice to pay proper attention to his family. His negligence had probably cost them their son. He couldn't change things now, and to fight the divorce would only cause them both more pain. The movers had packed up Tim's desk, the spare mattress in the garage, a rug his parents had given them as a wedding present (which Jennifer had never liked), a trunk full of sweaters and coats, two suitcases of clothes and a framed picture of his son, holding up his first baseball glove. By nine o'clock that Monday morning Tim was rolling out the rug in his new apartment in Chestnut Hill. There was nothing more to do. His marriage was over and now he was left with a mattress on the floor and surgery at noon.

Tim didn't waste any time getting back to work. Actually, he had never really stopped working. J.C. had urged him to take some time off, but Tim didn't need more time to think about his life falling apart. Work was the glue that was holding him together. People at the hospital avoided him, either out of pity or embarrassment. Few knew how to behave around him, so they stayed away. He did receive condolences from Dr. Taylor and Nurse O'Reilly, and, surprisingly, from Dr. McConnell. Tim knew that McConnell probably took some sadistic pleasure in seeing him suffer, but his words seemed sincere enough on the surface.

Going about his business as usual was not as easy as he had thought it would be. He was late to the operating room, didn't get to rounds until late morning, missed most of his office hours and his patient charts were sloppy. His paperwork at the hospital was piling up and he couldn't seem to get a handle on it. He was merely going through the motions of being a doctor, and it showed. He had lost weight and often did not bother to shave. People noticed and people talked. J.C. caught up with him one day and took him aside. He looked serious and didn't mince words.

"Tim, everyone feels terrible for you, but you have to pull yourself together. The medical group is complaining that you continue to take a big salary but you're not pulling your weight. They're tired of covering for you."

"The same people that I've carried for so many years?"

"Everyone knows what you've been going through, but it's been over three months now. McConnell's Chief of Staff. You know he's out to get you, and he won't miss this opportunity. He's already talking about reviewing your cases and cutting your salary."

"Would it do any good if I talk to him?

"I don't think so. Take a month off. Regroup, and come back fresh."

"I could take a year off, J.C., and everything would still be the same. I've lost my wife, my son is dead, and I'm living alone in an apartment. Where do I go from here?"

J.C. didn't know how to respond. Something had to be done, however, before the vultures started circling. McConnell had waited a long time to take part in the downfall of the great Dr. Tim Graves. J.C., as his friend, had tried to warn him. The rest would have to be up to Tim.

***

This Friday morning he dragged himself out of bed, as usual. Tim had spent the past six months barely dodging bullets. He'd managed to function just well enough to get by, but it certainly was not a stellar performance. He stared at himself in the mirror before turning on the shower. Tonight was the big party honoring Dr. Taylor on his sixty-second birthday, and he had to put in an appearance. It was rumored that this would be Taylor's last year at the hospital and the hospital administration had planned this event to show their gratitude for all that Taylor had brought to the hospital with his innovations in fertility and in vitro fertilization.

On Tim's part, extra effort in the grooming department

72

would be necessary. He was badly in need of a haircut, but he had two cases in surgery, plus office hours this afternoon, which he swore to his secretary he wouldn't miss. He would have to take his tuxedo to work with him and change at the office so that he could get to the Hilton in time for cocktails. That was one thing he could appreciate these days, free booze.

Tim was not looking forward to mingling with the crowd coming out for Taylor's big bash. The room would be filled with doctors, with their egos taking up the most space. Tim could predict the flexing of muscles and showmanship, as if the party was more about them being invited than the man who was being honored. Tim hadn't always been so cynical about the medical community, but having experienced firsthand the selfish reactions to his personal tragedies, his view was somewhat jaded. He realized that there was a world within the hospital that he had ignored for a long time, and it frightened him. This was a world of politics, and jealousies and retribution. This was a world in which the unscrupulous prevailed.

At ten past five Tim locked his office door. He had seen his last patient of the day and the secretaries had left to begin the weekend. Tim went to the closet where he had hung his tuxedo that morning. He draped it over the leather chair in front of his desk and noticed a folded piece of paper pinned to the plastic dry cleaning bag. It had not been there that morning. He unpinned the note and read, "Enjoy yourself tonight, and be good." It was from his secretary, Judith, who never stopped trying to cheer him up. Tim chuckled and shook his head. He would try to enjoy himself, in spite of the company.

Earlier that day he had almost changed his mind about going. The entire hospital was talking about the "big birthday party" and he heard that the local news station was going to be covering some of it. He thought that all the hype might be more than he could handle. But Tim didn't want to have to make excuses to Taylor about why he'd missed his celebration, the culmination of years of hard work. Taylor would know if he didn't go. He seemed to find out everything about everybody. Besides, Tim was grateful for Taylor's help over the years—during his residency, and especially his support in securing a faculty position. Tim had to show his respect, if not for Taylor's benefit, then to

73

honor his own sense of loyalty.

At a quarter to six, Tim was in a cab heading toward the wharf. The traffic was horrible, as expected, but the Irish cabbie managed to take advantage of the slightest opening, and they were in sight of the Hilton in record time. Limousines and news vans lined the entire block in front of the hotel. Tim noticed groups of people dressed in tuxedos and evening gowns making their way to the entrance, their heads bowed against the gusts of wind coming off the ocean. The cabbie cursed under his breath and looked at Tim through the rearview mirror.

"Buddy, I think you'd better get out and walk. We're not going to be moving any time soon."

Tim handed him twenty dollars and stepped out into the street. He wove his way through the cars to the sidewalk. He was reluctant to join any of the groups and slowed his steps accordingly. As he got closer to the doors, however, he was caught up in the crowd of people pushing into the lobby. Fortunately, no one had noticed him so far. He was grateful for that. He had to admit that he was hoping to have at least one drink under his belt before he attempted to "mingle."

Following the sound of music, Tim eased his way through one of the sets of double doors leading to the main ballroom. There were at least a hundred round tables covered with dark green tablecloths. Each table displayed an elaborate centerpiece of foxgloves, hyacinths, gladiolas, roses, and irises. The flowers alone must have set the hospital back thousands of dollars. There were small votive candles at each place setting, which created the only light in the room. After Tim's eyes adjusted, he was impressed with the atmosphere that had been created. The dim lighting flattered and enhanced. The women appeared younger, their features softened by the candlelight. For the men, the candlelight was equally forgiving. Against the wall at the far end of the room was a massive platform with two long tables flanking a center podium. Above this, on the wall, was an enormous black and white picture of Dr. Taylor. The picture had probably been taken thirty years ago, and it was a young, round faced Dr. Taylor who presided over the room. *Leave it to Taylor. He's reached a new high on the arrogance scale. Yet, somehow he can get away with it!* Tim went in search of that much-needed

74

drink. It was going to be a long evening.

As he waited in line at the bar, bits of conversation floated around him. One elderly lady was talking about her grandson, who had recently been accepted at Harvard Medical School. Her family had been neighbors of the Taylor family back in Newton, and she used to walk home from school with "little Malcolm." The young man she was talking with could not imagine that there ever was a "little Malcolm," and said so. There was a time when Tim might have joined in the laughter and interjected a witty remark that would have carried him from one conversation to the next for the rest of the evening. Jennifer would have been by his side, jumping into the conversations with him, charming everyone with her ease and humor. Tim realized that this was his first social event without Jennifer by his side. He felt naked, vulnerable, and even a little foolish. He should be laughing, joking, appearing to enjoy himself. He needed an ally. Where was J.C.? Tim scanned the room, but it was too dark to see very far. He decided to take his vodka and tonic and keep moving until he found his friend.

Tim moved self-consciously through the crowd. All the guests had settled into their drinks and chatter. If anyone recognized him, which they surely did, no one said anything to him as he passed. He reached the empty foyer outside the ballroom and still hadn't spotted J.C. He looked around for the men's room. He assumed it would be tucked around a corner, so he walked toward the end of the hall. As he turned the corner he spotted a little alcove on the left which probably led to some restrooms. An attractive red-headed woman looked up at Tim with surprised green eyes. She had been digging in her purse and had not heard him. She was standing in front of a pay phone and gave him an inquiring look.

"I didn't mean to startle you," Tim said. "I . . . do you know where the restrooms are?"

"They should be around here somewhere." She stepped out of the phone cubicle as she spoke and peered down both sides of the hallway. As she swung around to face him, she collided with Tim, who was also turning back. They both apologized and Tim backed away. He smiled nervously as he hurried off. She called after him, "Hey, do you have change for a dollar?"

Without pausing to check his pockets, Tim mumbled, "No," and continued walking. The woman shrugged, thinking his curt dismissal would have seemed rude, except that there was something about him. She wasn't sure what that something was, but it might be worth pursuing.

After dinner had been served and all the speeches were made, the orchestra started up again with some oldies. Most people left their tables, wanting a change of pace, and filtered onto the dance floor. Tim had found J.C. and Helen and retreated to the safety of their table. Now, he remained in his chair, watching his friend escort his wife to the floor. He was left alone with plates of half-eaten cake and empty coffee cups. He wasn't aware that the redhead had been watching him all through dinner. She had spotted him when she returned to her seat. His table was a few in front of hers and she had a clear view of him. She had noticed immediately that he did not have a dinner partner and he did not appear to be enjoying the festivities. Although she was there on assignment, covering the story of Dr. Taylor's accomplishments, the melancholy man she had encountered by the pay phone was far more interesting. After an hour or so of light conversation, she felt comfortable enough with Jan, the young female doctor seated next to her, to ask about him. She had introduced herself simply as "Meg," not revealing her occupation or her last name, in case Jan read the *Globe* and recognized her byline.

"I ran into a man earlier, and we had a conversation about the Cayman Islands. He'd never been there, but he was interested in my trip. Anyway, for the life of me, I can't remember his name and I wanted to give him the name of the place I stayed. Maybe you'd know him?"

"What does he look like?"

"He's sitting right over there," she nodded in Tim's direction.

Jan followed Meg's gaze. When she saw Tim she smiled and turned back to look at the curious woman sitting next to her. Her look suggested that she wasn't surprised that this attractive female would be asking about Dr. Graves. But Jan's smile quickly faded when she spoke, her voice taking on a serious tone.

"That's Dr. Tim Graves."

Meg had heard the name before, though she couldn't place it

at the moment. She didn't want to appear nosey, but the way Jan said his name, told her there was a story here. She decided to probe some more.

"I didn't get a chance to ask about his practice. What does he do?"

"He's a neurosurgeon. You've never heard of him? He's one of the best, or perhaps *the* best." Then she lowered her voice and added, "Though maybe not lately."

"What do you mean?"

The young doctor kept her eyes on Tim while she spoke. "He's going through some rough times. The talk is that it's affecting his work. I can understand why, but most people in this profession are not that forgiving."

Trying to mask her eagerness to learn all the facts, she urged Jan to continue.

"What's his problem?" she asked, innocently.

"He had a son, a bright boy with a lot of talent. About a year ago his son collapsed while he was playing baseball. He died. He had a cerebral aneurysm."

Meg shuddered, "God, that's awful."

"Yeah, and completely unexpected. But that's not the end of it. Shortly after that his wife just up and leaves him."

"Why?"

The young doctor lowered her voice to a whisper and said, "Apparently he hadn't told her that he himself had had a cerebral aneurysm when he was young."

Meg didn't make the connection. "So?" she asked.

"Well, those things could be hereditary. If he had told his wife and taken more precautions about it, if she had just known the danger, then maybe their son wouldn't have died."

"Can you take precautions? Does that work?"

"Oh, yeah. You could have the aneurysm clipped as soon as you know it's there. The problem is knowing whether to look or not. It you suspect an aneurysm, an angiogram can confirm it. Their problem was, they didn't look." She was beginning to sound as if she blamed Tim, too.

"You said it's affecting his work? How so?"

"Oh, he comes in late. He's not around as much. He's a lot thinner than he used to be. Maybe he's drinking a little too much.

You know the kind of things I mean."

Meg didn't like what she was hearing. She imagined the talk that went on behind Dr. Graves' back and wondered if he knew about it. She felt guilty talking about him. She politely excused herself and got up from the table. She made a wide circle of the room, ending at Tim's table. He was still sitting alone, watching the dancers on the floor of the ballroom. She stepped in front of him and said in a playful tone, "Did you ever find that restroom?"

It took a couple of seconds for her face to register with him, then for the first time in a year, he grinned. "Yes, I did. Do you need help finding it?"

"No, not right now." She continued to stand in front of him.

Tim felt awkward sitting while she was standing, so he motioned to the chair next to him. "Would you like to sit down?"

She immediately pulled out the chair. Tim adjusted his chair so that he wouldn't be sitting too close to her and kept his eyes on the dance floor. He wasn't sure what to do next. He felt he had nothing worthwhile to say, especially to this enticing redhead, but he decided there was no harm in some small talk. While he was trying to decide how to begin, she spoke up.

"I didn't properly introduce myself." She extended her hand and waited for Tim to take it. "I'm Meg Logan."

Tim took her hand and continued to clasp it, but didn't say anything.

"And you are . . . ?"

Tim dropped her hand and tripping over his words, managed to say, "Tim Graves. Timothy Graves. Dr. Graves."

Meg laughed, but Tim failed to see the humor. "Well, which do I actually call you? Or who do you really want to be?"

Her tone was glib, yet Tim sensed that she was making more than just a joke. It sounded like she knew him already, or knew something about him. That should have made him uncomfortable, but it didn't. Something about Meg made him feel at ease—and safe.

Meanwhile, Meg was losing her confidence. Perhaps Tim had no sense of humor, maybe he mistook her silliness as an insult. She wasn't trying to make fun of him. She just wanted him to lighten up. She felt her face heat up, blushing being the curse of all redheads. *Damn. I'm making a mess of this. Why doesn't he say something?*

Tim noticed Meg's smile fade and realized he had been staring at her. He shook his head and smiled.

"I'm sorry. My name? That was the question, right?" He looked at her with a hint of humor. "Please call me Tim. He's someone I still recognize." He noticed her reddening face and added, "Are you hot? I mean, you look like you're hot."

This caused Meg's blush to deepen and she couldn't help confessing her own foolishness. "I'm sorry. I'm just a little embarrassed. I mean, here I introduce myself to a total stranger and then I start trying to be funny. You obviously didn't think it was funny. I'm sorry." She nervously brushed her hair away from her face.

"No. It was funny. I'm the one who should be embarrassed. I'm just not very good at this . . . this socializing. Please, let's start over." He stood up and held out his hand. "Hello, my name's Tim. What's yours?"

Meg laughed and gave him her hand. "I'm Meg. Pleased to meet you."

"Maybe I should call you the blushing Meg," Tim said with a grin.

"Oh, I know. Isn't it awful?" Her hands shot up to cover her cheeks.

"It's kind of cute, and it matches your hair."

"Cute, no. Ridiculous, yes."

Even in the dim light Tim could see that she didn't wear much make-up. She didn't have to. She had sparkling green eyes and a wide smile. With her bright red hair, she was really quite captivating.

Meg felt Tim's eyes on her and decided to change the subject. She looked around the room and asked, "So, what is your relation to the great Dr. Taylor?"

"Nothing special." He picked up a spoon and started fiddling with it. "We met when I was a resident at Harvard and he was just starting to make it big. We've been crossing paths ever since."

"You did your residency at Harvard?"

"Med school and residency."

"Impressive."

"Not really," Tim shrugged.

"You're being modest. Harvard has some of the best neuro-surgeons in the world, doesn't it? The best department?"

"There are some superb neurosurgeons there, yes," he stopped short. He looked at Meg more closely, trying to remember if he had ever seen her in the hospital. "Why do you ask about neurosurgeons? What do you know about me?" The question sounded stupid, but Tim didn't know how else to ask.

Meg realized her mistake. She would have to come clean with Tim. "Okay, you caught me. I found out who you are before I came over here. I wanted to talk to you again, and I didn't know how else to go about it. I'm sorry."

"I guess it wouldn't be hard to find out about me in this crowd." He said it without emotion. He was past caring about who talked about him. "What else do you know?"

"I know about your son." Meg knew she was being bold, but there was no point in dissembling now. If she tried to be less than honest she knew that Tim would have no interest in seeing her again, and this was a man Meg would like to get to know. "I'm terribly sorry. I wanted to tell you that."

Tim hadn't expected her to bring Jonathan into the conversation. Nobody ever mentioned his name around Tim, as if the boy had never existed. It was painful, yet it felt good to hear someone talk about him. All the feelings of love and loss that he had tried to suppress came boiling to the surface. *How can a stranger get to me this way?*

"I appreciate your concern. Don't take this the wrong way, but I'm not used to people bringing up Jonathan's death. I've become somewhat of a pariah in this medical community." He looked up at her. "I suppose you know he died of a cerebral aneurysm. He collapsed playing baseball."

"Yes," Meg answered.

"We couldn't do anything for him. It was too late. The thing had blown up. I couldn't do anything to save my own son." Tim spoke evenly, but the pain on his face was obvious.

"Surely you don't blame yourself?" Meg knew that Tim did blame himself, and she knew why.

Tim hesitated. He wasn't sure how much more he wanted to say.

"I do. My wife certainly does."

"Your wife does what?" Meg was curious about Tim's wife. But she could tell by the look on his face she'd pushed too far.

"This is supposed to be a party. Besides, I've told you my darkest secrets, and I don't know a thing about you."

Meg braced herself for the inevitable questions and hoped that Tim would not be put off.

"What brings you to this party?"

"To tell you the truth, I'm here on business."

"What kind of business?" he asked suspiciously.

"I'm covering the Taylor story for the *Globe*." She waited for his reaction. There was none. "I'm a reporter and my editor sent me to do a story about Taylor and his last hurrah."

Tim was interested. "I knew there would be news coverage, but the *Globe*? Taylor's quite the celebrity."

"Sounds as if you aren't particularly fond of the esteemed Dr. Taylor," Meg said.

Tim shrugged this off. "No. He's fine."

"Actually, my editor is close to Taylor. His wife is one of Taylor's patients." She leaned closer to Tim. "My editor owes him."

"I see," Tim said slowly.

"So that's why I'm here. Although, you might say that Dr. Taylor and I have a history," she said with a chuckle. "He tried to pick me up in a bar once—God, it must have been almost twenty-five years ago!"

"So you have a personal interest too."

"I'll have to admit, I lost interest in the Taylor story once I heard about you— speaking from a professional standpoint."

Tim wasn't following her.

She decided to forge ahead. "Your story is very moving. I think a lot of people would be interested in hearing it."

"A lot of people already have heard it. I've been the subject of gossip around the hospital for months."

"No, it would make a great story. They look at you and see a broken man—a great neurosurgeon who had a great life, and who, now, finally, is falling from grace."

"Is that what they see, Ms. Logan?"

Meg heard the disdain in his voice, and she couldn't blame him. This was coming out all wrong. "No, but my point is I think that what people think they know is wrong."

She could see she was losing him. He was retreating before her eyes. He had opened up to her, believing she cared, only to find out that she wanted to print what he had told her. She had to convince him that she did care, and that she wanted to do the story precisely for that reason. "Look, I can see that you think I swindled information from you, pretending to care in order to get a story, but you're wrong. I want to write the story because I do care."

Tim watched her leaning into him, pleading with him with both her words and her green eyes. Those eyes were boring into him and he saw honesty in their intensity. Regardless of her motive, however, she presumed to know a whole lot more about him than he had revealed. "Why didn't you tell me about this before you asked about my son?"

"Because I wanted to find out as much as I could. But so I can help you. That was my first priority."

"Help me? Seems to me your first priority was to find out if I was worthy of a *Globe* article."

She shook her head violently and said, "No, no, no. Look, when I heard about you from some doctor over there, I was angry that this woman was talking about you like she knew what you were thinking and feeling. You were being judged and pitied, but not understood. I mean, where was her compassion? I got the impression that your so-called 'colleagues' revel in the aftermath of your tragedy. I want to tell *your* story, Tim. The neurosurgeon, the father, the devastation of losing a son. But how you're not broken." Meg reached out and covered his hand with her own. "You're a healer, Tim. That's what you do."

Tim was listening to her, dumbfounded. Just then, J.C. flopped down in the chair next to his and slapped Tim on the back, and out of his trance. Meg took her hand away and sat upright in her chair. She looked at Tim, who was looking at her.

J.C. winked at Meg and said to Tim, "When are we going to see you on the dance floor, Tim? If I were you, I'd ask this pretty lady to dance."

Tim hadn't danced with anyone but Jennifer, and after Jonathan was born they had rarely gone out dancing. Since Jennifer had asked him to leave, Tim cursed himself repeatedly for neglecting so many of Jennifer's needs—he thought that providing money to live comfortably was enough, but he had forgotten about the fun and the joy—the things his money couldn't buy.

Tim heard J.C. say something and felt everyone staring at him. They were expecting him to ask Meg to dance. He turned to Meg and saw compassion in her big green eyes. Tim decided it wouldn't be so hard to dance with her.

"Would you like to dance?"

She nodded.

As they reached the dance floor the band was playing the final strains of a slow Sinatra melody. Just as they stepped onto the floor they started pounding out the first chords of "La Bamba." Meg looked at Tim and laughed as he turned back toward their table. She grabbed his hand and pulled him into the music. The steps were coming back to him. Tim was dancing, and he was enjoying it.

When the song finally ended they were both out of breath. They decided to sit the next song out.

"It's been a while," Tim admitted.

"You're pretty good for a guy who's out of practice," Meg replied.

As they were walking back to their table Tim heard his name called out. When he turned around he found himself face to face with McConnell, all decked out in a tuxedo.

"Tim Graves. Good to see you here," McConnell boomed loud enough to cause heads to turn. Tim hadn't spoken to McConnell in years. They would occasionally pass each other in the hospital, but neither was inclined to speak. Tim thought McConnell was a jerk, and McConnell knew it. That McConnell had sent a sympathy card when Jonathan died had surprised Tim. It seemed so out of character.

"How's it going, McConnell?"

"I'm just great. I must say, though, I'm surprised to see you here."

"Oh?"

"I didn't think you'd be out celebrating so soon after your wife left you."

This side of McConnell Tim understood. He was a master at kicking a guy when he's down. He used any excuse to get his digs in, especially in public. This was a game Tim had no interest in playing, not now, not ever.

"Excuse me, McConnell, we have friends waiting."

Tim quickly walked Meg back to J.C.'s table, made his excuses and rushed toward the lobby doors. Suddenly it was all too much for him. He should not have come tonight. Meeting Meg had been like a breath of fresh air, but he couldn't drag her into the quagmire that was his life.

Meg watched helplessly as the doors shut behind Tim.

Eleven

On Saturday morning, Meg skipped breakfast. She had no appetite and no time. She arrived at the newsroom a little after five A.M. She loved Saturday mornings. Everyone was bustling to get the Sunday edition ready for print and there was a certain electricity in the air. Her plan was to spend the morning in the archives of the newspaper and on the phone, ferreting out every bit of information about Dr. Timothy Graves that she could get her hands on. She needed to know his background, where he grew up, where he went to school, what his interests were, what made him tick.

When she returned to her office shortly before noon, on her desk were two releases shuffled over to her by the features editor with a note that said, "Check it out." One release was about a zookeeper who read all the classics while on the job. The other was about a woman turning one hundred fourteen. *Boring!* Meg shoved them aside to make room for the fruits of her morning's labor. "I've got something better," she said aloud.

"But you never want to share it with a poor guy like me," said a voice behind her.

"Mike, I'm actually glad to see you," Meg said as she confronted Mike Argosa, assistant sports editor for the *Boston Globe*.

"Does that mean that we can step into my office and close the door?" Mike asked, with an exaggerated wiggling of his eyebrows.

"You can step into your office and close the door anytime you want. Maybe then you'd get some work done."

"Ouch."

"Seriously, I need your help." Meg knew she had to get past Mike's bullshit before she could get what she wanted.

"Let me guess. You need someone to keep you warm at night. Well, I'm your man."

"Funny. I need you to check your records concerning baseball players, or any athlete, for that matter, dying during a game. Specifically, dying of cerebral aneurysms." Meg felt certain that she had read about an athlete dying from an aneurysm that ruptured during a game, but for the life of her she could not remember where or when.

"Cerebral aneurysms?"

"Yeah, you've heard of them, haven't you?"

"Sure, but what the hell do you want with that kind of information?"

"It's just a story I'm working on and I'd really appreciate the help."

"And what do I get in return for this favor?"

"My deep and profound gratitude, from one journalist to another. Will you do it?"

"I'll see what I can find out, meanwhile, maybe you can come up with a better reward."

Meg had already tuned him out. She was thinking of Tim Graves. She wanted to write this story, if only so she could see him one more time.

After enduring McConnell's snide remarks last night, Tim decided he had better pull himself together. This Saturday morning was the perfect time to start. He would make rounds and then tackle the paperwork he had let pile up for weeks. He thought about the woman he had danced with. Meg with the big green eyes and the luxurious red hair. *She was right. It's time I stop providing grist for the gossip mills.* Last night was the first time in a long time that he actually felt good about himself. Tim went to the hospital thinking about dancing and how there was still some joy to be had in life.

At around three that afternoon, Tim's direct line to his office rang. He had been working at his desk for several hours, and the sudden noise made him jump. Tim picked up the phone, wondering who would be calling him here on a Saturday.

"Hey, Tim."

"J.C.?"

"Yeah. I tried you at home. I'm surprised you're in the office. What's going on?"

"Just trying to catch up," Tim said, yawning.

"Helen and I were worried about you last night. You left so suddenly."

"Sorry. I just felt a little claustrophobic. Thought it was time to get out of there."

"Yeah. So, Tim? When are you gonna finish up there?" J.C. paused. Tim was just starting to realize how odd it was that J.C. was calling him at his office on a Saturday afternoon.

"Another hour or so. Why?"

"I thought maybe we could meet for a beer, you know, at O'Houllihan's." J.C. cleared his throat.

"Okay. I can be there in an hour."

"Good," J.C. said, and he hung up.

Tim put down the receiver and stared at the phone. *I've never heard J.C. sound so glum.*

*　　*　　*

When Meg came back with her pastrami and rye from the corner deli, she found a note on her desk from Mike. He had written, "Good things don't come easy. I've got something for you in my office. M." Meg hoped that the "something" was worth a visit to the lion's den. He couldn't just leave whatever it was on her desk, that would be too easy, and "good things don't come easy." *What a prick. This better be good.* She dropped her purse into the bottom drawer of her desk and made her way through the labyrinth of desks to the sports room. A part of her enjoyed invading this all-male territory. They always welcomed her with enthusiasm, even though she was a mere woman. The sports room was always lively. Radios played constantly, with familiar voices doing commentary on a basketball, football or baseball game—depending on the season. One of the writers Meg had consulted with not too long ago called out to her from a corner. "Good to see you, Meg." She smiled at him and kept walking toward the door of Mike Argosa's office.

Mike was on the phone, but he waved Meg in and pointed to a chair across from him. She chose to remain standing, hoping to get the information she needed and get out quickly. She didn't have time to play games with Mike. She had only been in his office once before and nothing had changed. There were color posters of Larry Bird and Pete Rose, and a couple of other players she didn't recognize. Scattered around the walls in a haphazard fashion were framed photos of players from golf to football, some of them autographed. Meg could read one from where she stood. It read, "To Mike, my last friend—Bill Buckner." She held back a chuckle.

Mike was yelling into the phone something about the commissioner having his thumb up his ass. From the way he looked at her as he spoke, she knew he was trying to impress her with his macho language. When he finally hung up he breathed a deep sigh and leaned back in his chair.

"I get so tired of setting people straight," he said, grinning.

"Did you find something for me?" Meg asked impatiently.

"That depends."

"On what?"

"On what you have for me."

"Come on, Mike, cut the crap and tell me."

"Cut the crap? Gee, I thought all you people over at news were more refined than that."

"Look, I have a story to write. Now, what's the word?"

Mike sensed it would be futile to continue the banter, so he reached for a piece of paper sitting on the corner of his desk.

"All right. I only found one incident. In Wisconsin. A kid collapsed after a football game and later died at the hospital. Cause—cerebral aneurysm."

Meg grabbed the paper out of Mike's hand. The story had been written up in a local Wisconsin newspaper with the headline, "Honor student dies at football game." Scanning through the article, Meg saw that the boy was sixteen when he died, the same age as Jonathan Graves.

"This article is dated 1978," Meg stated, surprised.

"Yeah, seven or eight years ago."

"And this is the only one you found?"

"That's it." Mike locked his hands behind his head. "Is there anything else I can do for you?" he leered.

"I gotta hand it to you Mike, you do persevere, and thanks," she tossed over her shoulder. As she headed out of his office she was already planning her approach to this story. She didn't want to focus solely on the tragedy of Jonathan's death, but she felt that she had the beginning of a great human-interest story. A world renowned neurosurgeon, star pitcher at USC, loses his only son to a cerebral aneurysm on the baseball field—it seemed like a cruel joke; a wild pitch in an otherwise serene and well-ordered life. Meg knew this would be a captivating story for the public to read. She would have to come up with more background, talk to a few experts on sports injuries, lives saved/lives lost. Maybe pertinent for other parents who'd lost children suddenly in this way? This could be a public service story if she could come up with the right approach. She needed a big story to give her career a boost. But really, she wanted more than just to tell a story, she wanted to help Tim Graves start to recover from his losses and live again. She gave herself over to the fantasy of being a part of the new life Tim Graves made for himself, with her help.

O'Houlihan's was on Massachusetts Avenue, where it had been for over a hundred years. It attracted a fairly young, urban crowd, mostly students and fledgling professionals. By the time Tim arrived at four o'clock that Saturday afternoon, the bar was already crowded. The odor of stale cigarettes and sour beer reminded Tim why he rarely went to bars. To the right was a long bar of beautifully polished, dark hardwood with a brass foot rail. Every barstool was occupied, couples and singles drinking and talking. A table for two near the door became available and Tim grabbed it. He thought back to the last time he was in O'Houlihan's, the one and only time. It was the day he graduated from medical school when he and a few classmates had shared some beers. That was twenty-five years ago . . . and plenty had changed since then. Tim breathed in to see if he could recapture that sense of excitement and exhilaration of being a medical school graduate, but it was impossible.

A waitress came up to his table and asked for his order in her thick Boston accent, an accent that Tim had never fully accepted. He had yet to see J.C., so he went ahead and ordered two beers.

"What kind of beer?" she demanded.

"Whatever you recommend." Tim had no idea what to order. J.C. was the big beer drinker. Tim preferred wine.

The waitress shrugged and went back to the bar. A few minutes later the door opened and J.C. came bursting in. He spotted

Tim immediately and sat down in the chair across from him.

"I ordered a beer for you," Tim said.

"What kind?"

"I had a feeling you'd ask that."

The waitress brought two glasses of dark beer and set them down on the table. J.C. took a swig, saying, "I needed this."

"Busy, as usual?"

"Yeah. It seems like the longer I'm in practice the more referrals I get. I've already had to take on two younger members in the department."

"We're busy too. I can barely keep up with the work."

J.C. frowned and looked away. Then he leaned toward Tim and said, "There's something I have to talk to you about."

So Tim was right. Something was up. He waited.

"The talk about your problems at work has gotten worse. It's gotten to McConnell."

"That's not so strange. McConnell's nose is always in my business."

"Maybe so, but this is serious." J.C. hesitated for a moment before he continued. "He's making a big deal out of that patient you lost last week. The cerebral aneurysm you tried to clip. The residents were talking and said that you didn't use good judgment, that you came unglued."

"Hold on. That was a difficult aneurysm." Tim caught himself and looked around, lowering his voice. "It was inaccessible and large, with a broad neck. Just dissecting it out was hard enough. Trying to occlude it was even more complicated." Tim stopped. J.C. didn't say anything.

"Anybody would have gotten into trouble," Tim added halfheartedly.

J.C. rubbed the back of his neck. He still had more to tell.

"I believe you, Tim, but McConnell is out to get your ass. It doesn't matter if you're right or wrong. He's the president of the medical staff, which means he'll use everything in his power to even the score with you."

Tim knew very well what J.C. was talking about. McConnell's academic career hadn't turned out very well for him, so he compensated, like so many doctors do, by becoming involved in the hospital administration. Ever since Tim's residency, McConnell had been jockeying for position in the hierarchy of the staff. He figured that at least he would be influential in the medical staff affairs, if not in the operating room. McConnell learned quickly that the medical staff committees and, subsequently, the officers, wielded power, particularly over the administration. He had started out by serving on committees, and then he became the secretary, and finally medical staff president. Over his six to eight years of climbing the ladder he had learned the bylaws very thoroughly, and was well schooled in the procedures of dismissing members of the medical staff. McConnell was eager to put his power to the test.

J.C. let the other shoe drop. "McConnell's appointing an Ad Hoc Committee, today, to review your cases over the last three months. Word has it that Larken and Jenkins approved it. He's suggesting that there are several other cases where you screwed up. He's gathering up incident reports filed by nurses. Things like you arriving late to the operating room, late to clinics, flying off the handle . . . He's moving on this thing, Tim."

J.C.'s words pierced Tim's soul. He thought he had been through the very worst that could happen to a man, and now this despicable, vile excuse for a doctor wanted to strip him of the only thing he had left, his career. He was the first to admit that he had slipped in recent months, but even a mediocre Dr. Tim Graves was a competent and dedicated physician. This was not a case of doctors policing their own. This was the personal vendetta of one man.

"I've carried those people for so long, and now this? All my years of hard work and it comes down to three people to decide if I can continue to practice medicine?" Tim slowly shook his head.

"I did talk to Taylor before I came over here. You know he's always watched out for you." J.C. paused, and then added, "Anyway, he's on your side."

Tim couldn't help laughing bitterly at the picture J.C. painted. It reminded him of the neighborhood football games and how the kids used to pick sides. He never imagined then that thirty years later he'd still be watching people dividing into teams, preparing to do battle. Tim had a feeling that this time, for the first time, he would be the odd man out.

Tim heard J.C. clear his throat. He was sorry that his friend was caught in the middle. Tim hated involving other people with his problems, even his best friend, but he did appreciate J.C.'s insight. Tim realized that the politics he had spent his entire professional life avoiding were now coming back to haunt him.

"What do you think will happen next?"

"There will be meetings of the Executive Committee to review the results of the Ad Hoc Committee. Then the Executive Committee will make a recommendation. Don't forget, I'm on the Executive Committee and I'll have plenty to say in your favor."

"But?" Tim interjected.

"But, if the Ad Hoc Committee report is unfavorable, you could get suspended."

"What are the chances of that happening?"

"I don't know. McConnell will use everything he has against you, both real and imagined." J.C. waited for Tim to show some sign of emotion, but Tim did not react. He was going to need that old fighting spirit of his. This was not the time to be apathetic.

"He won't get away with it," J.C. insisted. "We're going to fight this thing and screw that son of a bitch."

Tim cracked a smile. If only he could feel some of J.C.'s optimism. Nothing ever seemed to get him down.

"Thanks, J.C. You're a good friend."

"I mean it, man. We're gonna kick some ass." He pounded his fist on the table, more for dramatic effect than serious conviction. This did get the attention of the waitress, and they ordered one more round.

The article said that the boy in Wisconsin had no symptoms that might have alerted his parents. *"...He just collapsed,"* the mother *reported, through her tears.* Standing in her kitchen, perusing the article, Meg wondered what could possibly alert a person to the fact that their head was about to explode. She was convinced that there must be some sort of warning, but she kept coming back to the same puzzle. If there are visible or physical symptoms, wouldn't Tim Graves, a world-renowned neurosurgeon, have noticed them and understood their significance? Meg was reluctant to blame Tim, but she had to wonder if he had missed something in his own son that might have saved his life.

She read through the article again. It described the Wisconsin boy as a quiet boy; a straight A student who worked hard and was well liked by his friends and teachers. The coach of the high school football team said the kid had been the best quarterback he had ever coached. *What a tragedy to lose someone so young and who had so much potential. Life is sometimes so unfair.* Meg looked more closely at the picture they'd chosen for the newspaper article. It was probably a school photo taken that same year. Meg brought the photo closer to her eyes and was surprised to notice something familiar about the boy. There was something so compelling about his face, so honest and innocent. *And so familiar. Sean. Why do I feel as if I know you?*

Twelve

"He got into some bleeding, lost control, and the patient died. He was abusive to the nurses and, basically, not in command of the situation." Larken waited for a reaction from McConnell, but none was forthcoming. He went on with the report. "A resident had to take over the procedure, but it was too late. Dr. Graves did not talk with the family afterward and they were understandably upset. Their grief has turned to anger and they are making noises about suing Dr. Graves and this hospital." Larken paused, looking toward McConnell and Jenkins. Jenkins, the CEO of the hospital, deferred to McConnell. As the president of the Medical Staff, McConnell's decision would carry a lot of weight.

McConnell sat in silence. Of course, what he wanted was an immediate suspension, but he would have to tread softly. He had been waiting years for the opportunity to ruin Tim Graves. He had to think carefully. Both Larken and Jenkins looked to him to make a responsible and impartial judgment, so he couldn't be overzealous. He could suggest trending the issue, which would mean careful observation of Dr. Graves, but what if he didn't mess up again? He would need the approval of the Executive Committee, and while there was much gossip about Tim throughout the hospital, he still had a strong following of friends to support him. McConnell decided to begin with a compromise.

"Well, it sounds on the surface to be very serious, but I think we need to know all the facts before we jump to any conclusions. Cerebral aneurysms are tricky, and there isn't a neurosurgeon anywhere who hasn't gotten into trouble with bleeding at some time in his career. Whether this was an oddball case, or whether it was a 'routine' cerebral aneurysm in which Dr. Graves lost his cool, I can't say based on this incident report. We have to have an in-depth investigation before we can make an informed decision." McConnell stopped, allowing all of his objectivity and fairness to sink in with Larken and Jenkins.

"What are you suggesting?" Jenkins asked.

"I suggest that we establish an Ad Hoc Committee, using three physicians, to review the case and interview all the people who were involved."

Jenkins sat back in his chair and drummed his fingers on the table. "Who will appoint these three physicians?"

"I will," McConnell said.

Jenkins took a moment to ponder the situation. Finally he spoke, "Well, that could be appropriate, but we should remember that Dr. Graves is internationally revered. He brings patients to this hospital from all over the world. As you say, these things sometimes just happen, even to the best. Maybe we should just forget about it until we see if there are going to be any repercussions."

Larken's eyes darted back and forth between Jenkins and McConnell. He knew just how much McConnell wanted to make an issue of Dr. Graves' lapse in judgment, but he did not want the appearance of a witch-hunt. He decided to speak to the issue instead of appearing to align with either side. Larken was the hospital Medical Director and had been retired from clinical practice for ten years. He was at the beck and call of Jenkins and had a reputation as a fence sitter. It was also widely known that he tended to drink more than was good for him.

"I think the medical staff should deal with this problem. All of these proceedings will be confidential and will be done discreetly, without damage to anyone's reputation. If we don't investigate this case, the nurses will think there's some kind of favoritism or cover-up going on. That there's no point in filing an incident report."

McConnell tried to hide his surprise. Larken was actually taking a stand and it was going to work in his favor. It was agreed. An Ad Hoc Committee was to be formed immediately to investigate the conduct of Dr. Timothy Graves. The members of the committee will be appointed by Dr. McConnell. All three men stood and shook hands. The meeting was over.

* * *

When Meg called at five-thirty, Tim's machine picked up. She

95

hung up. When she tried again at six-thirty, she again got his machine. This time she decided to leave a message, but was cut off in mid-sentence.

"Are you screening your calls?" Meg asked.

"Just lately," Tim replied. When he got home after his meeting with J.C., there was a message from McConnell. McConnell said he wanted to talk, and Tim knew that he merely wanted to be the first to deliver the bad news. He had been surprised when he heard Meg start to leave a message. He liked the sound of her voice in his living room.

"Am I bothering you?"

"No, not at all. How are you?"

"I'm fine, but I was concerned about your sudden departure last night."

"Sorry about that. All the people and the noise got to be too much. I needed to get away. It was nothing personal."

"I hope I wasn't the one you needed to get away from?" She was teasing, but there was a question in her voice.

"On the contrary . . . " He let the words hang between them.

Meg found him hard to read. It could be that he was just trying to be polite, but she sensed some interest and she decided to play her hunch.

"I'm going to take your word for it, because I enjoyed last night. I'd like to see you again sometime, if you would. Like to see me, that is."

"Do you eat dinner? I mean, would you like to have dinner with me sometime, or tonight? Or is it too late?"

Meg was delighted. "Dinner tonight would be wonderful. Shall we meet somewhere, say in an hour?"

Tim named his favorite restaurant and said he would wear a red carnation, in case she had forgotten what he looked like. *Fat chance.*

At dinner they found that they had much to talk about. It was as if they had known each other for years. There was something electric in the air, and they both were aware of it. Still, it was clear that Tim had something on his mind, though he made every effort to be the perfect companion, focusing his attention on Meg. She didn't want to spoil the mood, but she did want to satisfy her curiosity about something that had been bothering her.

"Who was that guy we ran into last night, just before you left the party?"

Tim hesitated and then said, "He works with me. He's a doctor."

"He acted so arrogant."

"That wasn't an act. He's an arrogant son of a bitch, and a mediocre doctor."

Meg was surprised. Up to this point, Tim had been so controlled. "Wow, you really don't like him, do you?"

Tim was disgusted with himself. It wasn't like him to be so indiscreet. After all, he barely knew this woman. "Sorry, I'm just . . . I've had kind of a bad day. Up until now," he hastened to add. He didn't want to get into the whole McConnell thing with Meg, or with anyone, for that matter.

Her reporter's antennae went up, but she decided to let it slide for the moment. She didn't want anything to ruin their evening together. There would be time to try to coax the story out of him. She decided to turn the conversation in another direction.

"Do you remember how I told you I want to write a human interest story about you?"

"That I remember."

"So?"

"So what?"

"So, are you going to let me do the story?"

"In the *Globe*? About me? Who would want to read it?"

"I've only scratched the surface of who you are and what you've done, but you seem to have had a remarkable life, and you've made remarkable contributions to the field of medicine. I'm certainly interested in learning more—readers will be too."

Tim looked doubtful. She pressed on. "My thought was to use your story as a human interest lead-in to the subject of sports injuries or deaths on the high school playing field. Who knows, we might even save a life or prevent a serious injury."

Meg stopped. Tim remained quiet, deep in thought. He would hate the attention. But then he thought about the Ad Hoc Committee and his impending suspension. Maybe a story in the *Globe* would create the kind of attention he needed—positive publicity. Also, the hospital always benefited from this type of story, and that could only help his cause. Even thinking this way was so foreign to Tim. He had always succeeded with hard work and fair play. He had never had to strategize about his future, or consider using the media to further, or protect, his career. Now he had to learn to play the game or risk losing everything. This article might be a first step. Besides, it would give him a chance to spend time with Meg.

"What do I have to do?"

"Just answer my questions, be open with me, let me dig around in your past. The usual."

"When will it be published?"

"That depends on how soon I get everything together. Probably next week or the week after."

"Okay, let's go for it."

"You won't be sorry, Tim. Your situation is so unique. I mean, virtually without precedent. People will want to read it."

"Virtually without precedent? What does that mean?"

"I mean, no one has achieved what you've achieved and no one has had to endure what you've endured. That's all." Meg was excited and felt herself getting too carried away. *Slow down, girl. You're beginning to sound like a reporter.*

"I am not unique. I went to medical school and became a doctor. I chose neurosurgery as my field and worked hard to become a good one. I am certainly not the only one to have done this. They also lose children and get divorces. Cerebral aneurysms are not uncommon. There are no mysteries here."

"I understand that, Tim, and I don't want to sound insensitive, but very few children die in the middle of their high school baseball games. That's all I'm saying."

"Oh, since my son died during a baseball game I make a good story?" His voice dripped with sarcasm. He felt that he had been duped. He had wanted to believe that Meg was a reporter with integrity, but it sounded like she was looking for tabloid material.

"No. I knew you'd misunderstand. I'm trying to tell you that your case *is* unique. There was one boy in Wisconsin who collapsed after playing in a high school football game and died of a cerebral aneurysm. That was seven years ago. There had been no other cases, before or since." Meg paused, "And then, Jonathan."

"Wisconsin?"

98

"A sixteen-year-old boy in Wisconsin, star quarterback. It was a tremendous shock for the family."

Tim was silent. He remembered wheeling Jon into the Emergency Room. He thought they would save him. He heard Jon complaining about headaches. *Just take a couple of aspirin, son, it'll go away.* Tim felt sick. He was having trouble breathing. He signaled to the waiter and asked for the check. He couldn't look at Meg. He couldn't think. He couldn't bear the pain of his loss. Somehow he saw Meg to her car and made his way home. She had looked so bewildered, and so hurt. He would call her tomorrow and try to explain. He could do no more tonight.

He was awakened by the ringing of the phone and automatically picked it up.

"Hi, Tim, how's it going? Hope I didn't wake you, but you didn't return my calls."

"What do you want, McConnell?" He was through with being polite to this guy.

"Got some bad news for you, buddy. I thought you should hear it from me."

"Save it. I already know what you're doing."

I knew I'd be too late. Damn. He had been savoring the pleasure of breaking the bad news to Tim, and someone had gotten to him first. He'd have to settle for a little twisting of the knife, then.

"I want you to know that this was a difficult decision to make, but it is a matter of great concern for the hospital. We have to protect our patients," he said condescendingly.

"You have a right to do that. Just don't make it personal, McConnell."

"If this were personal, Graves, I'd have already had you suspended."

"Just do it right. I'll go after you if you don't."

"Are you threatening me, Tim? You have changed. I always took you for a wuss."

Tim ignored his taunts. "Who's reviewing my case?"

"Oh, we've got the neurosurgeon from Tufts, Chief of Anesthesia and Chief of Medicine."

Tim ran his hand over his face. "You've done your homework."

"Actually, I just picked them out of a hat."

"The Chief of Anesthesia and I have been at odds for years, ever since our fight over dedicated neuroanesthesia. Marlow, Chief of Medicine, hates surgeons in general and me in particular. He blocked my academic advancement last year," Tim stated in biting tones.

"Really?" McConnell inquired, all innocence.

"And, as if you didn't know, the neurosurgeon at Tufts has been after my job for as long as I've had it. Sounds like a fair playing field to me."

"If you're clean, then none of that will matter, right, Tim?"

"There was a time when I thought that was true. Come to think of it, I changed my mind about that at about the same time I first met you."

McConnell couldn't think of anything else to say. He wanted to make Tim squirm, but Tim Graves never gave him that satisfaction. That's why McConnell hated him.

"We're meeting next week. I might call you as a witness, so be ready." He was about to hang up when Tim stopped him short.

"One thing, McConnell. How the hell did you ever get Larken and Jenkins to go along with this?"

"Go along with me? They practically suggested it." He hung up while he had the upper hand.

By Tuesday morning the hospital was buzzing with rumors about Tim Graves and his imminent suspension. Word leaked out among the staff that an Ad Hoc Committee, appointed by McConnell, was on a witch-hunt. Although the hospital staff always enjoyed good gossip, they managed to adhere to certain rules of decorum when participating in it. But when Tim arrived at the hospital that morning he noticed a blatant lack of discretion. People were talking openly about his predicament, and it embarrassed him, even though from what he overheard he was generally the object of sympathy rather than scrutiny. The rationale was that the hospital had to protect itself against lawsuits and poor publicity and Tim might just have to be offered up as the sacrificial lamb to the gods of hospital politics. What made the story so irresistible was that there had never before been any question about the ability or integrity of Dr. Tim Graves. Many people understood his loss and the stress he had to deal with in the past nine months, both personally and professionally, while others reveled in his pain. Unfortunately, his fate was to be decided by a small committee of his "peers," most of whom would gladly see him fail.

Tim went through his rounds trying to ignore the gossip, not an easy task. Finally, after checking on his last patient, he ducked into the doctors' lounge. He usually found it empty in the early morning, and he wanted some time alone before he had to face the rest of his day. When he pushed open the door he found J.C. peering into the refrigerator.

"Hey," was all the greeting he could muster.

J.C. knew from Tim's voice that the day had not begun well. He wanted to help his friend, but his hands were tied. All he could hope was that he could be the voice of reason when the time came to speak up at the Executive Committee Meeting.

"How are you holding up?"

"Okay, I guess. Everyone's talking about me, but what else is new?"

"Have you heard who McConnell got for the Ad Hoc?"

"Yeah, three of my very best friends, Hanson, Marlow and Swenson."

J.C. whistled. "Jesus, Tim, McConnell is pulling out all the stops. Amazing that some of our worst enemies are our fellow physicians..."

"That's just it," Tim interrupted. "Why doctors? We should be sticking together, working for a common goal, instead of working to destroy each other." Tim leaned in closer to J.C. "You know, in the twenty-five years that I've been a doctor, I've been more wary of my colleagues than of lawyers, accountants and the IRS."

The door of the doctors' lounge swung open and a young nurse motioned to Tim, "Dr. Graves, they're ready for you in room six."

Thirteen

Dr. Steven Graves had just turned seventy-eight years old. He had been retired for thirteen years—a fulfilling time, since he enjoyed the more leisurely pace after thirty-five years of a busy surgical practice. He maintained good physical condition with jogging, proper diet and keeping his weight down, unlike so many of his friends. When he went to his fifty-fifth class reunion for USC he learned that many of his teammates had died.

His routine was to get up at five-thirty in the morning for his two-mile jog, take a shower, and spend the rest of the day playing golf, gardening and reading. Recently he had noticed some pain in his jaw and left arm after about a mile. He wasn't too concerned, because it didn't seem to affect his heart rate and he didn't become short of breath. He knew the signs of a possible heart problem, however, and reluctantly went to see Dr. John "Jack" Stanley, who he felt confident could detect a problem with a minimum amount of fuss.

Steve decided not to jog in the morning before going to see Dr. Stanley, just in case. After describing his symptoms and receiving a cursory exam, he was referred immediately to a cardiologist for a treadmill stress test. At the conclusion of the test, he heard Dr. Steele say, "You're in great shape, Steve, but I'm afraid your stress test is positive. I had to run you all the way out to the end of the protocol to find it. Your ST segments have changed. Your last treadmill stress test was five years ago, and that was normal. This is a distinct change, and significant enough that I am going to recommend that you have an angiogram."

As a general surgeon, Steve had appreciated the enormous changes in cardiac surgery over the past fifteen years. Patients were having as many as six blood vessels bypassed. There were several heart teams who achieved outstanding results, but he had never thought he would apply these statistics to himself.

"When do you want to do the angiogram?"

"Let's go ahead and admit you this afternoon and we'll do it in the morning."

Steve was given instructions for his admission, shook Dr. Steele's hand, and left the office. The news had a sobering effect on him, but he was hopeful that whatever the angiogram revealed would be minor, possibly something that could be treated with medication. He had been a doctor for a good part of his life, but never a patient. Sally had always taken such care with his diet and encouraged him to exercise. She was going to be shocked.

He broke the news to Sally as soon as he got home and it was just as he expected. She felt responsible for his well being and thought that she had somehow let him down. Theirs was a close and loving relationship. Although Jonathan's death and their estrangement from Tim had tested their marriage, they supported each other one hundred percent.

"What about the boys, Steve? Are you going to tell them?

"Why don't we wait and see what happens with the angiogram. If it's negative, no harm, no foul." He grinned, but Sally wasn't amused. He convinced her, "No point in worrying them if we don't have to."

He and Sally drove to St. Vincent's. After a fitful night's sleep Steve was taken to the catheterization laboratory. Dr. Steele greeted him and without any fanfare positioned the catheters in the right location to shoot his coronaries. Steve experienced some chest pain during the angiogram, but this was relieved with nitroglycerine. It was tolerable, but not a pleasant experience.

Back in the recovery room, Steve and Sally were anxious to hear the outcome of the angiogram. "Well, I've got good news and I've got bad news," Dr. Steele told them. "The good news is that 90 percent of your blood vessels are in excellent shape. The bad news is you have at least a 65 percent left main coronary artery occlusion and a 90 percent proximal right coronary artery occlusion. I could dilate the right coronary artery, but I can't do anything about the left main, so I'm recommending surgery."

Steve was astonished. "I can't believe it. I feel great. Look at me. I'm in great shape for my age. If I hadn't been jogging to try to keep in shape, I wouldn't even have had those symptoms." The irony of his situation amazed him.

"You're right, and you're fortunate that we detected this problem so early. The angiograms don't lie and your symptoms are classic for angina. If you hadn't paid attention to your symptoms you might have suffered a full-blown heart attack while you were jogging. Dr. Kraemer is just finishing in surgery and I've asked him to stop in to see you before you go home."

When Dr. Steele left Steve gave Sally what he hoped was an encouraging smile. "I guess you should call the boys—all three of them." *It's time to patch things up with Tim. Life's too short.* Sally looked ashen. Steve reassured her, "This has become routine surgery, there's no need to worry. Go over to the nurse's station. Tell them who you are, they still remember me around here. They'll call Boston for you."

Sally was visibly shaken as she asked the nurse to use the phone. The nurse readily obliged and she reached Tim's office in Boston. She spoke to Judith, who transferred her call to the recovery room, where she knew Tim would be watching his fresh postop patient.

Tim knew something was wrong.

"Mom? What's happened?"

"Tim. Dad had an angiogram this morning and they want to do bypass surgery as soon as possible. He has two arteries that are blocked off."

"What do they mean by as soon as possible? Today? Tomorrow?"

"I don't know. Dr. Kraemer hasn't been to see him yet. When I know more, I'll call you back. We want you to be here."

"Let me know as soon as you know anything. I'll fly out this evening."

"Thank God you can get away."

"Of course." She didn't need to know why it was so easy to leave at the moment.

The nurse interrupted Sally's conversation to let her know that Dr. Kraemer was going in to see her husband. Sally hurried to Steve's bedside. Right away she saw that Dr. Kraemer was someone who inspired confidence. He and Steve had shared many mutual patients over the years and Steve had no problem placing his life in Dr. Kraemer's capable hands.

"I've reviewed your angiogram and you're going to need

surgery. It doesn't have to be tomorrow, but you should have it done within the week. You can take some time to think about it, but I'd advise you not to delay more than a few days. Just call my office and we'll get you on the schedule."

Steve and Sally nodded.

"By the way, Steve, I don't know if you're aware of this, but there has been some concern about a new disease that's transmitted through blood transfusions. Ordinarily, we don't use blood during an open heart procedure, but we have to have some available, just in case. I'm recommending that patients have family members donate blood for them, since we don't know what this disease is or how to treat it. The blood bank will allow you to designate your donors." Dr. Kraemer spoke some reassuring words to Sally and left.

"Let's take you home," Sally said.

*   *   *

The Ad Hoc Committee met Tuesday evening in the Board Room of the hospital. Swenson, Marlow, Hanson, McConnell and Larken all shook hands and sat down. McConnell was dying to present the case to the group, but he didn't want to appear biased. He decided to pass the buck to Larken.

"We're here to decide whether or not Dr. Graves acted below the standard of care, nothing more, nothing less." Larken reported the details of the complaint and sketched a picture of Tim's behavior based on witnesses and incident reports. When Larken was through with the presentation, the three doctors who were reviewing it shifted uncomfortably in their seats. They had a tough job ahead of them. Dr. Marlow, the Chief of Medicine, wanted to know how long they would have to complete their review.

"As long as you need," Larken replied.

"We have to acknowledge that aneurysms of this type are extremely difficult," Swenson remarked, looking around for some agreement, which he didn't get. "It's always tough to lose a patient on the table, especially one so young."

"What's your point, Swenson?" All eyes focused on McConnell. This was the first time he had spoken since the meeting began and his impatience was evident.

"I'm saying that every neurosurgeon has lost a patient while clipping an aneurysm. It's important for us to look at Dr. Graves' track record here, and not make a judgment on one case alone."

There was an uneasy silence, broken by Dr. Larken. "Maybe we should look at the numbers. That might be a good idea."

"Wait a minute. I thought we were supposed to decide whether or not Dr. Graves acted below the standard of care in this case. That means this case alone. It doesn't matter what he's done before or since," McConnell sputtered.

"You can't expect us to come to a fair conclusion if we don't use all the information at our disposal. Dr. Graves' overall performance as a surgeon is certainly pertinent. We need to know if this was an isolated case of extenuating circumstances, or if he has a pattern of erratic behavior," Swenson responded.

"I agree with Dr. Swenson." It was Marlow who spoke next. "Besides, I'm a little curious about his record."

"I'll get the numbers." Larken excused himself and left the room. *This is fortuitous. I'm glad I pushed to have the outcome data of all patients who were treated here over the past thirty years entered into the new system.*

Entering his office, Larken went straight to the locked file cabinet where he had taped a copy of his password to the inside of the top drawer. It was recommended to the doctors that they use their birth dates as access codes, but Larken had chosen a more secure (and difficult to remember) password. Individual physicians could access only their own patient information, but as Medical Director, he was one of only three people capable of accessing patient data of all the physicians in the hospital.

At his computer terminal he typed in his password and clicked on "patient outcome" and entered "Dr. Timothy Graves/cerebral aneurysms." It would take half an hour or so to collect the data and he decided to wait in his office rather than return to the Board Room. He was uncomfortable reviewing one of the world's finest neurosurgeons and needed some time to think. It seemed wrong to fry Graves over one case. He reached for his copy of the Bylaws of the Medical Staff and read through them again. It clearly stated that where the safety of a patient is

106

concerned, it is appropriate to review the case and the physician. On paper it sounded as if the Executive Committee was taking the appropriate action, but something in Larken's oversized gut told him the entire process was wrong.

When the computer indicated that the search was complete, he printed the results. He stared at them in disbelief. He had had no idea. Larken rushed back to the Board Room, where he found the others examining the cerebral angiogram that was displayed on a portable view box. Swenson looked up from the film he had been viewing and said, "You know, Sandy, this is one hell of an aneurysm."

"But when he got into trouble he decompensated, started shouting at the nurses, his hands were shaking, and the resident had to take over. I don't see why we even have to discuss this. His behavior deserves some serious attention," Hanson stated vehemently.

"I think we should all give some serious attention to this," Larken said, holding up the computer printout. He sat down and hitched his belt up over his belly. The rest of them returned to their chairs. They were eager to hear the numbers.

"Over the last fifteen years Dr. Graves has done 425 cerebral aneurysms." Larken stopped talking and looked around the room. *That number alone should knock their socks off.* "There were two deaths on the table, both of those happened nine years ago. One patient had a cardiac arrest from an air embolus and the other suffered a myocardial infarction."

"Postoperative deaths?" asked Swenson. He was stunned by Tim's record.

"Of the 425 patients, there were forty hospital deaths due to the extent of their underlying disease."

Swenson whistled and said, "Dr. Graves does not sound like somebody we should be reviewing in this committee."

The other doctors were speechless. They couldn't argue with the numbers: it was a near perfect record. This was making McConnell increasingly nervous. He was losing ground and if he didn't come up with something fast, they were going to drop the whole thing. Then Hanson saved the day.

"Let me reiterate that we're not going on past records. We want to know if this is something new, a new behavior that may continue. This is the present we're dealing with, and we have to remember that Graves' life has changed dramatically. Maybe he just can't cut it anymore, and he could become a danger to his patients."

"Only a person who's never been there could say something like that," Swenson scoffed.

"Wait a minute. I give general anesthesia for his cases all the time. I've been there."

"You've been there? You put a tube down the patient's throat and pass him gas. That hardly compares with the responsibility of the neurosurgeon."

Hanson turned red in the face and Marlow stepped in before things got out of hand. "Let's not get personal here. I agree with Dr. Hanson. We're dealing with one incident. While there is no question that Dr. Graves has an excellent record, we have to consider his most recent behavior and make a determination based on what we know today."

"I suggest we hear from a witness." Everyone agreed with Larken. They needed another voice. Larken called in the nurse who had been asked to be available for questioning. Linda Schott, attractive and slightly overweight, was the nurse who had filed the incident report. She settled in her chair and waited for the first question. It came from Hanson.

"Ms. Schott, can you tell us what prompted you to file this incident report?"

"Yes. I was the circulating nurse." She spoke clearly and confidently. "Everything seemed to be going well and then suddenly they got into some bleeding. Dr. Graves began to curse. His hands were shaking and he yelled at me to get some blood. I was upset, because I'd never seen him act like that before. When I got back with the blood the patient's pressure had dropped to forty and the resident was trying to clip the aneurysm. Instead, the resident clipped the entire middle cerebral artery. The brain swelled and the patient had a cardiac arrest."

"Where was Dr. Graves?" asked Swenson.

She hesitated and then said, "Dr. Graves was sitting on a stool, with his head in his hands."

"Had you ever seen him respond to a crisis in this way before?" asked Marlow.

"Never. He was always completely in control."

"Why do you think this time was different?"

"Well, I guess it has to do with his personal life, his son dying, the divorce, you know . . . He just hasn't been the same."

The nurse was excused. The men sat in silence, contemplating what they had heard.

Marlow finally spoke, "I don't think we need to drag in any more witnesses. I've heard enough." Everyone waited to hear what he was going to say. They all knew there was no love lost between him and Tim Graves. "Dr. Graves acted in a way that cost this patient his life. He should be suspended."

Hanson added, "I agree. Dr. Graves must be suspended."

Swenson shook his head. "I don't believe you guys. This is ridiculous. There are only a few neurosurgeons in the world who could have pulled off this surgery." He was getting angry and stopped to collect himself. He didn't want to appear to lose control. "This was a near impossible aneurysm to clip. You can't sew a thing like that. All you can do is suck, compress and pray. If it blows, like this one did, there's nothing to be done. We're just going to ignore the four hundred plus successful procedures and punish Graves for one case of bad luck?"

"I've seen Dr. Graves get out of trouble before. This is not his normal behavior," declared Hanson.

"I agree with Hanson. This might be a trend. One case of bad luck might need to another and another. I'm responsible for writing the report and I'm noting that this committee recommends suspension." Marlow's demeanor suggested he expected no opposition.

"If you write that, Jack, you better also write down that I disagreed with that decision," Swenson demanded.

"That will be duly noted."

Swenson pushed his chair away from the table and stood up. "I'm glad I work across town. I'd hate to work with you piranhas." With his statement hanging in the air, he stormed out of the room.

"What do you suppose his problem is?" McConnell asked. He loved watching other doctors butt heads.

Marlow answered. "He's like every other neurosurgeon . . . arrogant assholes. Tim Graves is no different."

109

Larken was astounded to hear that sort of prejudicial talk in a meeting such as this. They were a committee appointed to review the performance of a member of the medical staff. They were charged with being impartial and unbiased. Tim Graves' career was on the line and Marlow certainly sounded like he had a personal axe to grind.

"Wait a minute," Larken challenged. "Where do you get off making a statement like that?"

"Look, I didn't mean it that way. Tim Graves has changed. He needs help and I think this suspension will give him a good opportunity to work out his problems. We are actually doing him a favor. We might even add to our recommendation that he seek some sort of professional counseling before he is reinstated."

Larken threw up his hands. "Hold on. You can't assume that he will be suspended and you can't make that recommendation. We shouldn't even be discussing that possibility. You're not here to make recommendations. You're only supposed to file a report for the Executive Committee to review. That's it."

McConnell had to laugh. This couldn't have gone any better. He and Marlow exchanged a knowing glance. They both knew how much weight their "report" to the Executive Committee carried. Graves was as good as gone. The four remaining men adjourned the meeting.

Tim was already in Los Angeles when the Executive Committee held what was dubbed an "emergency session" to decide his fate on Thursday. J.C. Parker strongly objected to holding the meeting in the absence of the defendant, but McConnell persuaded the other members that the matter could not wait. With visions of lawsuits dancing in their heads, they were compelled to dispose of this unpleasant matter expediently. Under normal circumstances meetings of the Executive Committee were sparsely attended, but to hear the case of Dr. Timothy Graves, attendance was one hundred percent. By 12:30, every seat was taken.

McConnell sat at the head of the table, with his starched white coat and freshly trimmed hair. He was smiling and greeting everyone as though he were running for political office. Jenkins and Larken sat on either side of him. There was an excited buzz in the room as people got their lunch and settled in their chairs. J.C. spoke to no one. He had considered abstaining from the meeting on the grounds that Tim was not present to defend himself, but he decided he could do more good for Tim by being there and being heard. He looked over at Taylor and wondered if he would keep his word.

As the conversation died down McConnell called the meeting to order. He started with a sarcastic remark about the perfect attendance. He didn't want to stall the proceedings with any Larken bullshit about ethical procedure and moral guidelines. Instead, he dove right into the case, sparing no details. He tried to sound objective, but to those who knew him, his criticism came through loud and clear. Everyone knew he hated Tim Graves and they knew he would do his best to persuade them to suspend him. McConnell concluded his report and stole a glance at Taylor. He hoped Taylor had done his homework.

McConnell opened up the discussion, which began rather lamely. There were the usual questions about clarification of one point or another. The doctors seemed hesitant to offer any opinions. They all had their own agenda. McConnell winced as he listened to J.C. Parker sing Tim's praises. Of course he was on Tim's side, they'd been buddies for years. But, McConnell thought, perhaps that will work against Tim. Obviously J.C. would support Tim, he would do anything to protect his friend. Would he even lie for him?

"Dr. Parker, I'm not sure how credible your input can be. I mean, you've been friends with Dr. Graves since, when was it? Since medical school?" McConnell addressed J.C.

"That's right, but that shouldn't discredit what I say. If anything, it should make it more credible. I know Tim Graves better than anyone in this room." J.C. was looking forward to doing battle with McConnell. He'd wanted to punch out the guy for years, but he knew that public humiliation would be much more devastating to McConnell than any blow to the jaw. Now J.C. had the perfect forum and he wasn't going to hold back.

"Perhaps the Executive Committee should consider to what lengths a close, personal friend would go to protect someone. I'm not sure we can count on you to be totally objective, Dr. Parker." McConnell took the first shot.

111

"Give me a break, McConnell. Everybody knows that Tim Graves is one of the best doctors this hospital has ever seen. Now, whether I'm his friend, his colleague, or his damn dog, I'm not going through this lynching you call an 'emergency meeting' and not speak out in favor of a man who has devoted twenty-five years of his best work to this hospital."

There was an uncomfortable murmuring among the other doctors. Those who supported Tim were gratified to hear J.C. speak out, but those who wanted to bring him down did not want to be thwarted by the sympathy vote. They didn't want to sing Tim's praises, they wanted the dirt.

"Dr. Parker, I think you exaggerate. We know Dr. Graves is an excellent surgeon, but whether he is the best this hospital has ever seen, well, I'll have to call that into question. The 'best doctor ever' does not allow a third year resident to take over a major operation." This came from a young internist. There were mutterings of agreement around the room. McConnell smiled.

"Dr. Berry is right. How can we excuse such aberrant behavior, no matter who it is?" Another voice against Graves. McConnell was impressed.

"Aberrant behavior? Isn't that a little harsh?" J.C. questioned.

"Yes, isn't that a stretch?" Taylor finally spoke up. The room was very quiet. Taylor carried a lot of weight. "We're talking about a man who slipped up once, something that could happen to any one of us, and undoubtedly has in some way."

"This was more than a slip-up, Dr. Taylor. He yelled at the nurses and lost control of the operation he was performing," McConnell persisted.

J.C. jumped back into the fray. "I understand that last week you experienced a major complication during a 'routine' procedure and weren't exactly a gentleman about it, McConnell."

"My patient experienced a known and recognized complication, even though it was unexpected. We're talking apples and oranges here, and besides, I'm not the one on trial here today."

"What an interesting choice of words, McConnell, and how accurate."

"Dr. Parker, you know as well as I that when you're in an operating room, you've got to have control. The surgeon is the captain of the ship—he's got to maintain control at all times, even when he runs into trouble."

"I understand that, but what I'm not understanding is how your loss of control in the cysto lab can be excused, while Dr. Graves must endure harsh scrutiny and possible suspension."

"This meeting is not about me, Parker."

"Are you sure about that, McConnell?"

McConnell clutched the arms of his chair. J.C. Parker was getting under his skin. He was close to losing his cool, a tactical error he could not afford. Once again, Larken inadvertently came to his rescue.

"Gentlemen, please. This is about Dr. Graves. Let's stick to this case and stop acting like schoolboys. Dr. Graves has been written up by some of the nurses for his behavior. I think we should be considering whether this is the beginning of a new and disturbing pattern. We . . . the hospital, certainly cannot afford to have a repeat of this unfortunate incident. We don't yet know what the consequences of his actions will be to himself and to the hospital."

"I deal with Dr. Graves every day, and I have never, in my life, seen any rude behavior. He is always a perfect gentleman and his patients worship him. I understand he's been under stress because of his family situation, and he's handling it the best he can. I would think that is something we all can understand. I wonder if any of you could deal with what he has had to face." This came from the Chief of Pediatrics.

Taylor took over from there and began his own defense of Tim. As Taylor was talking about Tim's support of his infertility research over the years, J.C. saw that McConnell had regained his composure and looked surprisingly at ease. One would think that this praise of Tim would make him edgy. McConnell's urology practice and Taylor's fertility practice often intertwined, and they had always seemed to have a good working relationship. In fact, this was the first time J.C. had seen McConnell in direct opposition to Taylor. He wondered how it would all pan out.

Taylor had finished his words in support of Tim and the room remained silent for a few seconds. Then, the young internist who had spoken out against Tim earlier, started in again.

"I still believe that Dr. Graves deserves some kind of punishment for his actions. If we let this one slide, then we'll let countless others slide, and pretty soon the lawyers are slapping us with lawsuits left and right, the hospital is forking out more money to lawyers than for patient care, and we as doctors are chastised for not policing our own. I, personally, don't want to be footing the bill for the mistakes of others."

This was something with which they could all identify. Just dangle the threat of a lawsuit in front of a doctor and watch him cave. Whatever had been said in support of Tim was quickly forgotten in light of the harsh reality of dollars and cents. It was easy to sacrifice one for the good of them all. Good sense and common decency had to make way for politics and litigation. J.C. was speechless as he vaguely heard the comments circulating around the table. To his surprise, Dr. Taylor could be heard agreeing that a short suspension might be just what Tim needed to "get his act together." A motion was called for and the table was ready to vote. McConnell was back in the driver's seat.

"A motion has been called for the suspension of Tim Graves for a duration of twenty-nine days, after which he will be reinstated with a six month probation, requiring auditing of all his surgical cases. All those in favor, raise your right hand."

Fourteen

Meg waited impatiently for the elevator. She wanted to get a rough draft written today, do some revisions over the weekend, and get a working copy to her editor on Monday. She'd spent the past few days gathering facts and quotes from various sources, and was ready to put it all together. She had probably spent too much time in the research phase of the story, but every day there had been one more fascinating item about Tim Graves that she had to explore. Actually, talking with Tim's old friends, classmates, retired coaches and professors had frustrated her. Meg finally admitted to herself that her quest might have been to find the flaw that she hadn't been able to detect in the time she had spent with him. She had tried contacting Jennifer Graves, but couldn't get through to her by phone. Jennifer had no interest in talking to a reporter, but Meg knew that she most certainly could have revealed another side of Tim.

Meg gave a characteristic shrug as she stepped out of the elevator when it stopped at the tenth floor. The hum of the newsroom never failed to get her adrenaline pumping. "Better than caffeine," she told her friends. She headed straight to her desk and immediately noticed a photocopied article placed conspicuously in the center of her blotter. She dropped her purse and picked up the paper. Jane, her friend and fellow reporter, leaned over Meg's shoulder and whispered with a wicked leer, "Mike was looking for you. If I were you, I'd run for the hills."

"Thanks for the warning," Meg mumbled, without taking her eyes from the article. She sat down in stunned disbelief. This had to have come from Mike. She reached for the phone and dialed Mike's number.

"Mike, it's Meg."

"Meg, honey, you've made my day."

"Did you leave this article on my desk?"

"You see, Meg, I'm thinking about you all the time."

"So, it was you. Where did you get it?"

"Some local news in Texas, no big name."

"It came in yesterday?"

"Yeah. I ran across it by accident. I was looking something up, can't even remember what, and I found this."

"I appreciate it, Mike. I really do."

"When can you stop by and thank me personally?"

"I'm thanking you personally now, Mike." She hung up the phone and immediately picked it up again. She guessed Tim was probably in surgery, but she wanted to try to find him, anyway.

"Neurosurgery, may I help you?"

"Yes, I'd like to page Dr. Graves, please."

"Are you a member of his family?" the secretary asked.

"No, I'm a friend."

"Dr. Graves is out of town. He has a doctor on call if this is an emergency."

"Out of town? No, this isn't an emergency. Where is he?"

"I can only say that he's out of town. May I take a message?"

"When will he be back?"

"I don't know when he'll return. Would you like to leave a message?"

"No. No thank you." Meg slowly replaced the receiver. *Where did he go?* She picked up the phone and dialed a different number.

"University Hospital."

"Yes, I've been trying to page Dr. Graves, but he's not answering. Do you know where he is?"

"What number are you trying?"

"546-9870"

"That's Dr. Graves' office number."

"Yes, I know, they're not answering and my call was directed to you."

"One moment." Meg could hear the clicking of a computer keyboard. The operator came back on the line.

"Dr. Graves is out of town."

"Can you tell me where he went?"

"Is this a medical emergency?"

"This is his . . . cousin. I need to reach him."

There was a pause, then the woman said, "He went to Los Angeles. That's all the information I have."

"Thank you very much."

Meg knew that Tim's parents lived near Los Angeles. *But why would he go so suddenly?* Maybe something had happened to one of his parents. Her concern over his sudden departure had made her forget, for the time being, about the disturbing article. She had to find out where he was and make sure everything was all right. She was beginning to care a great deal about Dr. Timothy Graves.

*   *   *

Tim was restless during the flight to Los Angeles. He had to deal with his father's heart surgery and then return to Boston to face McConnell's inquisition. His career was in jeopardy and he had himself to blame. He had lost his edge and the vultures were circling, but he wasn't dead yet. Tim resolved that when he returned to Boston he was going to pick up the pieces of his life and start again. It was going to take more than McConnell to destroy what he had spent his life building. As he let his thoughts drift, the picture of a smiling Meg entered his mind. *There's another reason to pull myself together.* He was also trying to make sense of Meg's revelation concerning the boy in Wisconsin. Clearly, this was a coincidence, but he couldn't quite shake the nagging feeling that there was something more to it. The fact that Tim and Jonathan both had cerebral aneurysms was some kind of fluke. Most genetically transmitted diseases are not dominant and would not be transmitted to every offspring. He would have to tell Meg that there was no reason to go down this road for her story. If she wanted to do a story about Tim, the neurosurgeon, fine, but he doubted it would be interesting enough to make it past her editor. Maybe she would drop the whole idea.

At the Los Angeles airport Tim rented a car and headed for Glendale, and home. This was a nostalgic drive for him, passing the old high school, driving on the street that bordered the park, and turning into his driveway. He hadn't been home in eight years, but all the familiar feelings came flooding back. After giving a perfunctory knock, Tim opened the door of his parents' house and called out. His mother hurried in from the patio and threw her arms around him.

"I'm so glad you're here." She pulled back and looked at her son. It had been too long. How could she have let the distance grow between them? "We're out on the patio, come see your father."

Steve stood as Tim reached the patio door. They hugged and patted each other on the back. It was an emotional moment for Tim. His father had always been his role model, the source of his inner strength. All the hard feelings surrounding Jonathan's death were forgotten as he held him close.

"How do you feel, Dad? What do the doctors say?"

"I feel just fine. I only have angina after strenuous exercise. It's unfortunate that I have a left main lesion, otherwise, I could probably get by with medication. Dr. Kraemer and Dr. Stanley both strongly advise the bypass surgery."

"I asked around. Seems Dr. Kraemer is the best, and bypass surgery has become so routine, these guys do three or four a day. I hope they plan to use the internal mammary artery for one of your bypasses?"

"Yes. We discussed that. I plan to be around a long time after the veins wear out. That artery will still be going strong. I'm the second case of the day, so the team should be warmed up and ready to go when they get to me," he said with a grin.

Tim was relieved to find his father in such good spirits. That doctors were not the best of patients would be an understatement, and he was having trouble picturing his dad in the role. Steve Graves was used to being in control; undergoing heart bypass surgery could be very difficult for him.

"So, surgery is scheduled for the day after tomorrow, Friday. I'm glad you got here today."

"Jim and Bill told me they want family members to donate blood for you, just in case. We've already worked it out. I'm going to pick up Jim at his office and Bill's going to meet us at the hospital. We figured we'd all donate together and then grab a bite and catch up." As he spoke a strange look came over his father's face, but Tim was too anxious to notice. As he looked at his watch he realized he'd better get moving. He hugged his mother again and headed out to his rental car.

Jim's office was near St. Vincent's Hospital. He had established his practice in a prestigious law firm. He was a successful defense attorney and often represented doctors. As far as Tim could tell, Jim had everything he'd ever wanted. He had a wife he adored, two beautiful children, and he loved practicing law. How Tim envied his orderly and predictable life.

Jim was waiting outside his office when Tim pulled to the curb at exactly noon. Jim appreciated punctuality, and Tim was determined to do everything he could to help things go smoothly. Jim and Bill had remained close to their parents, while Tim had been in Boston since med school. It was his turn to be there for his family and take some of the burden off his brothers, at least for a short time.

"Good to see you, little brother."

"Same here." Two years older than Tim, Jim looked more like their father every time Tim saw him. He exercised religiously, was careful with his diet, and did not smoke or drink. That their father suffered from heart disease in spite of all his precautions had come as a shock to Jim. His brother had been very supportive of Tim and his problems over the past year. They had spoken by phone frequently, and Jim had offered legal advice along the way.

In answer to Jim's question about how things were going, Tim had to admit, "It seems like this bad streak will never end. The divorce from Jennifer has been a nightmare. Now I've got trouble at the hospital." He went on to relate the volatile situation at work. He was ashamed of the mess he had gotten himself into, and he didn't want Jim to think that he was "losing it" as a surgeon. He tried to explain what had happened without sounding defensive. Sharing his pain was difficult, but cathartic.

At the conclusion of his bitter monologue, Jim just shook his head. "That guy, McConnell, sounds like a real asshole. We have to hope that there are enough reasonable and responsible people hearing your case so a jerk like that won't prevail. If you need any legal help, you can count on me, any time." As they pulled into the hospital parking lot, he continued, "You know we all feel terrible about what you've been going through. Jonathan was a great kid and I know you'll never stop missing him. But for your own good, you have to get past the pain and move on. Getting this thing with the hospital behind you will be the first step, so after we get dad through his surgery, you should go back to Boston and hit them with all you have. I know what kind of a surgeon you are, and they're damn lucky

119

to have you. Don't let them beat you, Tim."

It was such a relief to talk with someone who was clearly on his side. As they passed through the double doors into the lobby, Tim looked around. The very walls of the hospital seemed to envelop him. *This is where lives are saved, and lost. I have dedicated my life to the practice of medicine and there aren't enough McConnells in the world to take that away from me.* They found Bill in the blood bank, already donating. With smiles, Jim and Tim rolled up their sleeves.

* * *

Steve was admitted to the hospital on Thursday afternoon. Tim and Sally stayed with him during the admitting process and went with him to his room. Jim and Bill promised to be there in the morning, in time to see their father before he was taken to surgery.

Tim had rarely experienced surgery from a patient's perspective. When he was in the Emergency Room with Jonathan he had feelings of total helplessness. He felt much the same today, watching his father being wheeled into the operating room. Tim tried to reassure his mother and brothers, but he knew there was always the possibility that this would be the last time they would see Steve Graves alive. All they could do now was return to the waiting area and watch the clock. Surgery was scheduled to begin at 10:30 A.M. and Dr. Kraemer said it would last several hours, but Tim knew that heart surgery could last much longer. There were too many things that could go wrong.

As they waited, his brothers passed the time talking about mutual friends and local gossip. His mother had lapsed into silence the moment Steve had been taken to surgery. Tim decided to leave her alone with her thoughts. Sitting around and waiting was not something he did easily. He decided to walk around.

He found a pay phone and used his credit card to place the long distance call. Meg answered on the first ring.

"Hi, Meg. It's Tim."

"Tim. Where are you? I tried to reach you and they said you're in Los Angeles. What happened?" She tried to keep the worry out of her voice. She didn't want him to think she'd been checking up on him, or that he owed her an explanation for leaving town without telling her.

Tim told her about his father. Although she was concerned for his father, she couldn't help feeling relieved that he really had left in a hurry, and for a good reason. More importantly, he was calling her now. He had been thinking about her, even when his father was ill.

"I hope the surgery goes well. It has to be hard to just sit back and wait. I know you must want to get in there and help."

It warmed his heart to hear Meg echo his exact feelings. They talked for a few minutes more, then Tim said that he should get back to his mother.

"Do you know when you might be coming back to Boston?"

"As soon as my dad is out of the woods, a few days, maybe a week. I'll let you know," before he knew what he was saying he blurted, "I miss you."

Meg's spoke in a hushed voice, "I miss you, too. I'm so glad you called, Tim."

"I'll call again, soon."

Tim walked back to the waiting area and sat down. Only an hour had passed, but it might as well have been days. The brothers tried to kill time reminiscing about their early years growing up in Glendale. After that topic had been exhausted, Tim read, dozed, and finally looked up to see Dr. Kraemer striding purposefully across the room. He greeted Jim, Bill and Tim, but spoke to their mother. "Sally, everything went very well. We did a triple bypass. Steve's heart is normal and we used the mammary artery on the left anterior descending, and veins from his left thigh for the circumflex and right coronary arteries. He came right off pump without any difficulty, and we're moving him to the recovery room now." They all breathed a sigh of relief as Dr. Kraemer continued. "We did run into some bleeding, which is perfectly normal. He was already a little anemic from his heart catheterization, so I gave him two units of blood in the operating room. We'll watch him carefully while he's in recovery, and it may be necessary to give him the other unit. It was fortunate that three of you were able to donate blood on such short notice."

Tim was surprised. "Wait a minute, you should have four units of designated donor blood available. Both my brothers and

I donated on Wednesday, and Mom donated yesterday."

"Well, in that case, one of the units must not have been compatible. That happens. You can check with the blood bank if you want, but I feel sure that one unit will be all that your father needs, and we still have one in reserve."

Tim turned to his mother and asked, "What blood type are you?"

"I'm O. I was typed when I was pregnant."

"This doesn't make sense. You're O, Dad's O. We should all be O. Why would one unit not be compatible?"

"I don't know anything about blood types. What does it matter now? All I know is that I'm glad Dad's doing so well." She quickly changed the subject and asked them where they wanted to go for lunch. Dr. Kraemer had said it would be several hours before they could see Steve, and Sally was ready for some fresh air and a change of scenery. There was a nice restaurant within walking distance of the hospital.

When they returned from lunch, they checked in at the desk and the nurse told them that they could see Dr. Graves for a few minutes. They decided that Tim would go first, with Sally. The nurse escorted them to the recovery room where Steve was just awakening from the anesthesia. He was still on a ventilator, but didn't seem to be having any discomfort. Tim gave him a "thumbs up" and left his mother at the bedside.

Outside the recovery room, Tim looked up and down the hall and asked a passing nurse where he might find the Blood Bank. She pointed to the stairs and said it was one floor down, just underneath where they were standing. Tim thanked her and descended the stairs. At the Blood Bank window Tim identified himself as Dr. Tim Graves and told the technician he was there to inquire about blood available for his father.

"Just a moment, doctor, and I'll check."

The technician sifted through some cards, pulled out four.

"Well, three units were compatible, O positive, but the O negative unit tested positive for antibodies and couldn't be used. Maybe you developed antibodies from a blood transfusion."

"I'm O negative? Are you sure?"

"Says so right here. Didn't you know?"

Tim just walked away. He climbed the stairs and stood at the door to the recovery room. Sally was just getting ready to leave. Steve appeared groggy, but aware of his surroundings. He gave Tim a weak smile. Tim told him to get some rest and they would see him later. He walked back to the waiting area with Sally and told Jim and Bill to go see their father. Tim looked so shaken, they wondered if something had happened to Steve. Tim assured them that their father was doing better than expected but that they should go see for themselves. He sat down facing his mother, wondering how to begin.

"Mom, there's something very strange. I went down and checked with the Blood Bank. Jim and Bill are O positive, but they tell me my blood type is O negative. How can that be? You and Dad are both O positive, so that's what blood type I have to have."

Sally stared at the floor and spoke in a low voice, "I don't know, Tim. There must be some explanation. It's probably just a simple mistake, a lab error, or something. I wouldn't worry about it. You heard Dr. Kay say that Dad won't be needing any more blood. Let's look on the bright side."

Tim struggled to remain calm. His mother was being deliberately obtuse. She was not a stupid woman, and it was not normal for her to be so evasive.

"Mom, look at me. There's something wrong and I want to know what it is. I *need* to know what it is. How can I be O negative? There has to be an explanation, and I think you know what it is."

His mother finally looked up at him and there were tears in her eyes. With a sob she said, "I didn't think I'd ever have to tell you this. We've never told anyone. You're not our biological son. You're adopted. Before you say another word, just hear me out, and know that I have always loved you, and I couldn't love you any more if I had given birth to you."

After a few false starts Sally was able to tell Tim the secret she had shared with only her husband for all these years. Steve had been doing his general surgical residency at Cook County in Chicago. He was called in to the Emergency Room late one night to see a patient with a possible ruptured appendix. The patient turned out to be a young woman who worked as a lab technician at the hospital. She was an attractive blond who was adamant

123

that Dr. Steve Graves be called. Complicating her condition was the fact that she was eight months pregnant. She had all the symptoms of a ruptured appendix and Steve rushed her to the operating room. She was very ill and it was necessary to call in an obstetrician to do an emergency Caesarean section while Steve removed the ruptured appendix. The doctor delivered a small, but perfect baby boy. Mother and baby were both doing well the morning after surgery, but later in the afternoon the young woman had some sort of episode and didn't survive. It was presumed that she had thrown a blood clot to her brain. It turned out the mother had no family. The father of the baby was never in the picture; apparently the baby was the result of a brief encounter. No autopsy was performed and arrangements were made for a quiet burial.

Steve Graves felt terribly responsible for everything that happened. He took it upon himself to make the burial arrangements, and he paid for them out of his own pocket. He went home that evening and told Sally what had happened. She had never seen him so emotionally devastated after losing a patient. He explained to her that this was a girl who had no one, no family, no friends, and she had left a baby with no one to care for him. It was then that he had the idea of adopting the baby. Once the idea took hold, he would not let it go. It was surprisingly simple, and during the two months the baby had to remain in the hospital, all the legalities were handled. Before they knew it they were bringing home their brand new baby boy, Timothy. Steve was just finishing his residency and he had already secured a position in Los Angeles. The family moved to Glendale to start their new life and that was the end of the story.

Tim stared up at the ceiling, unable to speak. *What more can go wrong in my life? My son died. My wife left me. I might lose my practice. Now my mother tells me I'm adopted, they're not even my real parents! Suddenly I have no past, the present sucks, and I don't even want to consider my future...*At that moment Jim and Bill returned from their visit with their father. They reported that he was fully awake and was demanding the removal of the endotracheal tube. "That's our dad," Jim said proudly.

Fifteen

Late Thursday night Tim walked through the door of his apartment, eight hours and twenty-five minutes after leaving his mother and father. The flight to Boston was delayed in St. Louis, but Tim had no memory of waiting in the airport. He didn't remember getting on or off the plane, picking up his baggage, finding a taxi and giving the cabdriver his home address. He was totally out of touch with reality and he wasn't sure he could find his way back.

His father had been in the hospital for five days and was now recovering nicely at home. His mother had refused any further discussion after the bombshell she had dropped on him. As far as she was concerned, the subject was closed, and she made him give his word that he would not mention anything to his father. She felt that it would hinder his recovery, and Tim did not want to be responsible for that. But he still had so many questions.

He dropped his bags on the floor and shut the door behind him. The light on his message machine was blinking. He didn't want to talk to anyone, but he might as well listen to his messages and get rid of them. He flipped on the lights in the kitchen and noticed the dirty dishes in the sink. He knew he should do something about them. He opened the cupboard above the refrigerator and pulled out a bottle of Chianti. He opened the bottle and poured himself a generous glass of wine. He took a sip and brought the glass with him to the living room, pressing the message button on the phone as he passed by. Easing down on the couch he stared at the plant on the floor in front of him. The leaves had dropped all over the carpet, leaving just a skeleton of twigs poking out of a wicker basket. *I can't seem to hang on to anything, even a poor, defenseless plant.*

The tape had finally rewound and Tim was startled to hear his mother's voice.

"Tim . . . it's Mom . . . I'm trying to find you . . . Uh . . . I

125

should have tried the hospital first."

BEEP.

"This is a message for a Dr. Timothy Graves. This is Herb Green. I'm representing Jennifer Graves in her pending divorce proceedings. I hope you have had an opportunity to look over the divorce papers that were mailed to you. Please call me at your earliest convenience. Area code 617- 566-7899. Thank you."

BEEP.

"Dr. Graves, I didn't want to bother you in California. I hope your dad is doing better. We're all thinking about you and hope everything is okay. I did want to let you know that there are some people here on my back about your overdue charts. I guess they need them immediately. Anyway, they've been calling me every-day. Okay, just wanted to let you know. I'm sorry,"

BEEP.

"This message is for Mr. Graves. This is Devin Jones, the landlord. I haven't received your rent check. I expect payment as soon as possible. Please call me at 787-6657. Thank you."

BEEP.

"Tim, it's J.C. I heard you left for Los Angeles. I tried calling your parents' house there but no one answered the phone. I hope everything's all right. Listen, McConnell's scheduled the Executive Committee meeting for Tuesday. Are you going to be back by then? I don't think we should have the meeting with you out of town, but no one seems to be agreeing with me. Anyway, I'll work on it. Take care, buddy."

BEEP.

"Hi, Tim. This is Malcolm Taylor. Your secretary informed me that you were out of town on family business. I hope it's noth-ing serious. Uh, the Executive Committee met yesterday, and I want to talk to you about that . . . in person. Call me when you get back from L.A. It's important."

BEEP.

"Tim, it's Meg. I'm just checking to see if you're home yet. You said you'd call again, but I haven't heard from you and I just want to make sure everything is okay. Please call me when you get back."

BEEP.

"This is a message for Dr. Graves. This is Herb Green again. I

126

called your office and they said you were out of town. Once again, your wife has filed for divorce and I am her lawyer. Please make some arrangements to contact me or allow me to contact your lawyer. My number, once again, is 617-566-7899."

BEEP.

"Tim, it's Meg again. I just wanted to tell you that the article was published in Wednesday's edition. It looks good. I'll save you some copies. Call me when you get back. Bye."

BEEP.

There was another message from the landlord and one from Stan, Tim's lawyer. Jennifer herself must have called him since Tim wasn't getting back to her lawyer. He never really believed that Jennifer would go ahead with the divorce, but now that he had been served with the papers he had better deal with it. The message from Taylor was cryptic, but it sounded like bad news. If there were any good news, J.C. would have called back.

Tim set his glass of wine down on the table and pulled a pillow to his chest. He curled up on the couch, hugging the pillow and closing his eyes. He needed to think, but his mind was numb. He was physically and emotionally drained and in spite of himself he sank into a deep, dreamless sleep. The ringing of the phone jarred him awake.

"Hello."

"Tim, you're home. How are you doing? How's your dad?"

Still groggy, Tim rubbed his eyes and tried to put a face to the voice on the phone.

"I'm sorry. Who is this?"

"Meg. Meg Logan. Tim, are you okay? You sound kind of strange."

"Oh, Meg. I got home late. What time is it? I must have fallen asleep."

"It's eight in the morning, Friday morning. Tim, can I see you today? I need to talk to you."

"Talk to me about what?"

"About what's been going on, and about something I read in the paper last week. Hey, did you read your article?"

"No, I haven't had a chance."

"I'll bring you a copy. When can we get together?"

Tim ran his hands through his hair. He needed a shower,

some clean clothes and some food. Then he had to organize his thoughts and come up with a way to get on with his life.

"I have to go to the hospital. I have patients to see and paper-work to catch up on. I really don't have time today. Can I call you later, Meg? I just don't know what I'm doing right now."

Meg could feel Tim pulling away from her, and she didn't understand why. When he had called her from Los Angeles they had seemed so close. What could have changed in just a few days? Something was seriously wrong, but now, on the phone, was not the time to pursue it. She would just have to be patient and wait for him to call her.

Tim headed for the shower. He knew he had to go to work. After a quick breakfast of coffee and toast, he called his office.

"Judith, I'm back. What's going on? Is the work piling up?"

"Dr. Graves." Judith was relieved to hear from Tim, but she was apprehensive as she continued. "Yes, you have a lot of paper-work to do, but you need to call Dr. Taylor right away."

"I know, I'll call him from the office, after my rounds."

"No, you need to call him now. I mean, he said it's urgent and I assume it has to do with your review. I'm sorry, but the talk around here is that you've already been suspended."

Even though he had been expecting it, Judith's words hit Tim like a ton of bricks. He might as well call Taylor, and get the offi-cial word.

Taylor had persuaded the committee members that he should be allowed to break the news of his suspension to Dr. Graves, much to McConnell's dismay. He had been looking for-ward to confronting Tim and rubbing his face in it. Nothing of their decision was to be made public until after Taylor had talked to Tim, but of course, news of his suspension had already leaked out. Taylor did not relish being the bearer of this kind of news, but he thought Tim would rather hear it from him than from that prick, McConnell. This was his last official duty before packing it in and moving up to Vermont. Taylor thanked God he had been able to avoid these entanglements in his own career. It almost seemed unfair that he had had it so easy, and here he was, about to suspend the one person who had contributed the most to his success. Taylor had done his best, but McConnell and his cronies were determined to make an example of Tim, and there was noth-

128

ing that he, Taylor, could have said or done to dissuade them.

Tim decided to forget about rounds and went straight to Taylor's office. If he really had been suspended, he would have no patients to see anyway, their care would have already been transferred to one of his partners. This is what hurt the most. He had always taken care of his own patients, and now he couldn't even do that.

"Hi, Meredith. I heard Dr. Taylor wants to see me."

"Good morning, Dr. Graves." Meredith favored him with a sympathetic smile. Tim remembered her from his visits to Dr. Taylor's office when he was a resident. She had worked for Taylor for years, and she still looked good.

"Dr. Taylor's not in yet, but you can wait in his office if you'd like." Meredith knew why Tim was there and she felt truly sorry for him. She had always liked him. He had always been pleasant to her, and seemed sort of humble—a far cry from the average egocentric doctors she dealt with every day.

"Thanks, Meredith. I think I will wait inside." The last thing he wanted was to be observed cooling his heels in Dr. Taylor's waiting room, waiting for the ax to fall. He stepped into Taylor's inner office. He had come full circle since he had first stood in this office. He knew his suspension would only be for a month or two, but he still felt like this was the end. He noticed a few packing crates stacked in a corner. Tim had forgotten about Taylor's early retirement and his move to Vermont, where he apparently planned to continue his research. His usually neat desk was nearly buried under stacks of old files and books. A yellowed newspaper clipping, sticking out from between the pages of a thick book, caught his eye. The print was different than that of the local papers, and his curiosity got the better of him. He pulled the newspaper from between the pages of the book. Tim froze as he read the headline, HIGH SCHOOL BOY SUFFERS BRAIN SEIZURE ON BASEBALL FIELD. *Another one?* Taylor could walk in any minute, and Tim didn't want to be caught snooping through his papers, but he had to read that article. He had a bad feeling about it.

Keeping one eye on the door, Tim continued to read. He was able to make out "Texas" and "cerebral aneurysm" before the door swung open. Tim pushed the clipping back toward the center of the desk and turned toward the door. Taylor looked from

Tim to his desktop and back to Tim again. He hesitated for only a second and then crossed the room, heading directly for his desk. He dropped a folder he had been carrying right on top of the newspaper clipping, and kept his eyes on the desk as he spoke.

"It's good to see you again, Tim, even though these aren't the best of circumstances. I wanted to meet with you in person, in fact, I insisted that we discuss it, just you and I." Taylor looked up at Tim, who was still standing. "Please, have a seat." He motioned to the chair and Tim slowly sat down, his thoughts spinning in his head. He was hardly aware that Taylor was speaking. He kept envisioning a boy's limp body on a baseball field in Texas.

Taylor continued talking and Tim tried to pick up the thread of his conversation. "Last week, while you were away, the Executive Committee made a decision."

"Bad news?"

"I'm afraid so, Tim."

"I guess that means I've been suspended."

"For twenty-nine days; then a six month probation period."

Tim's mind was still on the boy in Texas. *Why would Taylor have that newspaper article on his desk? From a paper in Texas?* Meg's words came back to him when she talked about the boy in Wisconsin. "Virtually unprecedented."

"J.C. and I did our best, but you know how it is. A bunch of doctors get together and it's a witch hunt."

"I understand, Dr. Taylor. You don't have to explain." Tim wanted to ask him about the article, but something made him hesitate.

"Look, Tim, I know this is a blow, but it's only for a month and then you'll probably be reinstated. Maybe it will work out to your benefit. You've pushed yourself to the limit for too many years, and with the added stress you've been under lately, you can use the time off."

Tim didn't like the word "probably" and he didn't want any time off. He needed to work. He wanted to work, not sit around twiddling his thumbs and wallowing in his grief. But to Taylor he just nodded his agreement and thanked him for all his support.

"You're right, I should use this time wisely. I have about a month's worth of paperwork to sort out. Maybe I can finally get my office organized." He chuckled for effect. Taylor chuckled, too.

"Yeah, I know what you mean. You should have seen this place last week."

"I noticed you're packing up. When's the big move?"

"End of this week. I'll tell you, Tim, when you've been around as long as I have, it's hard to retire, but to be honest with you, I'm ready to get out. Doctors have changed. Medicine has changed. I'm ready to do my own thing, with no one looking over my shoulder. I'll have a clinic up there in Vermont. Beautiful area. I'll continue my research, but I'm looking forward to a real change of pace."

Tim was anxious to end this meeting and sought a graceful exit.

"Well, I have to thank you, Dr. Taylor, for all your support over the years. I appreciate everything you've done for me."

"You've helped me too, Tim, and I'm sorry we have to leave on such a sour note, but you'll be back in there soon enough."

Tim stood up and extended his hand to Dr. Taylor, who shook it firmly.

"If you ever need anything, Tim, don't hesitate to call me. I'm leaving this place, but I'm not dropping off the face of the earth."

As if Taylor could ever "drop off the face of the earth." It seemed to Tim that he would still be standing, like one of those skyscrapers in the distance, long after everyone else had been forgotten. Tim headed out of the office and to the nearest phone. He needed to talk to Meg.

*   *   *

"Did you tell him?"

"Yeah, I told him."

"What'd he do?"

"He was expecting it."

"Was he upset?"

"What do you think? Of course he was upset."

"Tell me exactly what he said."

"You really get off on making this man suffer."

"Indeed I do. I enjoy watching Tim Graves suffer. Come on,

131

he thinks he's so hot. He deserves everything he's getting, and more."

"You know, McConnell, my work with you is done. I don't have to have anything to do with you from now on. But there is something I've always wanted to tell you."

"What's that?"

"You're a sniveling, whiny, incompetent son of a bitch. I never liked you, but I was forced to work with you."

"Are you sure you want to talk to me like that, Taylor? I'm still holding all the cards."

"Fuck the cards, and fuck you, McConnell. Our business is finished." Taylor slammed down the phone. He had played McConnell's dirty games and now he was finally going to escape. He hoped he was getting out in time. He thought back to the day more than twenty years ago when he had approached McConnell with what seemed like a simple plan. He knew that McConnell treated many male patients for infertility problems. The most basic test performed was a sperm count. He had devised a simple plan where McConnell would submit the specimen to Taylor's lab and the test would be performed there, at no charge. McConnell, of course, would continue to charge the patient's insurance company for the cost of the test. This would give McConnell additional income, and provide Taylor with specimens for his "research." Everything was fine until somehow McConnell found out that Taylor was using some of those sperm specimens for his fertilization program. That's when the blackmail had begun. From that day on McConnell demanded a "piece of the action" and Taylor was forced to pay him off to keep him quiet. He would gladly expose McConnell and his fraudulent billing if he could do it without revealing his own duplicity, but that would be too risky. He had waited too long for his retirement to jeopardize it just to screw McConnell.

Tim and Meg had arranged to meet at one o'clock at the Border Café in Cambridge. When Tim arrived he saw Meg already seated at a table near the window. He worked his way through the lunch crowd to her table. She wore a silk blouse of deep purple with a white linen skirt. She looked radiant. She jumped up when she saw Tim and threw her arms around him.

"I've been so worried about you."

They both sat down and he looked at her curiously.

"Worried about me? There's nothing to be worried about. You knew I was in Los Angeles with my dad."

"I know all that. But you left so suddenly, then I was so relieved when you called, but you didn't call again, and I guess, well, I don't know what I thought. Anyway, it's good to be here with you, face to face."

"Well, my dad's doing fine. Sorry I didn't call again. It was hard seeing him sick, and so much happened in such a short time. Actually, a lot has happened since we last saw each other."

Tim wanted to tell her everything that was going on. He just didn't know where to begin. The busboy placed some tortilla chips and salsa on the table. Neither of them ate. Meg ordered an iced tea from the waitress and Tim asked for a glass of water.

"Tell me what's going on," Meg urged.

"Well, to begin with, the Executive Committee at the hospital decided that I was a danger to their patients, so they suspended me for twenty-nine days."

"What?" Meg nearly came out of her chair.

"Yeah. I got into a bad case a few weeks ago and, well, anyway, they decided to make an issue of it, with the help of my good friend, McConnell. You remember I told you about him."

Meg nodded. She couldn't believe Tim's rotten luck. "Isn't there something you can do to appeal it? It seems so unfair. Surely they can't just disregard everything you have accomplished based on one case! Since when does the best neurosurgeon in the world get suspended? I know things have been tough for you lately, but certainly not enough to warrant this kind of treatment."

"I could try to appeal it, but why bother? It's all about hospital politics and people have already made up their minds. Anything I do now will only make a messy situation worse. The best thing I can do is just ride out the suspension and then get back to work."

Meg was surprised at how well Tim was dealing with this latest blow. She would have expected him to be livid, having his reputation as a surgeon being smeared by his so-called peers, but instead, he acted as if this were just a minor annoyance.

Meg slid her hand across the table and nudged his elbow.

"Tell me what else is bugging you. You're taking this way too well."

Glancing at the other diners to make sure he would not be overheard, Tim leaned close to Meg and said, "A strange thing . . . Dr. Taylor asked me to meet him in his office this morning. He wanted to be the one to let me know about my suspension, as a courtesy. Anyway, I got there early and his secretary let me wait in his office. I noticed this newspaper article on his desk, a clipping from a newspaper in Texas."

"Texas?"

"Yeah, and guess what the article was about?" He was about to answer his own question when Meg broke in.

"A high school boy in Texas collapsed while pitching in a baseball game. Diagnosis: ruptured cerebral aneurysm."

Tim's face had gone ghostly pale. "How the hell did you know that?"

"That's why I called you. The article came across my desk a few days ago and I thought of you immediately. It's amazing, isn't it?"

Tim took a moment to try to absorb all that Meg was telling him. "Yeah, amazing, but that's not the strange part. Why would Taylor have that article, clipped out of a Texas newspaper, sitting on his desk?"

Meg frowned. She hadn't thought of that. It certainly was strange for Dr. Taylor to have access to a Texas newspaper and to have that particular article.

"And then, when he walked in and saw that I was looking at the article he got real nervous. He started talking real fast and covered the article with a folder."

Meg and Tim stared at each other, both of them trying to make some sense of Taylor's actions.

"I thought maybe he was related to this kid, an uncle or something," Tim offered.

Meg shook her head. "I don't think so. The boy's name was Marcus Leon. Leon is Italian. The immigration people shortened it from Leoni when they came over. I don't think Taylor's anywhere near Italian."

"What about his family? What if there's a sister who married an Italian-American? Taylor has a sister, but I think she lives in Indiana. Unless she moved."

"Maybe it's a grandchild, or some distant relative, a cousin or a cousin's cousin," Meg ventured.

"Taylor doesn't have any grandchildren. He has one son who hates him. A civil rights lawyer in New Orleans. And I'm sure he's not married."

"What about Taylor's wife? Maybe it's from her side."

Tim pictured Joannie Taylor for a second, an attractive woman in her sixties. Very independent and very removed from her husband's life. Too busy collecting artifacts from all over the world. "An only child," Tim blurted out as he remembered it from a conversation he once had with Taylor.

"Well, that leaves us with no answers." Meg dug into the bowl of chips as the waitress came to take their order. Meg ordered the tostada salad while Tim stole a quick glance at the menu. He decided on the blackened chicken and handed the waitress their menus. He waited until she was on her way back to the kitchen before he continued.

"What is more puzzling is why Taylor felt the need to hide the article from me. It was so odd."

Meg had been asking herself the same question, and she thought she might have it figured out.

"Taylor knew your son died under similar circumstances, right? Well, maybe when he came in and saw you reading the article, he felt bad for you. Or he was embarrassed. Bad enough that he had called you to his office to tell you about your suspension, now you're staring at a reminder of your son's death. He probably didn't know what to say, so he chose to cover it up."

What Meg said made a certain amount of sense, but still didn't explain why Taylor would have the article to begin with. Something was telling him that there was more to it than that.

"I suppose . . ."

"I'll tell you what. I'll give you the names of both families, the one in Wisconsin and the one in Texas, and you can talk to them yourself."

"Why would I talk to them?"

"You all share the sudden loss of a child under similar circumstances. It might help you, and them, to talk about it. To talk about your sons."

135

He wasn't sure he agreed with Meg, but he had his own reasons for wanting to talk to the families. That these boys had all suffered rupture of cerebral aneurysms while playing sports was a frightening coincidence.

"Okay."

Meg smiled. She wanted Tim to move on with his life and talking to these families might be a first step. She'd get him the names as soon as she got back to her office, but for now, she was determined to enjoy their lunch together like two normal adults who felt a mutual attraction.

Their meals arrived, piping hot and smelling delicious. Tim realized that he was starving, and dug into his chicken with gusto. Being with Meg made him feel better about everything. He still had a lot of unanswered questions, but he no longer felt as though he had the weight of the world on his shoulders. He could allow himself to relax and enjoy a lunch; after all, he had twenty-nine days to get his life in order.

When Tim got back to his office Judith told him that Meg from the *Globe* had called and left two names for him. *That was fast.*

"Great. Now all I need is their phone numbers." He breezed down the hall and into his office. Judith was surprised to see him acting so chipper, considering he had just been suspended from practice. Whatever his mood, she still felt sorry for him, and decided that she would do everything she could for him. She reached for the two names she had written on a slip of paper. Getting these files to Dr. Graves right away would be her first task.

Tim needed to speak to J.C. Now that he had accepted his suspension, he wanted to get the inside scoop on what exactly went on in that Board Room. He especially wanted to hear what had been said by Taylor. J.C. returned his page promptly. He'd been anxious to talk to Tim all week.

"Tim, how's your dad?"

"He's better. They did a triple bypass. He came out of it all right. Looks positive."

"Thank God," J.C. paused. "I suppose Taylor gave you the news?"

"I wasn't surprised."

"It was a hatchet job, Tim. I didn't think it was ethical with you being out of town, but no one cared."

"What went on in there, J.C.?"

"They talked about how you decompensated, and how it might be a recurring problem."

"No, I mean, who stuck up for me?" Tim didn't care about the details. Anything they had discussed about the case was irrelevant at this point. Tim just wanted to know who, if anyone, was on his side.

J.C. took a second to think, then decided that Tim could handle the truth. "Taylor was on your side, although he waffled a little at the end, when it looked hopeless. Garcia, Pope. Jacobs sat on the fence, as usual . . . and me, of course."

"That's it?" Tim couldn't hide his shock. He could name a handful of doctors whose support he had expected. "What about Taylor? What did he say?"

"He was the most outspoken in your favor. He talked about his loyalty to you, about how loyalty among doctors has been lost. He mentioned how you helped him out in his own practice. What did you do for him, by the way, that made him so grateful?"

Tim had never mentioned his donations to anyone, not even J.C. It seemed silly to keep it a secret, even now, but Tim didn't really want to talk about it with his friend. He didn't want to tell him how he had earned his movie money as a resident. He decided to just let it slide.

"I was just a moral supporter, J.C., nothing major."

"Yeah, well Taylor's always watched out for you, even when you were a medical student."

"You mean as a resident," Tim corrected him. "I met Taylor in my first year of residency at Harvard."

J.C. realized that he had never told Tim about his meeting with Taylor after the Honors Day baseball game. It was so long ago that he'd almost forgotten about it. He remembered thinking it was such a big deal at the time, now it seemed like nothing. J.C. chuckled at his own youthful paranoia and said, "No, I mean med student. Do you remember that Honors Day game when you kicked McConnell's ass?"

"Remember it? Isn't that why I'm now sitting in an empty office with no patients to see?"

"Sorry, of course you remember. Anyway, after the game Taylor came up to me and asked me to go see him the next day. I went, and he asked me all about you. It was weird at the time, and I guess I didn't want to tell you about it, you know, give you something else to worry about, what with medical school, and all. Then I just forgot about it."

Tim was trying to absorb all that J.C. was saying. "What? What did he ask about?"

"Let's see . . . oh, about your pitching and about your days at USC. Oh, yeah," J.C. was starting to shout, then calmed himself. "That was the weirdest part."

"What was weird?"

"He told me that he actually talked to someone at USC about you." J.C. realized Tim was getting upset and he tried to back off. "Tim, it wasn't any big deal. He was just curious about you, I guess because he wanted to bring you into the residency program. That's all."

"What does my pitching at USC have to do with medicine, J.C.?"

"Well, that was my question, too. But you know, looking back on it, I think Taylor was just impressed with your talent."

"If that's all it was, then why didn't you tell me about it at the time?"

"Well, it was a stressful time, getting ready for interviews and everything. I was just a stupid kid. I didn't want to worry you, and it bothered me that he was digging into your personal life. I couldn't figure out why he was asking me so many questions about you, and when I told him so, he changed the subject and sent me on my way. My gut feeling was that something wasn't right, but how could I explain it? I just wanted to forget about it. Maybe I should have told you about it. I'm sorry."

Tim tried to seem nonchalant. "It's no big deal. Taylor's always been a little off the wall, and besides, he's gone now. Forget about it."

Of course, Tim wasn't just going to forget about it. He intended to talk to Taylor, but not just yet. He needed some time to think through all that he had heard. Something peculiar was going on, and it seemed to begin and end with Taylor. Before he could pursue his thoughts, Judith knocked on his office door.

"Here are those files you wanted, Dr. Graves," she said as she handed him two manila folders.

"What files?" Tim asked, confused.

"The files you asked me to get."

"I didn't request any files."

"Those names that woman left . . . you told me to pull the files, didn't you?"

"What woman? Meg?"

"Yes, I told you, the woman from the *Globe* left some names for you and you asked me to pull their files. Don't you remember?" She stared at Tim with concern. Maybe he wasn't doing as well as he had appeared when he came in.

"I asked you to get their numbers." Tim could hardly speak.

"I know, but I thought I'd pull the charts, in case you needed more information. The phone numbers are in there, too."

"These are from University Hospital?" Tim hadn't lifted his eyes from the files, which now rested in his hands. He kept his eyes focused on them.

"Yes, Dr. Graves." When Tim didn't respond, Judith asked, "Is there anything else?"

Tim finally acknowledged her, looking dazed. "No Judith, that's all. Sorry, I'm just tired. Thanks."

Judith gently shut the door behind her. Tim stared in disbelief at the files in his hands. *Two boys, one from Wisconsin, one from Texas, both born at University Hospital and both with a cerebral aneurysm.* He opened each file. Both babies had been delivered by Dr. Malcolm Taylor.

Sixteen

The records showed that Martha Leon and Sara Pitt had both given birth to their sons at the hospital in Boston. Tim checked the records of the two boys to see if they had ever been worked up for neurological diseases, but neither of them had any hospital records beyond their birth records. The fact that Taylor was the primary care doctor for these two women just didn't make sense. There was no explanation why a woman from Wisconsin and a woman from Texas would each give birth to sons in Boston, delivered by Dr. Taylor. Even if they had been passing through Boston on vacation or something and had gone into labor, they would not have received medical treatment from Dr. Taylor. He had a patient waiting list of over one year. Tim decided to call Meg about this latest revelation.

Meg's machine picked up his call, but he didn't leave a message. He needed to talk to a human, not a machine. Tim fidgeted in his chair. He thought about working on the stack of papers on his desk, but he was unable to focus. He looked at his watch. Five o'clock. He tried Meg's house again, but still got the machine. He wasn't accomplishing anything, so he decided to lock up and leave.

Tim walked down Longwood Avenue. He had no destination in mind, he just needed to walk, and think. When he got to Huntington he turned left and headed downtown. He tried to assimilate all the information he'd been bombarded with since his return from Los Angeles. He recalled his conversation with J.C. about Taylor, but could come up with no reason why Taylor would have taken such a personal interest in him so long ago. Tired of walking, Tim crossed the street to catch the Green Line. Depositing his fifty cents, he took the nearest window seat. He leaned back in the plastic seat and sighed. He stared into the darkness of the underground and was content to ride and let his mind wander.

When the train stopped at the next station Tim got off and climbed the stairs to the street. He walked down Massachusetts Avenue through Harvard Square. He realized he was close to where Meg lived, having been there several weeks ago when he dropped off some material for her *Globe* article—an article he had yet to read. As he approached Meg's house he saw that her front door stood wide open. She occupied the lower level of a colonial two-story house. A couple of history professors at Harvard lived on the upper level. Tim walked up the front steps and called Meg's name. There was no answer. He saw a purse on the floor just inside the front door. He cautiously stepped into the foyer and looked around. Nothing. His heart beating faster, he stepped into the living room. *Could she have surprised an intruder?* Calling her name again, he hurried to the back of the house and spotted a bag of groceries on the kitchen counter. He started back down the hall toward the front door when a door swung open and Meg charged right into him. She screamed and shoved him away. Tim stumbled backward, nearly losing his balance, as Meg exclaimed, "Tim, what are you doing here?" She bent down and retrieved her Walkman and earphones from the floor.

"I saw that your front door was open and you didn't answer when I called out. I thought . . . I didn't mean to barge in on you and scare you to death."

Meg picked her purse up off the floor and closed the door. She was laughing and blushing as she tried to explain. "I was listening to the news on my Walkman. I was in a hurry to get to the bathroom coming home from the store, so I just dropped everything. I thought I kicked the front door shut, but I guess not."

Tim laughed at his own foolish imagination and Meg joined in. He sat at the kitchen table while she unpacked her groceries.

"So, tell me, what brings you to my neighborhood? Did you get those names I left with your secretary?"

"Yes, and then something strange happened. I asked my secretary to get the numbers and she thought I meant to get their hospital records."

"So?" Meg shrugged.

"So, the mothers of those two boys had University Hospital records. Two women from two different states each gave birth to a son at the same hospital in Boston."

Meg leaned against the counter and folded her arms, looking at him quizzically.

"And?" she asked, knowing there had to be more.

"And, these two women had the same doctor."

"Who?"

"Guess?"

"I have no idea."

"Come on, Meg."

"Tell me, who?"

"Taylor."

Meg's eyes widened. "Taylor?" She appeared as confused as he was.

"What do you think about that?" Tim asked.

Meg didn't know what to think. Obviously there was a connection between Taylor, the women, the article on Taylor's desk . . . but what did it mean? "It's really not so strange, Tim, when you think about it. I mean, Taylor is a world-renowned expert in fertility. People come to him from all over the country— from all over the world, for that matter."

"Are you saying you think these women had infertility problems and they both went to Taylor for help?"

"Is that so hard to believe? People come from Italy and England to see Taylor. Why not from Wisconsin and Texas?"

"But the only record on these women was from their hospitalization for their labor and delivery. There weren't any surgical records. If Taylor helped them with corrective surgery the records would show it."

"Is surgery the only solution to an infertility problem? What if the man has the problem instead of the woman? Certainly it's not always the woman's fault?" There was a slight edge to her voice.

"You're right. Of course, that's it, then."

"What's it?"

"That would mean that the women were artificially inseminated in Taylor's lab. Those records would be in Taylor's own patient files, not the hospital's."

Meg had read a little about infertility, but she was still confused. She didn't quite understand the concept of artificial insemination.

"Tim, if the husbands of these women are infertile, does that mean that their sperm is useless?"

"Technically, yes. A man who is diagnosed as infertile can't reproduce in any way."

"So if these women were artificially inseminated by Dr. Taylor, where did the sperm come from?"

"They have donors who give their sperm." Tim remembered the jar, Taylor's locker, the fifteen bucks and his own insistence that none of his sperm be used to impregnate women. He replayed Taylor's promise in his head.

"So it's that easy." Meg snapped her fingers for effect. "Taylor inseminates these women, they go to their respective homes, and when it's time to deliver, they come back to Taylor, a doctor they trust, to follow through with the delivery of their sons. I'm sure it happens all the time."

"And then the two boys are discovered to have cerebral aneurysms?"

Meg thought for a moment, then shrugged. "Maybe he's passing out some bad sperm." She chuckled a little, but quickly stopped when she saw the look on Tim's face.

Realizing what she had said, Meg blushed to the roots of her red hair. "I'm sorry Tim. I didn't mean that the way it sounded. This has nothing to do with Jonathan."

"Oh, my God." The words were out of his mouth before he had finished his thought. *Of course, all of them star athletes, all of them with cerebral aneurysms, all of them dead. Taylor lied to me from the very beginning. He never intended to use my sperm for research. He had already done his research, and he wanted me. I must have met all his specifications as a "preferred donor" for his baby on demand business. How could I have been so naïve?*

Meg went to where Tim was sitting and knelt in front of him. She took his hands in hers and forced him to look into her eyes.

"You've got to tell me what's going on here? Suddenly you're in a different world."

Tim guided Meg to the chair across from him and took a deep breath. This was the moment of truth, and he knew if anyone in the world would understand, it would be Meg.

"I knew Taylor when I was a resident at Harvard and he was just starting to make it big. He asked me to help him out

143

with his experiments."

"What kind of experiments?" Meg asked.

"On infertility. He asked if I would donate sperm for his study. I didn't want to do it at first, but then he offered me fifteen dollars a shot."

"Fifteen dollars?" Meg asked incredulously.

"It was big money at that time. It meant a lot back then. Anyway, I agreed, and I donated my sperm over the course of one year, and then once again in my final year. I was embarrassed about doing it, and never told anyone. But I made Taylor promise that he would only use my sperm for research, meaning that he wouldn't use it to impregnate women. He knew that I felt very strongly about that, and it was under that condition that I agreed to donate."

"So what you're saying is that you think these dead boys were actually your sons? That would mean that Taylor broke his promise and used your sperm against your wishes, and, since he had that article from Texas on his desk, that he knows about the genetic defect."

Tim nodded. "What other explanation is there?"

The reporter in Meg took over. "These are serious accusations. You're going to need proof. All you have so far are speculations and coincidences. We need more."

"We?"

"If you want to get to the bottom of it, you're going to need my help. I am an investigative reporter."

Tim was gratified by Meg's confidence. He was just beginning to understand the implications of what he had discovered. He knew that whatever happened from here, lives would be changed forever.

"I think I should confront Taylor with my suspicions. Ask him outright if he used my sperm for artificial insemination."

"If Taylor lied to you before, what makes you think he'll tell the truth this time? First, we need to have proof. We need to determine if those two mothers actually did use artificial insemination to become pregnant. We're assuming that they did, but we have to know for sure, so that you can confront Taylor with the facts. That way, he won't be able to wiggle out of telling you the truth."

He knew Meg was right. If he did confront Taylor and he

denied everything, he would be back to square one. He also would have made the tactical error of alerting Taylor about his suspicions. Taylor was no fool, and certainly he was clever enough to cover his tracks if he felt threatened. Clearly, their best approach was to gather all the facts and then strike, if their suspicions were confirmed.

"Okay. Flying to Texas and Wisconsin to talk to the mothers of those poor boys makes even more sense now." *If there is the slightest chance that I was the biological father, then I am also responsible for their deaths. God help me.*

Tim flashed back to the story Sally Graves had told him about his biological mother. Since no autopsy had been done, there was no way to determine a cause of death. The supposition had been an air cerebrothromboembolism to the brain, but it didn't take a "brain surgeon," given the facts he now had at his disposal, to make the leap to suspecting a cerebral aneurysm. Therein lies his genetic history. The cerebral aneurysm did not begin with Tim, but was passed on to him by his birth mother. From there he had turned three young boys, promising athletes, into victims. The ramifications were mind boggling . . .

*   *   *

Meg met him in the lobby of the Biochemistry Building. She rushed up to him, brushing her hair out of her face and trying to keep her shoulder bag in place. She grabbed his arm and gave him a quick hug. To Tim she had never looked more beautiful.

"Thanks for meeting me here on such short notice. When I called Luther and explained the situation, he said he could see me at one o'clock. I want you to hear what he has to say."

They climbed the gray marble steps to the second floor and worked their way down the hall until they came to Luther Kennedy's office. A steel-framed desk with papers piled high took up most of the room. An obviously overworked secretary looked up from an overstuffed filing cabinet. There was no place for them to sit in the tiny office.

"I'm Dr. Graves and this is Meg Logan. Dr. Kennedy is expecting us."

"Dr. Kennedy should be along any minute. Why don't you

both have a seat in his office."

Tim opened the door to a room no larger than the reception area. There were some personal photographs on the bookcase, but otherwise the office was in total disarray. Papers and journals cluttered the desk and the floor. Tim scooped some papers off of the two rickety chairs in front of the desk and they cautiously sat down. Meg smiled uneasily at Tim. *This is where Tim's hotshot DNA expert works?*

Tim hadn't seen Luther for almost six months. They had been classmates in medical school. Luther was at the Honors Day game when Tim had struck out McConnell and from that day forward Luther had pledged his undying friendship. McConnell had been especially hard on Luther during his rotation in surgery.

Shortly after one o'clock Luther came bursting in. He was wearing a long white lab coat with the collar turned up. His name was stenciled on the left upper pocket, LUTHER KENNEDY, M.D., PH.D. He had brown curly hair and he wore thick glasses. Although Luther was a brilliant biochemist and scientist who had developed his talents early, entering medical school at age nineteen, he never took himself too seriously. He was not the stereotypical academic—he kept himself in good physical shape and had quite a reputation with the ladies.

Luther greeted Tim warmly and then directed his inquiring gaze toward Meg.

"Luther, this is Meg Logan. She's a reporter from the *Globe.*"

"Whoa, Tim, you're not thinking of publishing anything about me in the newspaper, are you?"

"Nothing like that. Meg is here strictly off the record, as my friend."

"Well, that's a relief." Luther swung around his desk and plopped into his desk chair, which leaned dangerously to one side. "What are the Sox going to do this year, Tim?"

Tim smiled at his old friend. "They've got good hitting and pitching. There's no reason they can't go all the way."

"I sure hope so. I've got season tickets this year. Say, want to go to a game sometime?"

"Sure," Tim replied. "Anytime you want."

Luther abruptly changed the subject. "So, Taylor's up to his usual tricks, huh?" Tim had told Luther just about everything when they had talked on the phone. He knew about the suspension, the sperm donation, and the fact that he could have passed on a fatal condition to at least two boys.

"What do you mean by that?"

"It's common knowledge that he's been buying and selling sperm for years."

"What?" Tim couldn't believe what he was hearing. If it was common knowledge, how come he didn't know about it? Was he that out of it? "Well, he told me that the sperm donation was for research only. In fact, he guaranteed me that he would not use it for any other purpose."

"Ha! Don't you believe it. His type of research is published in *Reader's Digest*. He's not a scientist, that's for sure. It would give me a great deal of pleasure to bring Taylor down. He's been luring residents over to the University Hospital for years in order to have a pool of donors for his clinical practice. He's made millions. The worst part is that the administration would just look the other way. What was good for Taylor turned out to be even better for the hospital. Nobody wanted to kill the golden goose."

Tim was shocked to hear this. How naïve he had been! He could feel the rage bubbling up inside of him. But first things first: He had to find out how far Taylor had gone in using his sperm.

"The issue right now is whether those two boys who died from cerebral aneurysms were my sons. Then I have to find out if there are any more out there I may have passed on this defect to." He looked at Luther, pleading. "Can you help?"

Luther warmed to his subject. "It is amazing, the changes that have occurred in biochemical analysis in the last ten years. Do you want the full story, or would you rather have the abridged version?"

"Why don't you start, and we'll see how much we can follow."

"Well, you know about DNA. It's a double helix molecule that was originally described by Crick and Watson at Cambridge. Watson was a professor here at Harvard for many years after their discovery. Won a Nobel Prize for it. Since that time, there have been many advances, both in using the knowledge clinically and in research. As you know, there are twenty-three chromosomes and when the egg and sperm join together, they become forty-six chromosomes with over 100,000 genes. If you were to stretch out the DNA in a single cell, it would go for six feet."

Meg broke in with a question. "How can you know exactly what one person's DNA is with all of those molecules? It would be easy to make a mistake."

"Very perceptive. Actually, we don't do that. We take only portions of the molecule, one part of a gene or allele, and analyze that. We have ways of separating them out. I won't bore you with the details."

"Bottom line here, Luther. What are the chances of testing my DNA and someone else's DNA to see if I am the father?"

Luther leaned back in his chair, took off his glasses, opened his mouth, fogged both lenses and rubbed them with a tissue. He held them up to the light and put them back on. Tim was familiar with this routine. It gave Luther time to consider his answer.

"I could tell you that you are *not* the father with one hundred percent certainty. It would be ideal to have specimens from all the parties in involved. What are the chances of that?"

"I don't know. It's dangerous enough barging into the lives of these families, possibly exposing a well-kept secret. Maybe there would be a chance of getting samples from the Medical Examiner's autopsies of the two boys. I'm just not sure what kind of cooperation I would get from the mothers in terms of giving their own samples. Maybe there are some kind of legal steps I can take."

"That was the point of a recent trial where I testified in a paternity analysis case. We have advanced our techniques to the point where we don't need both parents' DNA to identify the true father."

This was good news. But before Tim could get too excited, he realized the task still at hand. "But we still need to get a specimen from the offspring."

Luther nodded.

This prompted Meg to ask, "What kind of specimens do we need, Dr. Kennedy?"

"The most common specimen we do is a buccal mucosa swab. That's the tried and true way. Of course, anywhere we can get DNA is okay. You can use blood, cells from saliva, semen, even sweat."

Meg nodded. "What about hair?"

"Oh, yes, of course, hair. As long as the roots are included in the specimen, hair will give us a DNA sample. Absolutely."

"How long will the test take if we can get you a specimen?"

"About two weeks. We do a DNA right here in our own laboratories, but it's still an experimental procedure. Our techniques are as good as any. We're getting specimens in from all over the country and we're amassing a good data base. We'll have a shot at almost ninety-nine percent certain, if there is a match, that you'd be the father."

"Close enough for me," Tim said, and he looked at Meg, "Anything else?"

She couldn't think of anything that Luther hadn't already answered. She stood up to leave, as Tim shook Luther's hand.

"Thanks Luther. I don't have to tell you that this has to be kept absolutely confidential. I don't want anybody to know about it."

Luther put his index finger and thumb together and swiped them across his lips, "Mum's the word."

Outside the building Tim and Meg joined hands and headed toward the parking lot. Holding hands seemed natural, as though they had known each other always. But Tim was thinking ahead to the next step in their investigation, and how he could finesse contacting the parents of the two boys. As if reading his mind, Meg asked, "When will you be leaving, Tim?"

"As soon as I can."

Seventeen

The taxi made its way down the tree-lined streets of the suburban neighborhood. It was a warm morning and it was going to get warmer. Tim rolled down his window and gazed out to admire the homes. They were mostly two-story, wooden structures. They resembled the houses in Needham, colonial and early American, but these houses in Middleton, Wisconsin all had verandas and no two houses were painted the same. The lawns in this particular neighborhood were well-manicured, and Tim could tell which houses boasted of a young family by the assortment of toys left out in front. Tim couldn't hear the cries of any children on this early Monday morning. He heard only the distant sounds of lawn mowers starting up, and the weak breeze rustling the aspens. For a few moments he felt at peace in this place and couldn't help thinking how perfect it would be to raise a family here, before reminding himself that he no longer had a family.

The driver startled him out of his thoughts when he abruptly stopped the taxi. Tim peered out the window at the pale blue house in front of him. It looked like all the others, with a clean façade and a brick walkway, which stretched from the sidewalk to the front porch. There weren't any toys outside.

Tim paid the driver and stepped out onto the sidewalk. As the taxi drove away, he took a deep breath and tucked in his shirt. He had chosen to dress casually, with a white, short sleeved shirt tucked into a pair of tan slacks. He had to pull an extra inch on his belt when he had cinched it that morning. He knew he had lost some weight, and he felt better for it.

He had arranged to meet with Sara Pitt this morning, and on the phone she had sounded eager to talk with Tim about her son, Sean. Tim was anxious to hear what she had to say, and he had some questions for her. Tim had explained his own tragic situation, so similar to her own, and she seemed to have no qualms about talking to a stranger about it. He knocked on the front door, which was immediately answered by a petite brunette. Her black curls were piled high on her head, which gave her a few extra inches, but Tim could see that she was no more than five feet tall. She stared at Tim without saying a word. Her round dark eyes scrutinized him, and still she did not speak. Tim shuffled his feet, his discomfort growing as the silence continued. At length, he spoke.

"Uh, Mrs. Pitt?"

She took a step back at the sound of his voice, still clutching the door knob.

"You're Tim Graves?"

"Yes. Did you forget our appointment?"

"No, I didn't forget. Forgive me. Come in. I was just surprised that you looked so . . . so young. Younger than I expected."

Tim stepped into the house, which held the wonderful aroma of cinnamon. Sara Pitt ushered him into the living room and asked him to sit down. She excused herself, saying she would be right back. Tim settled into a comfortable armchair and glanced around the room. He guessed that the house was probably built in the twenties. The floors were made of a dark wood, which creaked with every step. A large oriental rug covered most of the floor in the living room, the colors muted by many years of wear. A brick fireplace sat at one end of the room, with a large mantle filled with framed pictures, candlesticks, and a lovely antique clock. He admired the bay window, which extended from the living room onto the front porch. There were cushions and throw pillows on it, and Tim imagined it to be a pleasant spot for reading when the sun streamed in during the afternoon hours. There was a grand piano in the corner behind him. Arranged on top were a few framed photographs . . . He tried to make out the faces of the people in the pictures, but they were too far away. Just as he was moving to take a closer look, Sara Pitt came back into the room carrying a silver tray. She set the tray down on an antique trunk, which served as a coffee table.

"Would you like some coffee?" she asked, as she began pouring some into a porcelain cup.

Tim had found the source of the sweet cinnamon smell. Fresh muffins had been placed invitingly on the tray. He eyed the muffins, remembering that he had skipped breakfast. Sara had already handed him his coffee, and he thanked her profusely as she placed a muffin on a small plate and passed it his way.

"I baked some apple cinnamon muffins this morning. I hope you like them."

"That's very kind of you." It had been a long time since someone had treated him with such genuine hospitality. He took a bite and mumbled his appreciation.

Sara kept her eyes on Tim. She had been shocked to see such a handsome, and all too familiar, face on her doorstep. She couldn't get over how much Tim Graves resembled the son she had lost. Or was she still seeing Sean's face wherever she looked? Sometimes she couldn't be sure. Regardless, her heart went out to this still young doctor who had lost so much.

"Did you fly in this morning?"

"Yes, I was lucky to get an early flight."

"I've only been to Boston a few times. It's a lovely town. My husband and I did the Freedom Trail a long time ago. I love all that history stuff."

Tim took this as an opportunity to question her about her trips to Boston. He didn't want to appear to be prying. He had to proceed with caution, so he began by telling her of some of his favorite spots.

While listening to Tim talk, Sara considered how much she was willing to tell Tim about her reason for being in Boston. She had given birth to her son there, the greatest moment of her life. Would he think it odd that her son was born in Boston when they had always lived in Wisconsin? She wasn't ashamed of what they did, but her husband was. He had made her promise never to discuss the circumstances of Sean's birth with anyone. When they discovered that they couldn't have children and that her husband was the problem, he was devastated. He viewed it as a threat to his masculinity. No matter how hard Sara tried to convince him that infertility had nothing to do with his virility, or worthiness as a man, he refused to listen. After many ugly scenes, he finally relented enough to agree to the artificial insemination, but only on the condition that they keep it a closely guarded secret.

Tim had to repeat his question about Sara's visit to Boston. She seemed miles away.

"You said you've been to Boston several times. Is that your

favorite place to vacation?" Tim was trying to keep the conversation light.

It would have been such a relief to be able to tell someone, *anyone*, the whole truth about Sean, but she could not dishonor her husband.

"Actually, we took one vacation in Boston, and our second visit, it's actually very funny. We were driving to visit my parents, who live in Maine. I was pregnant at the time, very close to my delivery date. It was probably foolish of us to take the trip, but we headed out." Sara paused to take a sip of coffee and she shakily replaced the cup. Tim noticed that she avoided eye contact with him as she continued her story. "Before we hit Maine, we decided to drive through Boston, maybe stay the night and see some of the sights. Well, as we were walking around downtown, near that Italian neighborhood, I think it was, wouldn't you know it, my water broke."

She stole a glance at Tim and couldn't tell anything from his expression. She just wanted to hurry up and get through this piece of fiction before she tripped herself up.

"So, they rushed me to the hospital and it was all over in a matter of minutes." She threw up her hands and slapped them back down on her thighs. End of story.

"Who was your doctor in Boston?" Tim couldn't stop himself from asking.

"Dr. Taylor. A wonderful man. Do you know him?"

"Yes. I'm surprised he was available. He usually doesn't take emergency deliveries."

Sara fumbled with her skirt and refused to look at him. "Well, I guess he just happened to be there when I came in. Lucky us."

Tim nodded.

Tim felt sure Sara was hiding something, but he couldn't risk insulting her by challenging her story. She obviously didn't want to talk about it. He had started out with such high hopes and so far he had nothing.

"Dr. Graves?"

"Please, call me Tim."

"Okay, Tim . . . You said your son died of a cerebral aneurysm—like Sean's?"

She was certainly justified in changing the subject; after all, that was the reason he had told her he wanted to see her to begin with. He cleared his throat and began telling Sara the story of Jonathan. It was good to talk about his son again. He so rarely did. Sara sat quietly, listening to what he said, occasionally adding some story of her own. They were united in their grief and their memories. It had been seven years since Sean died, but to Sara his memory was as fresh as if she had just sent him off to school that morning. An hour flew by and it was time for Tim to go. He would learn nothing more that could help him. Sara offered him a cup of coffee for the road.

"No, thank you. You've been very kind, but I should leave now." He stood up and started toward the door. Sara reached for the tray and said, "Just wait one minute and I'll wrap up some of these muffins for you to take. We can't possibly eat them all ourselves." She hurried to the kitchen before Tim could stop her.

Alone in the room, Tim's eyes wandered back to the pictures on the piano. He stepped close enough to see them clearly. There were several baby pictures, a family portrait of Sara, her husband and a toddler sitting on some grass near a lake. Another picture, the toddler holding a baseball, made Tim smile. But he was stopped cold by a portrait in a large silver frame. He looked toward the door to make sure Sara wasn't coming back, then reached over and picked up the frame. The face was of a young boy, probably twelve or thirteen years old, with blue eyes and sandy blond hair. His grin was broad and genuine. Tim couldn't breathe. The boy looked almost exactly like Jonathan, maybe just a little slimmer. *So, he was right. Sara Pitt had not told the truth...and neither had Taylor. This has to be my son.*

The floor creaked as Sara came down the hall to the living room. Tim quickly moved away from the piano and pretended to be looking out the window. Sara held out a small paper bag to Tim.

"Here you go. I wrapped them in plastic so they won't get stale."

"Thank you," he answered and reached for the bag.

She walked him to the front door and slid behind him to open it. Tim couldn't think of a thing to say. He couldn't get that picture out of his mind. He must have uttered some words of farewell, because he found himself out on the sidewalk. Belatedly, he thought about calling a taxi. He decided to walk until he came to a main street. His flight didn't leave for several hours. He had plenty of time to catch a cab. He needed that time to think. If Taylor had used Tim's sperm to impregnate his patients, then there could be other children out there. He had to find better proof than a photograph, however, or Taylor would find a way to deny everything.

The taxi left him at the airport in Madison a good hour and a half before his flight to Boston was scheduled to leave. He was thirsty and looked around for a snack bar or vending machine. He came across the airport lounge, which was empty except for the bartender. He sat at the bar and ordered a glass of orange juice. As he pulled out his wallet to pay, a piece of paper fell to the floor. The phone numbers of Sara Pitt and Martha Leon were on that paper. Sara Pitt seemed to be a dead end, but maybe he would have better luck with Martha Leon. What did he have to lose?

He threw a couple of singles down on the bar and headed to the nearest airport monitor. He found a flight departing from Madison to Houston, where Meg had said the Leon boy had lived. He checked his watch. He had fifteen minutes to get to Gate 21 and buy a ticket. He started running. He rushed up to the counter, gasping for breath. He noticed the passengers at Gate 21 were starting to board. The two attendants at the counter were shuffling papers and talking to each other and it took a moment for one of them to notice him. The brunette looked up at Tim and smiled, then frowned as he blurted, "I need to get to Houston immediately."

"I'm sorry, sir, but this flight is booked," the attendant seemed to be genuinely disappointed that she wasn't able to help this handsome man.

"Completely booked?"

"I'm afraid so."

Tim rubbed the back of his neck in frustration. The next flight wasn't for six hours. Now that he had made his decision to go to Texas, he wanted to get on with it.

"Can't I try stand-by?" Tim asked hopefully.

The brunette frowned again. "The plane leaves in ten min-

155

utes and everybody who bought a ticket has already checked in."

Tim walked away, shoulders drooping. Maybe he should just fly back to Boston. He could always get a flight to Houston from there. As he was mulling over his options, he heard a shout coming from the boarding area. An elderly man in a wheelchair was being pushed down the ramp, followed closely by his distraught wife. She told anyone within earshot that her husband was having a heart attack and he needed an ambulance. Apparently one had already been called, as Tim noticed a gurney being wheeled by two uniformed attendants. From where he stood he caught the eye of the brunette at the ticket counter. She motioned to him to come back.

"You're in luck, sir. Looks like there are two seats available now." The brunette nodded in the direction of the stricken man and his hysterical wife.

The flight to Houston was uneventful. As soon as the plane landed, Tim found a phone and placed a call to Martha Leon. He explained to her that he too had lost a son to a cerebral aneurysm and he was interested in talking to her about her son. Mrs. Leon was surprised that someone from Boston had heard about the death of her son, but she was not reluctant to meet with him. She gave him directions to her house and suggested he take the free shuttle into town and a taxi from there. By four o'clock Tim was knocking on her door.

The Leons lived in an urban quarter of Houston. It was an affluent neighborhood and the houses were large and well kept. Tim was greeted at the door by an attractive Latina woman. She left him standing in the foyer while she hurried off to another room. Tim wasn't sure if she expected him to follow her, but decided to wait where she had left him. In an instant she was back, clutching a large book in her arms.

"Please, come and sit. I want to show you some pictures."

Tim followed her into a pleasant room, furnished in Santa Fe style. Mexican throws covered sofas and chairs. Martha sat on the couch and opened the book. She appeared to be overcome with emotion, unable to speak. She patted the cushion next to her and Tim settled in beside her. He was anxious to see the pictures of Marcus.

"This is Marcus as a baby," she began. Tim stretched out his legs and tried to get comfortable. He sensed this was going to take a while, and he hoped that Martha would be more forthcoming than Sara Pitt had been. As she flipped through the pages, the words came more easily, and soon she was caught up in the life of her son, eager to share it with Tim. Tim searched the photo, but didn't see any real resemblance to Jonathan, not like the haunting image of Sean in Wisconsin. Marcus Leon took after his mother: olive skin, jet black hair and a round face. He did have piercing blue eyes, however, which seemed all the more vibrant peering out from his dark lashes. As Martha talked, Tim waited for an opportunity to bring up the circumstances of Marcus's birth in Boston and the connection with Dr. Taylor.

"Come see Marcus's room." She jumped up and grabbed Tim's arm. She pulled him up the stairs and down a short hallway, only releasing her grip when they were both inside the bedroom. A vase of fresh flowers sat on top of the desk. The room was spotless, the bed freshly made up, as though waiting for Marcus to return. A large poster of Albert Einstein hung on the wall, surrounded by posters of football players and pennants from various teams. Over the boy's bed hung an elaborate crucifix. Martha pointed to a trophy prominently displayed among many smaller ones on a chest of drawers.

"You see that. That's when he won the Most Valuable Player trophy." She stared proudly at the golden figure of a football player preparing to throw a pass. *This could have been Jonathan's room with Jonathan's collection of trophies*. The memories all but overwhelmed Tim. Tim's heart went out to Martha and he understood perfectly when she declared that she just couldn't bring herself to change a thing in this room. He wondered now how he could ever broach the subject that had brought him here to begin with. He didn't want to add to her grief. The ringing of the phone broke the spell.

She was annoyed at the interruption. "Excuse me for just a moment."

Tim heard her softly answer the phone, then immediately become more animated. She was explaining that she couldn't talk because she had a guest, then began to rattle on about who Tim was and why he was there. As she continued with her conversation, Tim took another look around the room, occasionally picking up a book to examine the title. Marcus had books on airplanes, dinosaurs and football, as well as science fiction and mysteries. There was a complete set of Funk and Wagnall's Encyclopedias that appeared well used. A large book, looking something like a scrapbook, caught his eye. It was entitled "My Life." Tim opened it and discovered that it was Marcus's baby book. Inside was a chronicle of his first steps, first words and all the other enchanting firsts in a baby's life. Taped to the back cover was a piece of ribbon, probably from a first gift, some shoelaces, several locks of hair, a copy of his birth certificate, and his hospital ID bracelet, from University Hospital.

It sounded as though Martha was ending her phone call and he started to slide the baby book back where it belonged. *Locks of hair. Luther had said even a strand of hair, if it still had the root, could provide DNA!* He quickly flipped to the back of the book. Clearly the locks of hair had been cut with scissors. *No roots.* Tim started to leave the room, when he noticed a door leading to a small bathroom. Pushing the door open, he could see that the bathroom, too, had remained unchanged. Listlessly, he opened and closed drawers and cabinets, with no real hope of finding anything. The drawer to the left of the sink jammed as he closed it. The handle of a hairbrush prevented it from closing. He grabbed the brush and stuffed it into his coat pocket just as he heard Martha hang up the phone.

Martha was reluctant to let Tim go, but he explained he had another appointment to keep. He wished her well and promised he would visit again if he ever returned to Houston. She was clearly to disappointed to be losing someone to talk with about Marcus—someone who understood her grief. Tim, too, felt a pang at leaving the woman all alone with her pain again. He knew what that felt like. But he was anxious to get back to Boston, anxious to get this hairbrush to Luther Kennedy. The hairbrush, hopefully, could provide Luther with hair follicles and skin cells from the scalp, enough DNA for Luther to analyze. Finally he had some concrete evidence, something that might lead him to the truth.

He decided to call Meg from the airport while he waited for the next flight to Boston.

"Tim, where are you? I thought you'd be back by now."

"I'm in Houston. At the airport. I just met with Martha Leon."

"Did you find out anything?'

"No. Both women were reluctant to talk." Tim qualified his assessment when he pictured Martha Leon, and added, "about their pregnancies."

"So, nothing new, then," Meg sighed in disappointment.

"Afraid not." Tim didn't want to tell Meg about the hair sample. No use getting her hopes up if nothing came of it.

Meg had been concentrating on one idea that had been bugging her. She had come up with some interesting facts that she wanted to share with Tim.

"Tim, if Taylor did use your sperm for *in vitro* fertilization without your consent, then essentially he stole from you."

"Yes, so what?"

"I've spent hours researching the law books, penal codes, whatever, and I even had my friend at Harvard Law look into it. We just can't find it written anywhere that the theft of bodily fluids is punishable. Stealing sperm is not against the law."

"That's ludicrous. Of course it's theft. He took my sperm and used it without my consent."

"No, he didn't steal your sperm, you gave it to him. He just used it for more than just research. Did you have anything in writing describing the purpose of your donation?"

"No, of course not. It was just something he asked me to do, he paid me for it, and I did it. I don't care what the law says. He stole it."

She couldn't argue with his feelings about it, just the facts. "I'm just saying—even if you prove that Taylor did all these things, there's nothing under Massachusetts state law that says you can file charges."

Tim was dumbstruck. "You think Taylor knows about these laws, or lack of laws?"

"Well, if he's really doing this, then you can bet that you're not the only one he's used. I'm sure he's made sure he was protected."

A heat of fury came over Tim. *That conniving son of a bitch. All this time he made me think he was my only supporter...speaking well of me at my hearing, calling me into his office for a pep talk, supporting me through*

159

my residency, giving me my job at Harvard. He was always there, in the background. How could I have been so blind? Is Taylor that unscrupulous? I can't wait two weeks for any DNA report.

"I'm going to Vermont. I have to confront him. I'll accuse him of stealing my sperm and see how he reacts. He'll have to explain away the coincidence of the cerebral aneurysms, the babies born in Boston, and everything else I hit him with. I'll know if he's lying. Maybe I can't control the past, but I can control the present—and the future."

Before Meg could respond Tim hung up the phone and headed to his boarding gate. The next person he wanted to speak to was Taylor, no one else.

Eighteen

When Tim called Taylor's clinic in Vermont he had received a recorded message indicating office hours and giving directions to the clinic. Not wanting to warn Taylor that he was on his way, Tim was glad he didn't have to make up some implausible reason for calling. He found an old map of Vermont and traced his route from Massachusetts. The drive would take about four hours. Tim knew Vermont fairly well from his years in medical school when he often visited his uncle in Norwich.

The drive along the highway was uneventful. As he got closer to the turnoff to the clinic, he began to pay closer attention to his driving. He navigated the winding road, rarely encountering another car. This was an isolated area, with only a few houses tucked in among the trees, which stretched as far as the eye could see. The expanse of green was mesmerizing. Taylor had chosen a perfect place to hide, thought Tim, more convinced than ever he was hiding from something. Tim missed the turn onto Stevens Road and had to drive several miles out of his way before he could safely turn around. He cursed himself for letting his mind wander. He would need all of his wits about him for the ordeal he faced. He could not afford these lapses.

Stevens Road was a series of sharp curves and steep inclines, leading Tim ever deeper into the woods. He found the number of Taylor's clinic on a green mailbox and turned into the driveway. Oddly, no sign announced Taylor's name or the name of his clinic. The driveway extended a good three hundred yards before any structures could be seen. He slowed down as he approached the house, his heart racing. The house was a two-story colonial with a short porch leading to an ornate wooden door. About twenty yards to the left of the house was a modern, one-story building with shuttered windows. It appeared as though this building was recently constructed. Cold and sterile-looking, it didn't fit this tranquil setting. Tim could detect no movement inside, and no lights showed from behind the shutters. He had parked his car under an ancient maple tree, and it was the only vehicle in sight. The place seemed suspiciously deserted for an internationally renowned fertility specialist and his soon-to-be world famous clinic.

Tim's plan was to merely drop in on an old friend and try to have a few moments alone with Taylor. Once they were alone, behind closed doors, he would hit Taylor with all he had. As he approached the front door he noticed a small wooden sign hanging above the doorbell. The first line simply read MALCOLM TAYLOR, M.D. and underneath, INFERTILITY SPECIALIST. The sign was written in an old style cursive that made Tim feel like he was entering a candy store, rather than the clinic of so prominent a physician. The humility was out of keeping with the Taylor Tim knew.

Tim tried the door. Locked. It was Tuesday morning and the recording had clearly stated that office hours were Tuesday through Thursday from eight A.M. to four P.M. Tim pressed the doorbell. Within a few seconds the lock clicked and the door opened automatically. He stepped inside and, in spite of himself, was charmed by the interior of the house. It maintained the same colonial charm as the exterior. Everything was old, authentic and very cozy. All the doors off the main hallway were closed and it wasn't clear which way to go. There was something very strange about this place. The door at the end of the hall swung open and a woman walked confidently to meet him. It was Meredith. She stopped a few feet in front of Tim, her eyes wide with surprise. She never expected to see Tim Graves again, let alone here.

"Dr. Graves. What a pleasant surprise." She had always had a little crush on him.

"Meredith. I didn't expect to see you here," he stammered. He was surprised that Taylor brought her along to Vermont. He had always complained about how scatterbrained she was. Actually, he was even more surprised that Meredith had agreed to go with Taylor. Life in Vermont could not be very exciting. *Taylor must be paying her big bucks.*

"Well, Dr. Graves, I might say the same thing about you. What brings you all the way to Vermont?" She folded her arms in front of her and shifted her weight to one leg.

Tim didn't hesitate. "Actually, I came to Vermont to visit some family and decided to stop by and see how things are going. What a great spot you have here."

"Yes. We're settling in nicely. Still a few kinks that need to be worked out, but we should be ready to start seeing patients next week."

Tim smiled and nodded. He wanted to see Taylor, not talk to his secretary.

"Is Dr. Taylor available? I mean, do you think he has some time to see me?" Tim tried not to sound too anxious. This was supposed to be a casual visit.

"He's here, Dr. Graves, but I don't know how much free time he has, he keeps a very busy schedule." She winked at Tim. "But I'm sure he can find time to see an old friend."

Meredith led the way down the hall and through the door she had left open. They entered a large room with leather couches and a huge reception desk. It was much like the well-appointed waiting room in Taylor's old office in Boston, perhaps a bit more homey. Meredith offered Tim some coffee, which he refused. His heart was pounding fast enough without the aid of caffeine. She invited Tim to sit down and make himself comfortable while she slipped through a connecting door. Along with the entrance door and Taylor's private office door, there was another door behind Meredith's desk. *All these closed doors. What are they trying to hide?* He thought about taking a peek, but calculated that Meredith would return before he had time. *It's probably just a closet. I have to get a grip on my paranoia.*

Meredith hurried back into the room and closed the door behind her. Her expression told him that Taylor hadn't been too happy to hear that he had a visitor.

"He's very busy, Dr. Graves." Meredith offered him a weak smile. She was trying not to show her distress, but she just couldn't understand Dr. Taylor's negative response. She had thought he would be pleased to see Dr. Graves, but he became very agitated and told her to make some excuse to get rid of him. She didn't know how she could turn away Dr. Graves so rudely after all these years. She remained standing with her back to the door and fidgeted with her skirt. She didn't know what else to say.

Tim sensed her discomfort and wondered, himself, why Taylor wouldn't see him. *He doesn't know why I'm here. Why would an impromptu visit from me be a problem for him? The last time they had met, Taylor acted as though we were best buddies? ...*

"I don't know what else to say. He said he's very busy and can't see anyone right now. It's so un . . . " Meredith stopped herself and shrugged.

Tim knew this was a bullshit excuse and Meredith knew he could see right through it. He decided to use her sympathy to his advantage.

"Meredith, what if I just walk in?"

She stared dumbly at him. "Oh no, you can't do that. I'd get into trouble."

"Why don't you take a coffee break?" Tim asked casually. It was a simple suggestion.

"A coffee break?"

"Sure. It's . . . what?" Tim looked at his watch. "Almost eleven o'clock. I'd say you're due for a coffee break, wouldn't you?"

Meredith understood what he was doing. She nodded her head and walked mindlessly to her desk. She grabbed her purse from the bottom drawer and headed for the door. As she walked out she looked over her shoulder. "You'll . . . "

Tim cut her off. "I'll cover for you."

Acting before he lost his nerve Tim approached Taylor's door and raised his hand to knock. He paused with his hand in mid-air and dropped it to the doorknob. He turned the knob and slowly opened the door. Taylor was sitting behind his desk with his back to the room. He seemed to be "busy" doing nothing but gazing out the window. Tim closed the door behind him and Taylor swiveled his chair around.

"What is it now . . . ?" He stopped short and gasped out loud as he caught sight of Tim.

"Meredith?" Tim finished his question for him. "She went on a coffee break, my suggestion. I figured you wouldn't mind chatting with an old friend, right, Malcolm?"

Tim had never called him Malcolm before, and the name hung in the air between the two men like an ominous cloud. Taylor was smart enough to sense trouble. He could see it in Tim's eyes and hear it in his voice. He tried to regain his composure and assume the demeanor of a harried scientist.

"Tim, it's good to see you. Meredith knows how busy I am, but she constantly intrudes. I'm afraid I took my bad temper out on you. I hope you don't think I was trying to get rid of you. I knew you'd understand. Have a seat and tell me what brings you here."

Tim didn't buy Taylor's sudden hospitality. He would have preferred to stand, but took a seat in the leather chair that Taylor indicated. Instead of taking his seat behind the desk, Taylor chose the chair next to Tim's and perched on the edge of the seat, a sort of "we're all on the same side" gesture.

"I'm here on some personal business. I have a few questions." Tim spoke confidently and without emotion.

Taylor shifted back in his seat and looked up at the ceiling. He didn't like Tim's coldness. Taylor was used to a confident, yet reserved Tim Graves, who was always respectful. He was used to a Tim Graves who came to his office only when he was invited, not one who barged in even after he had been turned away.

"Okay, you came all the way to Vermont to talk business. It must be important. You're not looking for a job, are you? Are they giving you a hard time about your suspension?"

"No one's giving me a hard time."

"That's good to hear. I was worried about you with all this time on your hands. I know you thrive on hard work."

"I need to ask you about those experiments you did a long time ago."

"What experiments?" Taylor asked, a little too quickly.

"The experiments you did on my sperm." Tim watched for any reaction from Taylor but his face remained expressionless.

"You mean the time when you donated for me?"

"That's what I mean."

"What else is there to know about it?"

"That's what I'm asking you."

"I'm afraid I don't follow. You remember as well as I do that you donated sperm for my genetic experiments. What more do you want me to say?"

"Is that all you did? Use my sperm for genetic experiments?"

"That was our agreement."

Taylor watched Tim carefully. He knew where the discussion was heading, but he'd be damned if he'd help Tim get there. Taylor had his reputation to protect, and he realized that Tim Graves was a dangerous opponent. He had always been a little unsure of him. Perhaps it was because Tim seemed so untouchable, so impervious to the corruption of the medical system. Taylor admired Tim's dedication to his profession, but it was that same dedication that daunted him—he knew that neither he nor anyone else could buy him off. Graves was too honest and too principled. Twenty-five years ago he had accepted Taylor's support in securing a position at Harvard, but even that was damn hard for him. Now there was nothing Taylor could bribe him with, and no reason for Tim to accept a bribe.

Tim stared straight at Taylor. "Did you use my sperm to impregnate women?"

Taylor knew what it would mean if Tim discovered the truth about those many years ago. He wasn't dealing with a guy like McConnell, who didn't even know the meaning of integrity. Instead, he was faced with a man who considered betrayal the first sin against man. Taylor's thoughts returned to McConnell. *Could that prick have opened his mouth and tipped off Graves?*

"Who have you been talking to?" Taylor asked calmly.

"I haven't been talking to anyone. Should I be talking to someone? Is someone else involved?"

"No, no. I didn't mean it like that, Tim. You know how rumors get started . . . someone wants to get to you, so they start making things up. You know what I'm talking about." Taylor thought he might have a chance to lie his way out, now that he was pretty sure McConnell hadn't blown the whistle on him. All he had to do was deny everything. Tim had no proof.

"You still haven't answered my question. Did you use my sperm, against my wishes, to impregnate your patients?"

Taylor rubbed the back of his neck and forced himself to laugh. "That's absurd. Why would I do that?"

"That's my next question. Why would you do it?"

"First of all, where did you get this crazy idea? All of a sudden, out of the blue, you decide to drive to Vermont with these ridiculous accusations. Accusations based on what, a hunch? Do you realize how you sound?"

"I'm not accusing you of anything. I only asked you a question. A question you still haven't answered."

Taylor slapped his hand on the arm of the chair. "Well it sounds like an accusation to me. You barge in here, uninvited, throw some bullshit accusation at me about stealing your sperm and then expect me to act calm." Taylor was losing his cool. Tim felt like he was finally getting somewhere.

"I don't want you to act at all. I want you to tell the truth." Tim got up and gripped the arms of Taylor's chair. Leaning in so their faces nearly touched, he said, "So far the only 'bullshit story' I've heard is that you were too busy to see me. Me, Malcolm? Your old friend? What are you afraid of?"

Taylor didn't move. He refused to meet Tim's eyes. He didn't know what to say. Tim pushed away from the chair and went to the window. With his back to Taylor he continued, "I saw a picture of Sean Pitt in Wisconsin. You know Sean Pitt, don't you, Malcolm?" Taylor didn't respond, just kept staring blankly out the window. "What a coincidence, I tell you. Looked just like Jonathan. You remember Jonathan, my son? Died of a cerebral aneurysm? Just like Sean Pitt. And just like Marcus Leon. How many more are there?"

Taylor remained speechless, unable to move. Tim walked over to the bookcase and kept talking.

"J.C. Parker tells me you were once very curious about my pitching abilities. You even called USC and got my stats. Is that how you get into a good residency program? If you have a good arm then it's a sure thing?" Tim looked directly at Taylor. "Marcus Leon and Sean Pitt had good arms. But then they died. You must have passed out some bad sperm, Malcolm"

"You don't know what you're talking about," Taylor whispered.

"Excuse me? Did you say something?" Tim returned to the desk and decided to sit in Taylor's chair. The two men were now sitting face to face. Taylor spoke again, with more conviction.

"You don't know what you're talking about, Tim."

"You mean I'm wrong and I don't know what I'm talking about, or I'm right, but I still don't know what I'm talking about?" He cocked his head to one side in a sarcastic gesture of confusion.

"It was an experiment," Taylor began. "It was all an experiment. I didn't lie to you about that."

"What kind of experiment?"

Taylor sighed and put his head in his hands. "I wanted to see if it would work. If I could provide my patients with the best possible genes. I don't know, maybe it got out of hand."

Tim's anger grew. It sounded like his hunch was correct. This was close to a confession.

"Do you realize what you've done to me?" Tim couldn't think of where to begin.

"Tim, I never meant to deceive you. It just evolved, and I thought it wasn't a big deal for you."

"Who gave you the right to decide how I feel?"

"Tim, you really don't understand."

"You son of a bitch. I don't have to understand."

"Tim, what I did for those women . . . I gave them life. I gave them sons and daughters. For most couples having children is easy and natural. For these couples it's a struggle. An excruciating struggle, day in and day out. You might feel robbed, but think about how they feel."

Tim couldn't believe what he was hearing.

"We're not talking about stealing a couple of cookies from the cookie jar, for Christ's sake. You stole a part of me. You created another human being from me. This is not your fucking right, Taylor. I don't give a shit about the grieving, childless people of the world. The fact is you tried to play God. You know what that makes you, don't you Taylor? That makes you the devil. And I'll see you burn in hell."

Taylor burst into laughter. He heard Tim's speech, but he didn't care anymore. He wasn't afraid, because he knew something that apparently Tim didn't.

"You can't touch me, Tim. You can't do a thing."

"It's theft. You stole from me."

"I paid for it. That's not theft. That's called capitalism."

"I got a total of a hundred bucks. Gee, Taylor, how much did you get?"

"Do you feel cheated, Tim? The scales tipped a little too much in my direction? Well, after all, I did work harder than you did. At least you had a few seconds of pleasure. But, if you want more money . . . "

"I don't want your money."

"You make me out to be some kind of black market baby merchant. I offered those people hope and they embraced it. Should I complain if people are willing to pay for my expertise?"

"You thought you were saving the world from unbearable pain by allowing them to bear other people's children? My children?"

"Sometimes, Tim, the means justifies the end."

"Then how do you justify condemning a child to death before it is even born?"

"What the hell are you talking about?"

"Marcus Leon, Sean Pitt, were they mine?"

Taylor weighed the cost of telling him. If he lied, Tim would find out anyway. Maybe he would even go to the families. Taylor didn't need that kind of publicity.

"Yes, they were yours."

"Then you killed them."

"Tim, I don't know where you're headed with this, but I wish you'd get on with it. I'm a busy man."

"They both died of cerebral aneurysms. That's something I gave them. You must know that these types of neurological diseases can be inherited."

"I didn't find out about your medical history until I read about it in the *Globe* recently. Needless to say, I was shocked, but you can't blame me for their deaths. If anything, you should blame yourself for lying about it."

"If you will remember, there was no health questionnaire for me to fill out when you asked me to donate my sperm. Why would there be? You only wanted it for your research. You did health screenings only on potential donors for your infertility program. I had no reason to reveal my medical history. It doesn't concern anyone but me. You're the one who committed a crime, not me."

"Your secret sure did hurt your son." Taylor regretted this low blow as soon as the words were out.

Tim cringed. His secret had cost Jonathan his life. Even though Tim's parents had concealed his adoption and they could have alerted him sooner to the possibility of a family history of cerebral aneurysms, Tim still blamed himself for his son's death.

169

He would always blame himself for that. And now he was responsible for two more sons and two more deaths.

Tim was weak with anguish. His anger had turned to despair, but he still had to try to make things right.

"Tell me how many more are out there."

Taylor hadn't expected this. He squirmed in his chair and muttered, "Tim, I can't . . . even if there were . . . "

"You tell me who else is out there," Tim repeated, and then added, "They are my children and they are in danger."

Taylor heard something more than anger in Tim's voice. He heard desperation. He had spent thirty years dealing with desperate women, women who would pay thousands of dollars just for a twenty percent chance of having a healthy, biologically linked child. Whatever anger Tim felt toward Taylor was diminished by his need to know the truth, a truth that Taylor had to hide from Tim at any cost. He had to lie to protect himself and all those patients who had been promised anonymity.

"There's no one else, Tim. Just those two. I tried, but only two came to term." Taylor turned away from Tim when he spoke. He couldn't bear to look him in the eye.

"Do you swear to that?"

Taylor hesitated and then said, "I swear."

Tim accepted Taylor's answer without comment. He walked to the door and opened it slowly. Tim paused in the doorway and without looking back, said, "You're a liar, Taylor. There are more out there, and I'll find them. And then I'll be back. You and I aren't finished yet." He walked out of the office, through the waiting room, down the hall and out the front door. He got into his car and turned the key. He rested his head on the steering wheel as conflicting emotions threatened his equilibrium. *Not now. Not yet. I have to keep a clear head. One thing I do know, the answers are all right here. I just have to find them.* He put the car in first gear and rolled slowly down the gravel driveway.

As soon as Tim left, Taylor was on the phone to Boston. He paged McConnell and told the operator it was an emergency. McConnell called back in a matter of minutes.

"What's going on, Malcolm? What's the big emergency?"

"I was just paid a visit by Tim Graves. You haven't been talking to him, have you?"

"What the hell would I have to say to the guy? What did he want with you?"

"He was snooping around." No point in getting McConnell on his back too. "Nothing to get worried about."

"Sounds like you're worried enough not to trust me anymore."

"I've never trusted you, McConnell. Nothing's changed that."

"Graves got to you, huh? Don't tell me you're developing a conscience in your old age."

"Fuck off, McConnell."

"Hostile, too."

"Look, Graves is on suspension. That means no privileges. You know what I'm saying, don't you?"

"No access."

"Just make sure it's enforced, okay? Those guys get lazy."

"Sure, whatever you say."

"You're sharp, McConnell. Sharp enough to keep your mouth shut, I hope."

Taylor hung up. He'll never understand what possessed him to get involved with a prick like McConnell in the first place. But there was no escaping him now. He had to keep his eye on everyone.

The half moon offered just enough light for Tim to push through the shrubbery without using a flashlight, though he kept one in his pocket, just in case. He'd left the Manchester Inn at midnight, and was now standing in front of Taylor's clinic at twelve-thirty A.M. The only sound Tim heard was the crunch of gravel under his feet. There was a dim light burning outside of the modern building, but Tim didn't plan to go near there. He knew that Taylor would want to keep his secrets close, which meant that Tim should be able to find everything he needed in or near Taylor's office.

He worked his way around the periphery of the house. Fortunately, rural Vermont was not considered to be a high crime area, and Tim had not detected any type of alarm system when he was there earlier in the day. Of course, he was no expert, and he might accidentally trip some type of silent alarm, but he was willing to take his chances.

The windows on the bottom floor rested low to the ground, which would make it easy for Tim to jump up on the sill and climb inside. He could only hope that no one had discovered the window that he had unlatched. He congratulated himself on his quick thinking as he was leaving Taylor's office. He slipped on a pair of the surgical gloves he had found in his car. He counted the second window from the front of the house and stood underneath it. He nudged the bottom frame upward, but it didn't budge. *Damn.* He tried it again, pushing it with more force this time, but it still wouldn't give. Somebody had locked it.

Tim squatted on the ground and rested his back up against the house. Plan A had seemed so perfect, he had neglected to prepare a Plan B. Shattering a window would make too much noise. Taylor would be asleep upstairs, and Tim really didn't know how many other people resided in such a large house. The house had several entrances, and could very well be divided into separate apartments. As he stared at the house he began to lose hope. Ever since Taylor's confession, Tim could think only about finding any other children he might have. All the answers were in Taylor's files, somewhere in this vast house. Tim preferred the ranch-style houses he had grown up in. He had come to hate these houses in the East with too many rooms. Many were three levels, not to mention basements and attics. Suddenly he had an idea. He stood up and crept around to the side of the house. He stopped in front of small grate at ground level. It was a vent that led to the basement. *Maybe there was another way into this old house.*

Tim took out the screwdriver he had bought earlier at the local hardware store. He had wanted to come prepared for his first breaking and entering, but all he could think of to buy was the screwdriver and the flashlight. He started prying at the edges of the grate. It popped off and Tim caught it before it hit the ground. The opening was small, it would be a tight fit. He directed the light from his flashlight through the opening and peered around. The cement floor was just a short drop and with the exception of a few boxes the basement appeared to be empty. There was a stairway on the other side of the room. Tim pulled back and stretched out on his stomach. He eased his legs inside and squeezed the rest of his body through. He was grateful for his recent weight loss. The old Tim might have been stuck halfway through the opening. The basement was cold and damp, with a high ceiling. He flashed his light into the few boxes scattered around and was not surprised to find them empty. Taylor would have been a fool to store important documents in this dank area.

Tim climbed the stairs and paused at the door. It most likely opened on to the kitchen. He turned off his flashlight and gave his eyes time to adjust to the darkness before trying the door-knob. *Please, God, don't let it be locked.* The knob turned easily and he slowly pushed open the door. A window at the far end of the room let in some of the faint moonlight and Tim was able to make out the shapes of a refrigerator, stove and a small table with two chairs. He hoped Taylor was not inclined to come downstairs for a midnight snack.

Tim quickly crossed the kitchen and entered a short hallway, which led out into the same main hall which he had passed through yesterday morning. He was right where he wanted to be. He located Meredith's office without any difficulty. Taylor's office door wasn't locked and he cautiously moved inside. Tim hadn't noticed any file cabinets when he was there earlier, but he hadn't really been looking for them. This time he scrutinized every corner, but the only furniture was Taylor's desk, a few bookshelves, some chairs and a coffee table. There weren't any file cabinets to be seen. Next he turned his attention to Taylor's desk. All the drawers opened easily and he discovered nothing of interest. A half-smoked cigar and some postcards sent from Rome were his biggest find. *If he doesn't keep his files in his office, then where the hell could they be? Could he have destroyed everything before his move to Vermont?* To destroy all of his records would make no sense. This was Taylor's life's work and he planned to continue his research. *No, they have to be somewhere close.* His mind raced with possibilities. He couldn't search the entire house. He had no idea how many people were here. He decided to look in Meredith's office and check out the door he had noticed behind her desk.

This door wasn't locked, either. Tim had to push Meredith's desk chair aside in order to open the door wide. He flashed his light around inside. It was just a closet with a few winter coats hanging in it. *Another dead end.* He shut the door and then paused.

173

There should be a closet for office supplies. Why would anyone place a desk in front of the only closet in the office and then keep nothing but a few spare coats inside? To Tim's well-ordered mind, the coat closet should be near the front door, and this closet should be accessible and should contain office supplies. He opened the closet door again and pushed the coats aside. Using his flashlight, he inspected every corner of the closet. Bingo! He spotted the faint outline of a doorway, so well blended with the wood paneling of the closet walls that it was easily missed. He searched for a knob or latch to open the door, but found nothing. *There has to be a way in.* He tried prying at the edge with his screwdriver, but stopped when the wood started to splinter. The last thing he wanted was to leave evidence of his unauthorized visit. He carefully looked around the small closet, walls, ceiling, floor, but found no secret lever. Maybe he was wrong about this even being a doorway, or perhaps it had been at one time and was now sealed over. Glumly he left the closet and turned to Meredith's desk. *Might as well be thorough and take a quick peek through Meredith's desk.*

Tim opened desk drawers and found nothing out of the ordinary, just the usual secretarial supplies. The middle drawer became stuck as he tried to close it and he had to pull it all the way out to get it back on track. As he pushed it in his fingers brushed across an irregularity on the underside of the drawer, some kind of button. He depressed it and heard a sound behind him. A section of wall in the closet slid open. Not believing his good luck, he dashed into the closet and was amazed to find himself standing at the head of a short stairway. A wave of disappointment hit him. *I went through all this only to end up back in the basement?* But as he descended the stairs, he discovered a room lined, wall to wall, with file cabinets. If he was in the basement again, this was a separate area, clean, and carpeted, with no lingering dampness. He was forced to hunch over as he looked around. The ceiling was unusually low. The room was pitch black and it was awkward using his flashlight. He decided to take a chance and turn on the overhead lights.

Tim approached the first file cabinet and was not surprised to find it locked. Undaunted, he went back to Meredith's desk and searched the drawers for keys. He was not disappointed. After several tries, he found the right key and opened the first set of drawers. As expected, they were filled with patient files. He unlocked each cabinet, just to get an idea of what he was dealing with, hoping to stumble across something useful. After five minutes of searching, Tim stopped and sighed. This was going nowhere and he was losing time. The only thing he had discovered so far was that Taylor could populate the entire continent with the amount of patients he had cared for in the last thirty years. He found the drawer containing the L's and pulled the chart of Martha Leon. The file confirmed that she did receive artificial insemination, but gave no details. It merely indicated that the procedure was done in Taylor's office and that it was successful. Tim moved on to the P's and found the chart of Sara Pitt. Same information. He still hadn't found out anything that he didn't already know.

Tim slammed the drawer shut in frustration, forgetting the need for silence. He had placed his flashlight on top of the cabinet and it rolled off and hit the floor. Muttering under his breath, he leaned over to pick it up and spotted a metal ring buried in the carpet. The pattern in the carpet successfully disguised it and he would not have noticed it had he not been close to the floor. Tim pulled on the ring and a trap door revealed a ladder. *Gotcha, Taylor!* Pausing to turn on his flashlight, Tim turned off the lights behind him. Holding the flashlight in his mouth, Tim cautiously backed down the ladder. He laughed out loud when he saw two medium sized file cabinets pushed into the corner of this very small space. *Now I'm back in the basement. Taylor must have had part of it partitioned off to protect his precious files.* He eased the trapdoor shut and pushed on it to assure himself it would open easily. He fought his claustrophobia and went to work. If Taylor had gone to this much trouble to hide these files, they must contain something important, something damaging. He pulled at one of the drawers and smiled. Obviously, Taylor didn't expect anyone to find these, he hadn't bothered to lock them. His heart sank as he saw just more labeled files. He had been so sure he was on to something. As he flipped through the files he did notice something peculiar. The files were labeled with men's names. All of them. They were not alphabetized, and Tim stopped when he came across the name of Lance Johnson. Lance had been two years behind him at Harvard. He played on the intramural ice hockey team at Harvard and had been All League goaltender at Dartmouth College. Tim started at the beginning and read the names more carefully. Keith Karr, Rob Green, Danny Anderson and Howie Lowell. Rob played as a running back for the University of Michigan football team. Danny brought the Princeton baseball team to two Ivy League championships, hitting the most homeruns in a season of any college baseball player in the country. Howie Lowell ran the fastest hundred meters in college track and field. Keith played basketball at Cal Berkeley and turned down an offer from the Cleveland Cavaliers because he wanted to go to medical school. Tim couldn't believe it. He opened up Keith's file and found a list of about ten names with red dots next to five of them. Were these the women who received his sperm? He flipped the page and found Keith's medical records and vital statistics. He turned the page and found a transcript from Berkeley.

Taylor had recruited athletes with brains as his donors because they were talented and healthy. He could sell their sperm for big bucks to desperate couples who wanted to be sure they were getting good genes. Taylor seemed to have all his bases covered. He was sowing seeds for all seasons. He put Keith's file back. He hadn't figured out Taylor's filing system, but he knew he would find his own chart in there somewhere. He opened the last drawer and had his hands on his file within seconds. He hesitated, unsure if he was ready to know the truth. What he found would change his life forever. He thought of the families who could be destroyed if he were to reveal their secret. He reminded himself that he was doing all this in an effort to save lives, if any more lives remained.

With new resolve he opened his own file. Of the eight to ten names listed, three of them had red dots beside them. He had guessed that the red dots indicated a successful pregnancy and delivery. Sara Pitt and Martha Leon had a red dot next to their names. The name after the remaining red dot read "Maria and Tony X." There was also an "SF" with a question mark beside it. Tim had no idea what that meant. He focused on "Maria and Tony X." Obviously, they had not wanted to reveal their name. He wondered how he could ever locate them. There were probably a hundred Marias and Tonys on the Eastern seaboard alone, and they could have come from anywhere. Finding them would be impossible.

His concentration was broken by the sound of a door opening and the floor creaking. He stuffed the file back in the drawer and carefully closed it. He started up the ladder but heard footsteps approaching. He backed into a corner and held his breath. A voice directly over his head boomed, "I wouldn't try anything if I were you. This gun is loaded."

Tim tried to melt into the darkness and refused to breathe.

"Who the hell is in there?" Taylor shouted. Light flooded into Tim's hiding place as the trapdoor was partially opened. *This is it. Taylor's caught me red-handed.*

Suddenly the trapdoor slammed into place. Tim could hear Taylor mumbling something about "that dingbat Meredith leaving the closet unlocked again" and then he heard the closet door being closed and the lock clicking into place. He waited silently for a good five minutes, and then cautiously crept up the ladder. He raised the trapdoor and turned on his flashlight. At the top of the stairs, the door remained closed. He crossed the room and climbed the stairs. Just as he had feared, the door was locked from the outside. He was trapped.

Tim sat on the steps and contemplated his options. If he waited until morning, and if Meredith was the first one to the office, and if she would agree to smuggle him out, he might have a chance. On the other hand, if Taylor were the one to discover him, he had no idea what might happen. Taylor would surely know that Tim had discovered his secret files and he would be desperate to keep that knowledge from getting out. Tim had no idea what a desperate Dr. Taylor might be capable of doing. His only hope was to find another way out. He tried the door, but it was solid oak and would not budge. He decided to go back down the ladder and examine the walls more carefully. Maybe there would be a way to break through.

A careful survey of walls and ceiling revealed nothing. The file cabinets took up most of the space and reached almost to the ceiling. He tried to maneuver the cabinets away from the wall, but they were heavy and they could only be moved inches at a time. Tim was tired, thirsty, and covered with perspiration. He would certainly make sure he was better equipped if he decided to make a career of this. Finally he had one cabinet moved far enough away from the wall that he could squeeze behind it. Shining his flashlight over the surface he discovered a grate embedded in the wall, just like the one he had slipped through what seemed like hours ago. It was not so easy to pry off from the inside, but using his flashlight as a hammer, and his screwdriver as a chisel, he was finally able to chip away at the plaster and pop out the grate. He grasped the ledge with both hands, and pulled himself up. Using the file cabinet to push off, he propelled himself up and out.

Tim allowed himself a few moments to lie on the soft grass and breathe in the sweet, fresh air. *That was too close.* He forced himself up and carefully replaced the grate. He followed the wall around the house and found the place where he had entered the basement. He replaced that grate as well. *Better to have Taylor blame poor Meredith for carelessness.* Tim sprinted from tree to tree and stayed in the shadows until he reached the main road where he had parked his car. He wouldn't feel safe until he was out of Vermont and back in Boston. Then he would call Meg and tell her about Maria and Tony X. There had to be a way to track them down.

Nineteen

By the time Tim arrived back in Boston it was almost six A.M. He thought about Maria and Tony X for most of the drive, and his frustration grew. Tim knew that even if the mystery couple had come from another state, if Taylor had orchestrated the conception and birth of their child, there would be hospital records. Of course, the possibility existed that the couple had not returned to Boston for the birth of their baby, but he had to start somewhere. Taking a look in the hospital database would be the first step. If he drew a blank there, then he would have to think of something else.

Tim turned left on Huntington and headed for the hospital. He wanted to look at the database as soon as possible, and now would be the perfect time. He parked in the doctor's lot and hurried through the side entrance. He headed straight for the record room. This early in the morning he shouldn't attract any attention. He found a computer terminal tucked into a corner and typed in his name to log on. He entered his password and a message appeared on the screen, ACCESS DENIED. Tim tried his password again with the same result. His suspension restricted his hospital privileges, but he hadn't thought that would include his access to the database. *Damn.* He thought about calling J.C. to get his access code, but decided against it. J.C. knew nothing about Tim's discovery, and Tim wanted to keep it that way for awhile. He didn't want to drag his friend into anymore of his problems just yet. He guessed that most doctors used their birth dates for a password, as he himself did. He tried J.C.'s birth date. ACCESS DENIED. Tim clenched his fists and cursed Taylor. Taylor! *What an idiot I am. It won't do me any good to access my databank, or J.C.'s. I need to get into Taylor's databank.* Taylor's birth date was easy to remember. It was the day he met Meg. He entered the numbers, with no luck. *Of course Taylor wouldn't use such an obvious password. He was too creative for that. He would use something significant. Something...*Tim typed in

179

"wedge" and the screen blinked and then lit up with the database menu. Tim clapped his hands, then looked around to make sure he hadn't been heard. The record room was empty. Tim chuckled at the irony of using Taylor's access code, but soon became serious when he paused to consider how he might begin the process of elimination. He decided that he would call up all the babies delivered by Taylor during the seven years, beginning with his first donation. He had donated to Taylor late in his internship year, so he could at least narrow the field a little by calling up just the births that occurred after his first donation and nine months after his last donation. Tim typed in the command. The computer processed the information and produced a list on the screen. During those seven years there had been 714 births at the hospital where Taylor was listed as the attending doctor. Tim sighed in despair. He wouldn't get anywhere with a list that long. He had to eliminate more names. He typed in a command to search the 714 names and keep those records with the names "Maria" and "Tony" in the parent/guardian field. The computer ran a search and flashed a message NO MATCH FOUND TO FIT YOUR SEARCH. He tried again, using "Maria" and "Anthony," with the same result. He decided to run a separate search, one for "Maria" and one for "Tony." Between the two, the computer spit out eight names. *At least that's a more manageable list.*

Tim checked the records of the eight people listed and wrote down addresses and phone numbers. There were three girls and five boys. He logged off the computer and stuffed the list of names and addresses in his pocket. His plan was to begin his search immediately and he wouldn't stop until he found what he was looking for. He headed out to the doctor's parking lot and got in his car. He removed the street map of Boston from his glove box and studied it. He located South James Street, the first address on his list. *I'm in luck. It's not far from here.*

Tim drove up and down the street, but he couldn't locate number 137. He pulled over to the curb and double-checked the map. There was only one South James Street in Boston, and he was on it. He rolled down his window and waited as an early morning jogger approached his car.

"Excuse me. Do you know where 137 South James Street is?"

The man squinted at Tim and shook his head slowly.

"137?" the man repeated.

"That's right. I can't seem to find it."

"Well, do you see that dead end down there?" The man pointed a hundred feet to the end of the street.

Tim looked in the direction he was pointing and saw a fence separating the street from a park. Tim nodded.

"Well, I live in the last house, and my number is 128. Ain't no 137 on this street."

Tim thanked the man and scratched his head. His enthusiasm had waned considerably. He was tired, he was hungry, and he was discouraged. It was time to call in reinforcements. It was time to call Meg.

"I can't believe you broke into Taylor's house!" Meg exclaimed. They sat together at a coffee shop on Newberry Street. Tim wolfed down waffles and eggs as he told Meg all that had happened to him. Meg hadn't touched her coffee, she was so enthralled by Tim's story. She kept her eyes glued on Tim while her jaw dropped more with each detail. She had never trusted Taylor, not from their first encounter at Julianne's when he had tried to pick her up. Her heart went out to Tim. She could tell how desperate he was to find his last living child, if that child was still alive.

"So now I have these eight names I can check on. But the strangest thing is I've already tried the first address, and the house doesn't exist."

"What do you mean?"

"The address I took down from the hospital records was either wrong or falsified, or something. I was on the right street, but the numbers only go up to 128. The address I have is 137.

"Maybe it was a correct address in 1966, but they've torn some houses down, or something."

"I didn't even think of that." Tim felt foolish. He really wasn't equipped for this kind of sleuthing.

Meg continued, "Why don't you give me the name and address and I'll check it out. The *Globe* has extensive cross-referencing. Maybe I can find a more current address."

Tim gratefully jotted down the name and address and handed it across the table to Meg. It was such a relief to share this burden with another person. He knew he was in way over his head, and he could certainly use Meg and her resources.

Meg glanced at the slip of paper. "Tony Vincent Girardi," she read aloud. "Sounds Italian."

"Sure does."

"Well, I'll look into it and see what I can come up with."

Tim kept his eyes on Meg. He realized how much he was coming to rely on her. He wanted to tell her, but couldn't find the words.

"I really appreciate your help, Meg."

Meg thought she detected a note of intimacy in his voice. She was flattered that he had asked her to help him. She loved the whole idea of chasing down a mystery. But more important, she loved the excuse to spend time with him.

"Sure, I'm enjoying it. But I wonder how it's affecting you. How are you holding up?"

Tim hadn't had time to do much more than react to all that had happened. He had not examined his feelings, but now that Meg asked, he realized that in a way he felt rejuvenated. Out of all this sorrow, perhaps he would find that he had a child, and he might have a chance to make a difference in that child's life. He would never consider insinuating himself into another family, but if he could prevent another tragic death, all that he had been through would at least have some meaning.

"Okay I guess. I don't know. Hard to say. I just know I'll feel better when I get to the bottom of this list."

Meg nodded in agreement. She knew Tim couldn't possibly express the emotional highs and lows that he had experienced. He would need some time to sort things out. She just hoped that she'd be around for that. They finished their coffee in silence and Tim paid the bill. He told Meg that he would go home for a few hours and try to sleep, then he would set out on the trail of the other names on the list. He gave her a quick hug, which stayed with her all the way back to her office.

The *Globe* library had two walls filled with current directories of residences. Meg pulled out the Massachusetts directory F–G and flipped to Girardi. There were three listings: S. Girardi, L. Girardi, and Girardi's. Tim had told Meg that the mother's name was written as "Anna" in the hospital records. Taylor's records had the name Maria and Tony X, but nothing with those two names together had shown up on the database. Meg was puzzled. No match for a P. Girardi, T. Girardi, or even a V. Girardi. The "Girardi's" listing was probably some type of business. Meg read the address. It was on Salem Street in Boston, in an area called the North End, where all the first Italian immigrants into Boston Harbor had established themselves. Maybe it was a family business and somebody there would have some information on Tony Vincent Girardi. Meg hadn't been to the North End in months. She used to take visitors to Boston there all the time for a taste of the famous cannoli at Meoli's Pastry. Meg's mouth watered at the thought. *What the hell.* She grabbed her purse and headed for the elevator.

Meg hopped on the Green Line at Park Street station. She got off at Haymarket and walked under the Mass Pike overpass into the North End. The streets and sidewalks were spotless in this part of town. The Italian flag adorned many shops and there seemed to be a café on every corner. Old men gathered together, some standing and some sitting on chairs that had been dragged out of their stores. The men talked animatedly about the day, politics and the past. Young people sat in the cafés, sipping espresso and laughing.

Meg longed to join one of these carefree groups. She wished that she had the time to sit, relax, and take pleasure in a simple cup of espresso, but it seemed that she was always on a mission: for the *Globe*, or for herself, and now for Tim. In truth, she wouldn't have it any other way. She turned down Salem Street and started searching for number 18. She didn't see the number, but she did spot a sign with the name "Girardi's" written in thin black cursive on a white background. It was barely noticeable, and it only caught Meg's eye because she had looked up to a window above the store to stare at a beautiful young woman shaking out a rug. Girardi's turned out to be a deli. The front window displayed smoked mozzarella hanging from thick twine, surrounded by thick salami sausages. Meg opened the door and a string of bells attached to the inside announced her arrival. The smoky aroma of cured meat assaulted her senses. Once inside she was surrounded by baskets of bread, jars of olives and delectable cheeses.

She seemed to be alone in the store. She stepped closer to the counter, standing on her toes, and peered over. At the far end sat a man holding a newspaper up to his face. Meg cleared her throat to get his attention. As he lowered the newspaper, Meg was able to see the man's features. He was at least eighty years old and he stared at her through thick glasses. The old man took his time folding his newspaper carefully and placed it on the small table next to his chair. He slowly pushed himself to his feet and shuffled over to Meg. He looked her up and down and finally smiled.

"What can I do for you, *bella*?" His voice, strong and deep, did not reveal his age.

Meg enjoyed his appraising look. It was not meant to be insulting, and it made her feel young and pretty. She thought a little flirting might help her get the information she needed.

"Well, actually, I'm looking for someone." She tilted her head playfully and flashed her most ingenuous smile. She should have been ashamed to be resorting to feminine wiles to woo an eighty-year-old man, but she was enjoying herself.

"Oh?" The old man raised his eyebrows. "And tell me, who?"

"I'm looking for Tony Vincent Girardi."

The old man's good humor disappeared.

"Who are you?"

Meg wondered at his change in tone. "My name is Meg Logan." She decided to skip the part about being a reporter for the *Globe*. "Do you know Tony Vincent Girardi?"

The old man seemed more puzzled than angry. "No. Why do you want him?"

Meg was suddenly inspired. "I'm embarrassed to say . . . I was reading this book. Gosh, now I can't even remember the name of it. Anyway, in the book the young, gorgeous hero who fell in love with the princess . . . his name was Tony Vincent Girardi. And then, here I am strolling down the sidewalk, and what do I see? Girardi's. It was too much of a coincidence. I know it's sounds silly, but I was so enthralled with this character in my book, and then, here you are. I'm sorry to trouble you. I just thought it would be fun to ask." She giggled and shrugged her shoulders.

The old man didn't know what to think. The young woman

looked innocent enough, but she made no sense. Before he could think any further the door to the shop opened and a tall man wearing an open collared black shirt walked in. He was very striking, with graying hair and a lean, muscular build. Meg didn't want to stare, but it was hard not to notice him in such close quarters.

"*Buongiorno, signore*," the man spoke to the proprietor, nodding at Meg as he passed. "*Chi é questa?*"

The old man threw up his hands and muttered, "*Boh.*" They both looked at Meg, who was studiously reading the label of an olive jar.

"*Allora, come sempre?*" asked the old man.

"*Si*," the tall man replied.

Meg wasn't sure if she was the subject of their exchange, but she waited patiently as the old man started cutting bread and meats for a sandwich. While he was busy behind the counter Meg took a minute to look around. Apart from the food counter there was little else in the shop. The walls were covered in Boston Red Sox paraphernalia—pennants, flags and posters. Meg noticed more than one poster of a Red Sox pitcher. She recognized him from television interviews and newspaper stories but she couldn't remember his name. *Somebody Santori*, she thought. He was Boston's rising star and it was obvious that the old man was quite a fan. It made sense he'd be a hero in this section of the city.

Meg turned her attention back to the man in the black shirt. He was rattling off something in Italian and the old man was nodding his head, interjecting in rapid Italian every now and then. They appeared to be old friends. The old man finished making the sandwich, placed it in a brown paper bag and handed it to the younger man.

"*Grazie. Sta bene.*" He turned to Meg and said, "Good day," and walked out the door. Meg was impressed with his courtliness, but noticed that he hadn't paid for his sandwich. He hadn't even offered to pay. The old man was wiping down the counter with a white cloth.

"Do you often give away free lunches?"

The old man looked startled, as if he had forgotten she was there.

"He's family, that boy." He paused and then asked, "Do you

185

still want to talk to Tony Vincent Girardi?"

Meg was taken aback by his question, which sounded more like an invitation. She didn't even know whether the man existed, and she was being offered an opportunity to talk with him. Of course she wanted to.

"Yes," she replied eagerly.

The old man threw the cloth on the counter and placed his hands on his hips.

"So talk."

"I . . . excuse me?"

"You want to talk to Tony Vincent Girardi, and here I am."

Meg's heart sank.

"You're Tony Vincent Girardi?" she asked, trying to hide her disappointment.

"*Si, bella.*"

Meg didn't know what to say next. She obviously had the wrong person. She searched her mind for a graceful exit.

"Well, you're just as handsome as I imagined my hero to be." She winked at him and favored him with an impish grin.

"You're a dangerous woman, I can tell." He shook his finger at her and laughed. He tried to coax her into having a sandwich, but Meg said she had to get back to work. She edged her way out the door and waved gaily. He waved back, saying *"Ciao, bella."*

Meg headed back up Salem Street. All she had found out was that this Tony Vincent Girardi was not the one Tim needed to find. She followed her nose to Meoli's and ordered two cannolli to go. They wrapped the cannolli up in a white box tied with a yellow ribbon. Meg decided to drop by Tim's apartment and share the desserts with him. Despite her failure to uncover anything new, she felt happy to be carrying a pretty box of sweets to share with the man she . . . *Slow down, Meg!* She wondered if Tim had made any progress on his end.

Two shots rang through the air. When the people on the street heard the gunfire some scrambled behind parked cars while others stood rooted to the spot, unsure what to do. A woman screamed as she saw a young black man dash out of the store and tear off down the street. He carried a gun in one hand and a paper bag in the other. As he ran, he stuffed the gun in the waistband of

186

his pants. The screaming woman ran across the street and into the shop. The body lay on the floor behind the counter, where a pool of blood was slowly forming on the white linoleum.

"Oh, *Dio mio*," the woman cried, unable to move any closer to the body. Two arms wrapped around the woman and tried to drag her away, but she refused to budge. More people pushed into the shop to witness the horror.

"Vincenzo! Vincenzo!" the woman moaned tonelessly. She finally allowed herself to be guided out the door and onto a bench. She leaned into the gray haired man in the black shirt.

Meg was about to cross under the overpass to get back to Haymarket Square when she heard the commotion. People were shouting, but she couldn't make out what they were saying. She turned and saw some men running down the street. A police car, with its sirens screaming, roared around the corner. She followed the crowd rushing back into the North End. People were blocking the sidewalks as the police tried to push them away from the scene of the crime. As Meg got closer she saw that the focus of the crowd seemed to be just outside Girardi's deli. She elbowed her way through to the door, but a policeman held her back.

"I'm with the *Globe*," she tried to explain.

"Ma'am, this is a crime scene. We can't let you in."

"Please, can you just tell me what happened? I was just here, just a few minutes ago. What's wrong?"

At that moment an ambulance arrived and Meg watched as paramedics hurried inside with a stretcher. The crowd waited in silence. Soon the paramedics appeared, still carrying an empty stretcher. She heard one of them say to the policeman waiting by the door, "This is a case for the coroner."

Meg craned her neck, trying to see around or over the policeman blocking the doorway. "Who the hell is it?" she muttered in frustration.

"Vincent Girardi," said a soft voice behind her. Meg spun around and caught her breath. It was the tall man who had been in the shop with her. He eyed her suspiciously, as if he thought she might have had something to do with his death. Meg could only stare at him, at a complete loss for words. Finally the man turned around, worked his way through the crowd and disappeared.

Meg was frozen in place. She looked down and saw that she was still carrying the box of cannolli. She grieved for the charming old man that she had known so briefly, but she felt that somehow it would be dangerous for her to stay here.

* * *

Meg didn't find Tim at his apartment in Chestnut Hill and she couldn't reach him by phone. She had him paged through the hospital, but when he didn't return her call Meg guessed that he wasn't carrying his beeper around now that he was on suspension. She wondered if he had flown off somewhere to check out another name on the list. Maybe he'd had better luck. Tony Vincent Girardi had been a dead end—literally.

Meg decided to just go home and wait to hear from Tim. She flipped on the television set to see if the evening news carried the story of the shooting in the North End. While the sportscaster reported on the successful Red Sox game with the Chicago White Sox that afternoon at Comiskey Park, Meg headed into the kitchen to fix herself a scotch and soda. She hit the play button on the message machine as she passed it. One message from her mother complaining about how Meg never called her. One message from the dry cleaner reminding her to pick up the clothes that had been hanging on their rack for six weeks. One message from her editor about an overdue story. And one message from Tim. Meg rushed to the machine when she heard Tim's voice. She hit the replay button and listened intently.

"Hi, Meg. It's me, Tim. I'm in Maine. I decided to drive up here and check on another name on the list. I haven't had any luck, yet. Anyway, just wondering about you and how the Girardi thing went. I'll call you again later. Hopefully, I won't be here very long. Bye."

Damn. Meg wanted to tell Tim about Girardi. Now all she could do was wait for him to call back. Patience was not one of her virtues. She needed to report the events of the day to someone. She even thought about calling her mother, but wasn't up to hearing about how she was wasting her life. How she should be married and raising a family, not trying to make it in a "man's world."

Carrying her drink to the couch, Meg sat down to watch the local news. She switched channels, watching all the major network stations, hoping to catch the story of the shooting. By the time Dan Rather came on, Meg gave up and switched off the television. *That poor man. He lived his life minding his own business, working hard probably every day of his life, only to be shot down in his own store in broad daylight. Where's the justice in that?* Her thoughts drifted to Tim. Here he had flown to Wisconsin, flown to Texas, driven to Vermont and now Maine in an attempt to find the truth. He certainly didn't deserve all this heartache. With each thought of Tim, the desire to speak with him grew stronger. Meg allowed herself to give in to the alcohol and her own exhaustion. She kicked off her shoes and curled up on the couch. As she dozed off she fantasized about herself and Tim, walking along a beach somewhere. They were holding hands and Tim was laughing at something she had said. They were carefree and happy . . . so happy.

Meg struggled awake, realizing she had spent the night on the couch. Her neck was stiff and she was going to be late for work.

The phone was ringing as she stepped out of the shower. She rushed to pick it up.

"Hi, Meg."

"Tim! Thank God I woke up late. Did you find anything new? I have a story to tell you about that Girardi guy. You're not going to believe what happened."

"Slow down. I can barely keep up."

"Sorry. You first. What did you find out?"

"Well, I talked with the Thompson family. Taylor did deliver their son. Apparently Mrs. Thompson was treated by him for an infertility problem, but the problem was with her, not her husband. She had surgery and got pregnant right away. End of story." Tim tried not to sound discouraged. After all, this was good news. He had located a healthy child, a child who was not his own.

"I know how frustrating this is for you, but you are making progress. We just have to keep looking. Now, let me tell you what happened to me yesterday."

Tim listened in amazement as Meg related her encounter with Girardi and the subsequent shooting. She told him how she had spent the evening glued to the television, expecting to hear a report of the shooting, and how surprised she was that there was no mention of it.

"My God. You weren't hurt, were you?"

"No. I had already left the store when it happened. I ran back when I saw the crowd. The whole Italian community must have been there. He seemed like such a sweet old man—a victim of another random act of violence. You know what is weird, though? If the address you took down was false, and the only Tony Vincent Girardi in Boston is—was—over eighty years old, then how do you explain the hospital records?"

"Is he the only T. or P. Girardi you found? What about a V?"

"The only one so far. I haven't looked out of state yet."

"I wonder if we'll ever get to the bottom of this. The whole thing seems impossible to figure out."

"Come on, Tim, perseverance. Besides, what else do you have to do with your time?" Meg was hoping to cheer Tim up but she got no response to her teasing.

"Tim? Are you still there?"

"Sorry, I was just . . . " he trailed off.

"You were just what?" Meg asked anxiously. "Are you all right?"

"Yeah, I was just thinking about that name, Girardi. All of a sudden it sounds familiar, like I've heard it somewhere before."

"Where?"

"I don't know. I'm just thinking out loud. It's probably nothing. Anyway, I need to go to New York and check out another name. I'll call you later."

"Tim, I'm worried about you. You haven't slept. You're probably not eating and you're driving all over the place. Just be careful, okay?"

"So you're really a softy behind that tough exterior."

"What tough exterior? What do you mean?"

Tim just laughed and said, "Gotta go. Don't worry about me."

Is that what he thinks of me? That I'm tough? She glanced at the clock and ran to the bedroom. She didn't have time to figure out what Tim meant. She had to get to work before her so-called tough exterior would be chewed out of existence by her editor.

Twenty

"Stai zeet," he snarled over his shoulder at Lenny, the guy in the back seat. He and the driver were laughing at some joke about a priest and a nun. The short man in the front seat wasn't laughing. Paulie Strata rarely laughed, and he sure as hell didn't find anything funny about the other two goons in the car. He'd been assigned by the man himself to do this job personally, and of course he couldn't refuse such an honor. But when he found out who was going along with him, it was hard to keep his mouth shut. These two always screwed up, and everyone knew it. Paulie figured the only reason they were kept around was because they were big and ugly. People in their line of business thought big and ugly could get the job done, but Paulie thought the issue of size was highly overrated. *Hadn't anyone ever heard of David and Goliath? It's in the Bible, for Christ's sake!* Size doesn't mean shit when you've got brains and a 57 Magnum in your pants. Paulie was five foot three. He carried a Magnum, and a switchblade strapped to his ankle. Another advantage to being short—easy access to concealed weapons.

Paulie had been the unofficial head of his family since high school and during the ten years they lived on Salem Street. When their mother died, *God rest her soul*, Paulie and his brothers moved in with their aunt and uncle down the street and rented out their apartment to a young couple who had just moved to the United States. They collected four hundred bucks a month for it. Eventually they were able to buy up every apartment in the building. Paulie and his brothers were landlords, but they were more than that to the neighborhood. They were your best friends, or your worst enemies. Paulie had never bought into the melting pot idea. He believed that if you wanted to stick to your own kind then you damn well should be able to. He only rented to Italians, mostly from Sicily, and he promised them protection and privacy. This meant "talking to" unwanted solicitors so that they never came back, running groceries for the elderly women too infirm to venture up and down stairs, knocking some sense into a teenage kid hanging out with the wrong crowd, and discreetly arranging for an abortion for one sixteen-year-old girl who feared the wrath of her father. These things Paulie did in his role as landlord, but he was looking for more glamour and less grunt work. That's how he got to be where he was now, doing "favors" for Tony Santori.

Paulie had impressed his way into the Santori business, a story he relished telling, and retelling. He had watched Santori's business for months before he decided to make his move—watched who came and went into their building on Washington Street, watched who brought what in and out. One day he walked right into the Santori building and knocked on the unmarked door behind the stairwell. When a clean-shaven, big-guy type opened the door, Paulie said, "I stole twenty thousand dollars from Tony Santori. I'd like to speak to him, please." The muscle guy stared at Paulie incredulously, but something about Paulie's demeanor told him this was no joke. He called to someone inside the room. In the business, the higher up you are, the farther you are from the front door. The goon repeated what Paulie had said while Paulie stood, unmoving, staring at the new man. They frisked him, taking away his gun, but missing the switchblade around his ankle.

Paulie was led through a series of doors and rooms before they finally came to a small courtyard surrounded by trees and more big guys in cheap suits. Paulie recognized Tony Santori immediately. He reclined on a chaise lounge, impeccably outfitted in a navy pin striped suit, crisp white shirt and maroon tie. Gold cufflinks glittered in the sunlight. This was a man who exuded self-confidence and power. Paulie watched while one of the men approached Santori and respectfully waited to be acknowledged. Santori impatiently beckoned him closer and the man whispered a few words in Santori's ear. Santori nodded and Paulie was pushed forward.

"You have something to tell me?" Even though Santori remained seated, he and Paulie were nearly eye to eye.

"I stole twenty thousand dollars from you last night. I came to return it." He reached toward his breast pocket. All the men came at Paulie, guns cocked. Paulie held his hands out, palms up. One of the men called out that he was clean. Paulie reached again inside his jacket and pulled out a brick of hundred dollar bills, neatly wrapped in cellophane. He held the money out in front of him and let it fall to the ground. The money hit the cement with a thud. Paulie stared at Santori, no one saying a word. Finally, Paulie broke the silence.

He told Santori that there were problems in his organization if he could lose twenty thousand in one night, and not even know it. Paulie suggested that he should get better protection, and that he, Paulie, could provide it. Tony Santori was impressed by the short man standing in front of him. *Here's a guy who ripped me off, returns the money and wants to work for me. The kid's got balls.* Santori knew Paulie was the guy who ran the building on Salem Street. He had heard good things about him—how devoted he was to his tenants, a good *paesano*. He hired Paulie on the spot, gave him back his piece and let him do his thing.

That was ten years ago, and now Paulie was a made man. He was Santori's favorite and nobody could touch him. Just to seal the bond, Tony Santori offered Paulie his cousin's hand in marriage. Sofia was from Long Island. She had asked her cousin Tony about "the short guy who never smiles," after observing him at a family celebration. Sofia was intrigued by Paulie, and didn't much care if he was four inches shorter than she was. It didn't bother Paulie that Sofia towered over him. His stature had never been of any consequence to him and besides, Sofia was as hard as nails and he liked his women tough. He wasn't interested in a trophy wife that so many of the guys kept around. The best part of their marriage, however, was that it made Paulie a part of the Santori family. Being a made man gave him status. He was literally untouchable.

Tony trusted Paulie enough to handle his personal business, and that was the job he had to do today. He just hoped the other two goons wouldn't screw up. The three of them sat in the Cadillac across the street from a red brick apartment building. They had been parked there since midnight. Paulie checked his watch. Two fifteen and still no sign of Leroy Washington. In the back seat, Lenny was getting antsy.

"Hey, Paulie, how do we know this is the guy, anyway?"

193

"How many niggers you seen in East Boston?"

Paulie was right. If a black man walked through the neighborhood at any time of the day, he'd be noticed. The guys would know his name, address and where his mother lived, all before he made it to the other side of the street.

From the apartment building they were watching, a woman screamed. They heard a crash, something hitting a wall and shattering. A man cursed in Spanish.

"Pigs," Paulie muttered. "Fucking pigs."

Lenny suddenly pointed in the direction of the building entrance. Leroy Washington appeared in the doorway. His informant had described him well, but he was younger than Paulie had expected. Leroy was wearing a sweatshirt zipped up to his neck, brown pants and black sneakers. He kept his hands in his sweatshirt pockets and looked up and down the street.

"Kinda hot for a sweatshirt, don'tcha think?" offered Lenny.

"That's to hide the dope, dumbshit. Don't you know anything?" Paulie sighed. He couldn't believe the morons his boss had working for him.

Leroy skipped down the steps and headed down the sidewalk, away from where the Cadillac was parked. The driver, Mario, pulled out slowly and edged the car alongside the curb. Leroy walked fast, unaware of the car inching up behind him. They were nearly even with him before he turned his head and saw the car. His face registered fear. The streets of Roxbury were deserted except for Leroy and the occupants of the car. He had a deal to make and these guys were pissing him off. He started running as the Cadillac lurched ahead of him. The car screeched to a halt and Lenny flew out of the back door, landing in Leroy's path. Leroy tripped to a stop. There was no way around the massive bulk in front of him. He turned to run the other way and came face to face with Paulie, hands in his pockets, coolly observing Leroy

"Hey, Leroy. What's happening?" Paulie's tone was calm and nonthreatening.

Leroy squinted at the short man standing in front of him. He had never seen him before.

"Who the hell are you and what do you want?" Leroy blustered.

Paulie took his hands out of his pockets and held them, palms out, in a gesture of peace.

"We just want to talk to you, Leroy." Paulie tilted his head toward the Cadillac idling at the curb. "Why don't you take a ride with us?"

Leroy weighed his options. He flashed a glance at the car and then looked back at the giant of a man standing behind him.

"I don't gotta go nowhere with you, man." He shook his head emphatically. "If you got something to tell me, tell it to me right here."

"Come on, Leroy. We just a need a little of your time."

Lenny took a step toward him. Leroy looked from the short man, to Lenny, to the car.

"Look man, I got a buy to make. I just want my coke. I don't want no trouble."

"You can have your coke as soon as we're through." Paulie signaled to Lenny, who grabbed Leroy's upper arm and muscled him into the back seat of the car. They made a U-turn and headed out of Roxbury. Paulie rode in the front seat, and stared straight ahead as he spoke to Leroy.

"You were seen in the neighborhood last week, and again yesterday. What were you doing there?"

Leroy was shaking violently, both from fear, and from his desperate need for a hit.

"I weren't there, man. Must have been some other dude."

Paulie turned his head slightly. "All I want is the truth, Leroy. I know you were there. I want to know why."

"I didn't want to hurt nobody."

"What were you doing in the neighborhood, Leroy?" Paulie repeated the question in the same flat voice.

"Nothing, man."

"Leroy, people know you. Don't insult me by lying. Just tell me the truth and we can get this over with."

Leroy mulled this over. He knew he'd get the shit beaten out of him for lying and it seemed like these guys already knew everything, anyway.

"All I wanted was some money for coke." His voice quivered.

"Take it easy, Leroy. Just tell me what happened." Paulie's

soothing words reassured Leroy.

"I walk in and tell him to put the money in a bag. He gets pissed off and grabs for my gun." Leroy wiped his sweating brow with the back of his hand. "I had to shoot the old man. He was going for my piece."

"So what you're saying, here, Leroy, is it was kinda like self-defense?"

Relieved that Paulie understood how it was, Leroy agreed, "Yeah, man. Self-defense."

"Okay."

Leroy breathed easier. He loosened his grip on his legs. He looked out the window and nothing looked familiar. They had only been driving for ten minutes, but they were far from Roxbury. He wondered if they'd drive him back, or just drop him off. He started worrying about how he would find his way home.

"I'm sorry the old man died. I didn't mean to shoot him. Like I said, it was self-defense, you know? He shouldn't have gone for my gun. Why didn't he just give me the money? I just wanted the money."

"We know, Leroy." Paulie motioned for Mario to turn off. He pulled into a vacant lot and stopped the car. They sat in silence for a few seconds. Leroy was looking from one man to the other, waiting for someone to make a move. Finally, Paulie spoke up, "Okay, Leroy. This is where you get out. Lenny, do you have the keys to the car?"

Lenny reached into his pants pocket and pulled out a set of keys. He handed them over the back of the seat to Paulie. Leroy was glad to hear that they were letting him go, but he still didn't know where the hell he was.

"Hey, man, thanks. Where are we, anyway? How do I get back?"

"I'll take you back, Leroy. My car's right over there." Paulie nodded toward Lennie and Mario. "These boys are tired. They need to get some sleep."

Paulie stepped from the car and opened the back door for Leroy. Leroy climbed out, silently scoffing at Paulie's courteous gesture. *These guinea spics wouldn't last a day in Roxbury with their gentleman shit.*

Paulie walked toward a car parked in the corner of the

deserted lot. It was a dilapidated tan Ford. He unlocked the passenger door for Leroy and then walked around to the driver's side. He got in the car and slammed the door. Leroy was adjusting his seat belt when Paulie pulled out the Magnum and held it to his left temple.

"This is for Vincent Girardi." Before Leroy could react the bullet exploded in his brain. His head slammed against the passenger window. Paulie pressed the barrel to the nape of Leroy's neck and fired again. The body slumped forward. Paulie pulled the body back and pressed the gun to Leroy's throat for the third shot. Three shots to the head. A holy trinity.

Paulie got out of the Ford, taking a handkerchief from his breast pocket and wiping splattered blood from his cheek. He tucked his gun back in his waist, stuffed the handkerchief in his back pocket, and tugged on his shirtsleeves. He cracked his neck and walked back to the Cadillac. The job was done.

Twenty-one

The moment Meg stepped off the elevator she knew she was in trouble. The newsroom appeared to be abandoned. She was met with silence and empty desks. Obviously, the meeting had already begun. Normally it was no big deal to be late or occasionally miss a meeting. The editors knew that reporters on assignment would not be able to attend every morning brainstorming session. Unfortunately, Meg was not on assignment and her latest story was seriously overdue. She had spent too much time on Tim and his problems and had neglected her own job.

Meg tiptoed to the editor-in-chief's office. The walls facing the newsroom were made of clear glass, but fortunately there were enough bodies, sitting and standing, squeezed into the tiny office, that hopefully her late arrival went unnoticed. All eyes were trained on the man behind the desk. They were discussing some well-known actor who had died the day before in a car accident. Meg slid along the windowed wall and edged her way behind her friend, Lou, who stood just inside the doorway. He felt a tug on his coat and turned to see Meg smiling guiltily. Lou rolled his eyes in an expression of utter boredom and turned back to face the desk. Meg stood in the background, feigning interest as their editor droned on. She jumped when she heard her own name.

"And we hope that your tardiness, Meg, means you were combing the streets this morning for a spectacular story and that you have something inspiring to share with all of us."

Attention shifted to Meg as she stepped out from behind Lou's back and gave an innocent shrug of her shoulders. She had nothing to offer. *You want to hear about how a well-known doctor has been running a baby farm using stolen sperm?* Since that story wasn't ready to be told she searched her mind for something to say. Suddenly the whole Girardi incident popped into her head. If the TV stations hadn't picked it up last night, it must still be fresh. She could turn the story into a great feature story. She could address the issue of Italian-Americans and the dissolution of boroughs in Boston as each new generation moved out and older generations died off. She wondered why she hadn't thought of it sooner. She had been too preoccupied with Tim to concentrate on her career. She had better not make that mistake again, or she would be out on the street.

"Well," she began, "actually I do have an idea for a story. Yesterday I was in the North End and witnessed a shooting in a local store. The man . . . "

"Old news," muttered one of the reporters sitting up front. He was always the first to arrive and the last to leave these sessions, hoping to gain favor with the editor.

Meg was taken aback. *They all knew about Girardi.*

"I'm afraid, Meg, that we've already discussed that topic. We're doing that story in conjunction with a line on the Mob—'alive and well in the Bay State'," the editor stated impatiently.

"Another body in Somerville—I'm telling you, this is not news," a reporter in the back piped up. He strongly opposed the decision to run a column on it.

"You're missing the point, Meyers. It's a local story, but more importantly, it's RACIAL." The schmoozer up front tried to have the last word. "Anyone knows that if you want to get the blood boiling—if you want to sell newspapers—just mention race."

"Gentlemen," the editor interrupted, "please. We've covered all this. The story's running."

Meg was totally lost. *What about race? What do they mean "another body in Somerville"?* She would have to find out on her own. She had called enough attention to herself. She didn't need to ask any more stupid questions. The editor brought up a few more issues for discussion and the meeting was adjourned. Everyone was making their way back to their desks, and Meg stuck close to Lou, who was talking to Hank, the natural disaster man. They were heading toward the coffeepot. Taking a sip from her Styrofoam cup, Meg decided to casually steer the conversation back to the shooting.

"Hey, Lou. What was all that about race and bodies in Somerville?"

"What do you know about it?"

Meg sighed in exasperation. A reporter could never expect a straight answer from another reporter. They were much too territorial.

"Tony Vincent Girardi was shot to death in his store in the North End. He was an Italian-American citizen with a strong connection to the community." She stopped. That was all she seemed to know.

"Early this morning the body of a black man was found in the front seat of a beat-up Ford in Somerville. He'd been shot in the head three times. A typical hit." Lou sipped his coffee, eyeing Hank.

"Word on the street is that this black guy was the shooter. Santori's boys administered their own brand of justice," Hank added.

"Santori? You mean Lefty Santori, the top man in the Mob?" The two men nodded.

"But what does that have to do with the Girardi shooting?"

"It's obvious. They wanted to avenge his death."

"Because he was Italian?"

"Because he was family," Lou said.

Meg was still baffled. "Family?"

Lou and Hank exchanged incredulous glances. Lou decided he would be the one to enlighten her.

"Girardi was Lefty Santori's father-in-law. Mrs. Santori's *papa*."

Finally Meg put it all together. All the Red Sox paraphernalia and all the pictures of that pitcher, what's-his-name Santori, on the wall of Girardi's delicatessen. He was proud of his grandson.

"The son pitches for the Red Sox, right? What's his name?"

"Joey Santori. Meg, for a reporter, you're really out of it. You need to brush up on your Mafia info. You never know when it will come in handy."

"Thanks, Lou. I'll keep that in mind."

"What were you doing in the North End in the middle of the day, anyway? Did you get that cannolli itch?" Hank wanted to know.

This was not the time to even try to explain the "story" she had been working on. Instead, she answered Hank's question with one of her own.

"Who's covering the story?"

"Bailey—we're sending an Irishman to tackle the Italians," Lou quipped.

"Is he going to actually interview Santori and his gang?"

"I'm not sure. I know he's going to try to get to the grieving Maria Santori. I think he's going to work the familial angle and downplay the organized crime. That would be his only chance of getting an interview."

"Maria Santori? That's the daughter's name?" Meg couldn't believe what she was hearing.

"Yeah. Why?"

Tim had told her that the "parents" of his putative son were named Maria and Tony. It might just be a coincidence that Girardi had a daughter by the name of Maria. But, they still hadn't come up with an explanation concerning the Girardi name appearing on the hospital records, along with a phony address. Perhaps the address wasn't the only thing falsified on those records. *Maybe someone is being protected.* If this has anything to do with the Mafia, then it would make sense that someone needed to be protected. Tony Vincent Girardi might have been the alias for someone else connected to the Santori family. Meg heard Hank say her name, breaking her train of thought.

"What?"

"I asked you what's wrong. You look like you just saw your dead uncle."

"I don't have a dead uncle."

"Forget it. I've gotta get back to work."

"Me, too." Lou gulped down the last of his coffee and tossed the cup in the trash can.

"Oh, Lou," Meg called to his retreating back. He turned around.

"Lefty Santori. Is that his real name?"

"Do you mean is Lefty his real name?"

"Yeah."

"No."

Meg waited for him to continue, but he just stood staring at her.

"Well, what is his real name?"

"Ha! So you don't know that, either."

"Okay, you win. You are the most informed reporter, on your way to winning the Pulitzer. Now, please, enlighten me."

"Tony Santori. His real name is Tony."

The family in New York proved to be another dead end. Tim drove back to Boston feeling hopeless. He was beginning to realize that even though he might cover all the names on his list, he might not find his son. This could just be the first of many lists and many disappointments. He just had to persevere, with enough faith to keep him searching and enough skepticism to keep him grounded.

He called Meg from a rest stop and arranged to meet her at the Fool's Tavern in Cambridge. She sounded excited when he talked to her, but she hurried him off the phone and told him she would meet him later. He tried not to doubt her, but there were times when he questioned his judgment in trusting a reporter. She had never given him reason to think that she might betray him, but recent events were not conducive to trusting relationships. Although they had not known each other very long, he had never felt closer to a woman, not even with Jennifer. While he drove Tim thought back to the first time he and Meg had met.

They were at Taylor's party. He remembered how beautiful she looked and how soft and giving her body was when they danced. He fantasized about taking her in his arms again, just to hold her. There had been no women in his life since Jennifer. There had hardly been any women in his life before Jennifer. Looking back, Tim wondered at the limits he had imposed on his life. He devoted himself wholly to his profession. He built his private practice into one of the most well respected in the nation. In his career, Tim had been a powerhouse, but in his private life he had failed miserably. Now his career was in a shambles, he had lost his family and he had few friends. He could always count on J.C., but J.C. had his own life. The one bright spot in his life was Meg. She had offered her help and her friendship, and had asked nothing in return. Tim had a second chance at life and he had to make the most of it. His foot pressed down harder on the accelerator.

The clock in Harvard Square read eight-fifteen when Tim drove into town. They had arranged to meet between eight and nine, so his timing was perfect. On a Thursday evening the bars were doing a brisk business. The crowd at the Fool's Tavern was very young to Tim's eye, but he didn't mind. It was refreshing to be surrounded by young people. Television sets at each end of the bar were showing the sold-out opening game of the Red Sox and Yankees four-game series. Meg spotted Tim first and rushed over to greet him. She wore a T-shirt tucked into a pair of form-fitting jeans. She looked young and sexy, blending right in with the crowd.

"Follow me," Meg said, leading him to a secluded corner where she had managed to secure a table. When they were settled in their seats and had ordered a pitcher of beer, Tim told her he had hit another brick wall in New York.

"I'm just about ready to give up. We seem to be on a wild goose chase."

"But you've only just started looking. You can't expect to have all the answers in a matter of days," Meg protested. She still hadn't decided whether or not to tell Tim about her suspicions about Girardi and the Santoris. She could see that Tim was desperate to find his son, but she was afraid to suggest a connection to the Santoris, for fear Tim would barge in without stopping to think. From what she knew of Lefty Santori, you didn't want to piss him off. If Meg were to suggest that Joey Santori might be the son he was seeking, there was no telling how Tim might handle the information. She could picture him walking up and proclaiming himself the real father of Lefty Santori's only son. He would definitely be out of his league with that bunch of thugs. She would have to wait until she had all the facts before telling Tim anything.

"You're right. I've never been a patient man. I have to admit, this whole thing has made me a little crazy." Tim noticed the far-away look on Meg's face and asked, "What's wrong? You look worried."

Meg was still lost in her imaginings of hit men pounding on Tim's door in the middle of the night. She snapped out of her reverie and forced a smile.

"Deadlines, you know. I'm sorry. Back to you. No luck in New York, but there are more names to check out, right?"

Tim eyed her curiously. She sounded nervous, and strange.

Was she hiding something?

"Is there something you want to tell me?" he asked.

"Like what?"

"I don't know. Did you find something out today?"

"No, I . . ." Meg searched her mind for a plausible answer. "I'm still shaken up over that Girardi thing."

"Did they find out who did it?"

Meg hesitated and then said, "The police are still investigating." That wasn't a lie. The police were always investigating something.

A group of young people at a nearby table erupted in cheers as Tim Long, the Red Sox catcher, drove in two runs with a double in the last of the eighth. These were the first runs of the game. Both Tim and Meg turned their heads to look. Without being aware of it, Tim scrutinized the faces around him. He was subconsciously searching for his son in the face of every young man he encountered. It was unbearable to think that he could be in the same town with his own son and neither of them would know it.

"I think we should change the subject, mmm?" Meg lifted her eyebrows playfully.

"That's just what I was thinking. But then I wondered *how* to change the subject. It's like a black cloud following me everywhere I go. It's all I think about."

Meg nodded toward the television set hanging above the bar. "How 'bout them Red Sox?"

Tim smiled. Together they watched the top of the ninth as three Yankee batters in a row struck out. At least things were going right for Tim's favorite team.

Meg kept her eyes on the television set. She was hoping to see a close-up of Joey Santori. After learning about Tony and Maria Santori, she had rushed to Mike's office. She wanted to see every photograph ever taken of Joey Santori by the *Globe*. She wanted to observe every angle of the pitcher's face. She was hoping to see a resemblance to Tim. Mike obligingly took her to the sports photo archives, accompanied by the usual come-ons and innuendoes. For once, Meg barely noticed him. She examined at least a hundred different pictures of Joey Santori. Meg was convinced there was a strong resemblance to Tim; the strong jaw line, the dimples on both cheeks, the almond shape of the eyes, even the boyish grin which stretched from ear to ear. But what proof did she have?

Meg kept her eyes on the screen while Tim nursed his beer. He was lost in the memories of his residency and his encounters with Taylor. Tim kept replaying scenes in his mind, putting them together with what he now knew. Taylor had manipulated him from the beginning. The crowd drowned out the sound from the television, but Meg continued to watch intently. The game had ended and the announcer was on screen, interviewing Tim Long. She was hoping to catch an interview with Joey Santori, who was standing directly behind Tim Long. The announcer finally moved over to talk to Joey Santori. Meg strained to hear what they were saying.

"I'm going to see if they have any munchies at the bar. I'll be right back," Meg jumped up from her chair.

"I'll go," Tim started to get up.

"No, it's okay. I need to stretch my legs."

Before he could protest further, Meg was gone. Tim watched her hurry toward the end of the bar. He still thought she seemed on edge about something. She slid onto one of the barstools and focused on the television. He was surprised to see her watching the Red Sox post-game interviews. He hadn't realized she was so interested in baseball. Apparently she had forgotten about her quest for munchies. Tim looked at the screen. Joey Santori. Hell of a pitcher. Tim hadn't followed baseball much lately, but he had watched Joey Santori a few times. The man was a machine. Tim thought he had the potential of being the best left-handed pitcher to come along since Koufax. Santori perfected every type of throw imaginable, and he always kept his batters guessing. Then there was his fastball, clocked at ninety-six miles per hour. The most amazing thing about Joey Santori was his age, only twenty years old. With his broad shoulders and long, solid legs, he was truly on his way to being a superstar. Tim expected that the Red Sox player would be pitching his way into the record books for many years to come.

Meg remained at the bar watching the interview with Santori. When she felt a man's hands on her shoulders, she let out a startled cry and pushed herself away from the bar. Turning around she saw Tim and gasped again.

"Tim, you scared me. "

"Sorry, I just thought I'd come over and check out my competition."

"What?"

Tim gestured toward the television. Joey Santori was talking about his pitching strategy. He was holding a Dixie cup in his right hand, periodically spitting into it. He appeared subdued, and he cut the reporter off with a dark stare when he asked a question about his grandfather.

"You like him, huh?"

"He's good, isn't he?"

"The best." Tim watched Santori spit again into the Dixie cup. "That's unfortunate."

"What is?"

"He's chewing tobacco. It's a dirty habit, and bad for your health. He should know better."

Meg had already noticed Santori chewing tobacco. She was more interested in the Dixie cup. All day she had been wondering how she might get proof of his identity without having to confront the Santori family. They most certainly would not welcome a reporter from the Globe snooping into their personal lives. The Dixie cup might be the answer.

"You're right. Spitting into a cup isn't very glamorous." Meg smiled broadly for the first time that evening as she said, jokingly, "How about 'depositing your buccal mucosa?' Does that sound a bit more glamorous?"

Tim laughed. "Buccal mucosa. You remembered."

Yes, she remembered.

They spent the rest of the evening having a pleasant dinner and talking about inconsequential things. Tim walked Meg home, half hoping she would invite him in, but afraid, too, of where that might lead. They shared a lingering kiss on her front porch and then she gave him a little push back toward the street. With a toss of her gorgeous hair she disappeared inside her house. Tim slowly walked back to the bar to retrieve his car and drove back to Chestnut Hill, too tired to think.

With regret, Meg watched from the window as Tim walked down the sidewalk. Their kiss had sparked a desire in her, a desire she hoped Tim had felt, too. Tonight, however, she had more important things on her mind. Checking her watch, she realized that it was almost midnight. It wouldn't matter that she woke him up. Mike would do anything for her, and she wasn't ashamed to take advantage of that fact. The phone rang four times before a groggy voice answered.

"Hi, Mike. It's me. Sorry to wake you."

"Who is this?"

"You don't know? Mike, I'm hurt. It's Meg."

"Meg? There's only one reason you'd call me at this hour. You've finally come to your senses. You need me . . . can't live another moment without me."

"Actually, I need a press pass to the Red Sox game tomorrow. And a locker pass."

"You're calling me in the middle of the night because you want a pass to the Red Sox game? Why? Do you want to write for Sports now?"

"I just need it. Can you do it for me?"

"A locker pass. They don't allow women in the locker room."

"They'll allow you in there."

"Oh, so you're asking me out. This is a date."

"Please, Mike."

A short pause. "Okay. Meet me at the office at five. The game starts at seven. What's this all about?"

"I'll tell you later. Thanks."

Joey had struggled through the game, but nobody knew it. He allowed no runs, three hits and two walks. After the game everyone was talking about Joey Santori's phenomenal performance in the face of his grief. Some skeptics shied away from showering too much praise on a mere twenty-year-old, but the press believed in Joey Santori and theirs was a powerful voice. They scrambled to their typewriters, word processors and microphones, touting the story of "one of the greatest pitchers in baseball today." Meanwhile, Joey just wanted to be through with the game and away from the ballpark. All he could think of was his Papa Girardi and his brutal death.

When the locker room finally cleared of reporters, Joey took a shower and got dressed in dark slacks and a white shirt. He did not live the life of a rising superstar, shying away from the latenight, post-game parties or even acknowledging the women who literally threw themselves at him after every game. Instead, Joey spent his off time at home, with his family. He chose watching TV with his sisters over attending a ritzy party given by some advertising executive. Joey loved his family as much as he loved baseball and he refused to allow his major league status to interfere with those strong bonds.

His father's car arrived to take him to his aunt's house, where the family was gathered. Paulie held the door for him and they hugged before Joey stepped into the black limousine. Inside, Joey sat with Paulie and four bodyguards.

"Good game," Paulie said as they pulled out of the Fenway parking lot.

"Were you in the box?"

"No, we had it on T.V. at home."

Joey nodded. He understood why no one in the family came to the game. It was a time for mourning in the Santori family. He had been reluctant to pitch tonight, but he had a responsibility to his team. His family respected that.

"Any news?" Joey had been frantic to discover who had done this terrible thing to the grandfather.

Paulie looked out the tinted window. He never discussed family business with Joey or his sisters.

"It's been taken care of," Paulie said, still looking out the window.

Joey knew what he meant. He didn't judge his father's "business" decisions, nor did he try to change them. Lefty Santori never brought his work home to the dinner table. None of his children were involved in the family business—and this was with their father's blessing. Joey and his sisters were privileged—and protected. They knew little of Lefty's business and were not touched by it. That's the way Lefty wanted it. Lefty's father came from Sicily with nothing and worked his way up in the "family." His American-born mother took care of the home and the children and didn't get involved with the family business. Lefty was loyal to his friends and family, a trait Joey admired. That he was ruthless with his enemies—well, that, Joey figured, came with the territory.

The limousine pulled up to a brick building and the four

bodyguards stepped out first. Joey and Paulie followed them into the house and up the flight of stairs to the second floor. They rang the buzzer and an old, wizened woman opened the door.

"Ah, Joey *mio, che piacere vederti.*" The old woman held out her arms and Joey hugged her gently. She pulled him into the room where about thirty people were gathered. The space was crowded with relatives from both his mother's and father's side. He had greeted and hugged just about everyone by the time he made it across the room to the study, where his father was talking to his Uncle Gianni. Lefty Santori stood up as Joey entered the room. He held out his arms to his son.

"Joey! You pitched a great game," he bellowed as he kissed him warmly on both cheeks. More kisses and hugs from Uncle Gianni.

"Come, sit. Tell us some stories of the game. We need to laugh."

Joey could see that his father was trying hard to hide his anger and sadness. He was deeply committed to his family and the death of his father-in-law had shaken him badly.

"Where's Ma?" Joey asked.

"She's in the kitchen with Aunt Celeste and your sisters. They're preparing the food for this crowd."

"Ma shouldn't be cooking."

"She wanted to cook. It helps her."

Maria Santori always showed strength and courage...a woman had to be strong to be married to a Santori.

"Come on, son, tell us about the game."

"Not much to tell, Dad. You saw—I walked two guys and they got one hit. But my mind wasn't on the game. I kept thinking about everyone here...and about Papa."

"You didn't let your team down tonight, and that's important." Lefty was proud of his son. He himself had been hopeless at sports and he hated to exercise. Maria had insisted that he buy a stationary bike and he pedaled a few miles every night, but he would never enjoy it. Joey had pure talent and Lefty thanked God for the gift he had given his son.

Joey sat with his dad and his uncle for a few more minutes and then made his way to the kitchen. He found his four sisters leaning against counters, talking to their mother, who was busy stirring some spices into a rich tomato sauce. She saw Joey and rushed over to give him a hug.

"Oh, Joey. You must be starving after the game. Come, we'll feed you first."

"It's okay, Ma, I'll wait. What are you doing in the kitchen, anyway? You should be resting."

"She insisted," Cecilia, his eldest sister, exclaimed. "You try to get her to sit down."

"She kept popping her head in until we finally gave up and gave her an apron," Anna, his youngest sister, added. Anna and Joey were the closest in age and in everything else. They spoke to each other at least once a week, even when Joey was on the road. She had just gone through an ugly break-up with her boyfriend, and her baby brother was the only one who could comfort her.

"Joey," his mother said with a frown. "I saw you on the television. You were chewing tobacco again."

"Aw, Ma. It's okay. Everybody does it. Stop worrying all the time."

Joey stayed in the kitchen with the women until it was time to eat. His spirits lifted as everyone gathered around the table and served themselves pasta and roast pork. As he listened to the boisterous talking and laughter, Joey counted himself one of the luckiest people on earth. He couldn't imagine anyone having a better family than his. And tomorrow they would all be together again, to bury Papa Girardi.

Twenty-two

Meg met Mike in the office and together they took the T to Fenway. Mike had secured two places in the press box and one pass to the locker room. Since Joey Santori had pitched the night before, he wouldn't be playing, but he would be suited up and in the dugout.

Meg had read in the paper that they held the funeral for Tony Vincent Girardi that morning. All the North End shut down their businesses to honor the man who had given so much to their community. The services were held in the Sacred Heart Church in the North End, and over four hundred people were there to pay their respects. Those who could not squeeze into the church stood outside on the sidewalk and in the street, listening to the service from the speakers hooked up especially for this event. There were those in the crowd who did not know Girardi. They attended the service out of respect for the family, and probably out of fear. Tony Santori might wonder at a man who chose not to attend the funeral of his wife's father. And he would know who didn't show. Just a quick scan of the crowd and Tony Santori would remember the faces he hadn't seen.

Meg shivered at the thought of Lefty Santori and his mob. She knew little about them, and didn't know how they operated, but she knew they were capable of executing a man and leaving his body in a car, to be easily found, and getting away with it. She wondered that such a ruthless man could have raised a son of such honest talents who seemed so genuinely kind.

"You haven't said a word since we left. I thought this was going to be a stimulating date, if you know what I mean." Mike winked and squeezed Meg's arm.

Meg jerked her arm away and resigned herself to the fact that she was at a baseball game with Mike Argosa.

"This is strictly business, Mike, nothing more. I wouldn't voluntarily go to a baseball game. In fact, this is the first Red Sox game I've ever been to," she retorted.

"What? How many years have you lived in Boston?"

"All my life. What's your point?"

"And this is your first Red Sox game! I don't believe it! We've got to educate you, girl."

"How many times have you been to the symphony, wise guy?"

Mike stared at her blankly.

"Just as I thought."

"It's baseball. Our national pastime. How can you not like it?"

"Mike, if you love the game so much, why don't you shut up and watch it?"

"God, I love it when you're feisty!"

Meg controlled her frustration by reminding herself that she was here for Tim. He had called earlier to say that he was driving to Springfield to follow up on another lead. Meg felt guilty for letting him drive all around the Northeast and not letting him know about her suspicions concerning Joey Santori. He seemed even more depressed when he called today, which added to her guilt. But she just couldn't risk telling him what she knew until she had solid proof. Hopefully, being here tonight would bring her closer to the proof she needed. Meg looked at Mike, sitting next to her. He wore a dirty Red Sox cap and a T-shirt that was stretched to the max by his soft gut. She sighed deeply. *If I'm guilty of misleading Tim, then I'm more than paying for it now with this creep.*

Mike poked her in her side with his elbow.

"See, now it gets interesting," he started to explain. "If he walks, then it's bases loaded. The pitcher has to know that this batter has a weakness for swinging straight down the middle. So, while he shouldn't be swinging at anything, unless it's perfect, he'll be swinging at the middle. The pitcher has to throw a change-up to screw him up and make him swing. They don't want this guy to walk with Freddy Twine on deck. He'll rip one out of the park, and then it's four to one. The Sox never come back when they're down by more than two."

Meg rolled her eyes. It was only the third inning. *How long do these games last?*

The Red Sox managed to hold off the Yankee offense and win

212

the game by a narrow 3-2. As soon as the umpire called the last out Meg jumped out of her seat, dragging Mike with her.

"What the hell are you doing?" he shouted.

"I need to talk to Joey Santori," she called over her shoulder as she pushed her way through the crowd of reporters, all heading in the same direction. They made it to the press area just outside of the locker room. The players hadn't come off the field yet, though a few were starting down the tunnel toward the locker room. Meg craned her neck, trying to see over the head of the photographer standing in front of her. She couldn't see Joey Santori, yet, but she heard reporters calling out to him, "Question, Joey," and "Answer some questions, Joey?" "Please, Joey." "How do you feel, Joey?" They kept prodding at him until finally Joey stopped in front of one of them, holding up a hand for silence.

"I'll take a few questions, but you guys should be talking to Sawyer. He pitched a great game."

Meg was pushed up against the wall as Mike was trying to get close enough to ask a few questions. Through an opening in the crowd in front of her Meg was able to get a glimpse of the Dixie cup in Joey's hand. Her heart fluttered in anticipation. Now all she had to do was figure out how to get that cup away from him.

Joey fielded some questions about his pitching, the future of the franchise, and he answered "no comment" to questions regarding his contract. The rest of the Red Sox players filed past and walked on into the locker room. Few members of the press took time away from Joey to interview any other players. Joey Santori, with the scandal surrounding his family, was the news of the day.

"Joey, we're all sorry about the death of your grandfather. How are you handling it? Will the stress affect your pitching?"

"If you caught the game last night, you'd know that there's nothing wrong with my pitching. Nothing's changed."

"How is your family doing, Joey?" another voice called out.

"We're getting through it okay." Joey started edging his way toward the locker room door. As far as he was concerned, the interview was over.

"What do you think about Leroy Washington, the man found dead in Somerville, and the allegations that he was the one who shot your grandfather?" a sarcastic voice shouted out.

Joey just wanted the nosey bastards to shut up.

"No comment."

"Do you think your father is involved in the death of Leroy Washington?" the same voice persisted.

Now the prick had gone too far. Joey never, ever, discussed family business with the press, or anyone else. Most of them were smart enough to limit their interviews to the subject of baseball. He had no idea what was behind these questions. He had never heard of Leroy Washington.

"Who wants to know?" Joey asked, scanning the faces in front of him.

A hand shot up, and a short, balding man stepped forward. From the self-satisfied smirk on his face he was enjoying Joey's obvious discomfort.

Joey leaned down so that he was in the man's face, "No comment. And no more questions."

"Shit," Meg muttered to herself. "Now I'm never going to get close enough to get that cup."

Just as Joey had reached for the knob of the locker room door, the relentless reporter tried again.

"Are you sure you're wearing red socks, Joey? Or are they black socks?" he quipped, referring to the Black Sox scandal of 1919 when gamblers corrupted the Chicago White Sox and sullied the reputation of baseball. This reporter was pulling out all the stops.

Joey swung around to face the man who couldn't seem to mind his own business. He could handle most insults, but not when it came to his family. Joey stared the man down, fury clouding his judgment, and asked through clenched teeth, "Just what are you getting at, *asshole?*"

All eyes went from Joey to the reporter and back again. The photographers waited, cameras poised, for the perfect shot.

"I mean," he began, looking around him for support. Everyone held his breath. "Should we be worrying about you guineas polluting the Boston Red Sox?"

There was a collective gasp and then silence.

Joey lunged forward and tackled the reporter to the ground. They landed on the cement floor with a dull thud. A few of the men closest to them grabbed at Joey's arms, trying to pull him off the struggling man beneath him, but Joey would not be stopped. Meg stood back, away from the scuffle. Cameras clicked and flashes popped. This was front page news.

Joey straddled the man on the ground, holding his face to the cement with one hand while pinning his arm behind his back with the other. The man was still. Increasing the pressure on the man's head, Joey spoke with deadly calm.

"Don't you ever insult my family again."

The locker room door opened and one of Joey's teammates poked his head out.

"Jesus Christ, what the hell is this?"

More players pushed out from behind the door and rushed over to Joey.

"Come on, Joey, get off this guy," one of them implored. The others continued to coax him until he finally released the man and got up from the ground, dazed.

"Okay, everybody. The show's over. Go on home," one of the players yelled over his shoulder as they led Joey away.

No one bothered to help the man on the ground to stand up. Everybody who witnessed the scene deplored what he had done, even though he had handed them the scoop of the month. They had nothing to say to him as they hurried off to file their stories and develop their photographs, all of them worrying about deadlines. After only a few minutes Mike and Meg were left standing alone in the hallway.

Meg considered asking the balding reporter for his shirt. As Joey had lunged for the man his Dixie cup of spit had splashed onto the man's sleeve. All the buccal mucosa Meg needed was in that cotton fabric, but the guy was already stumbling down the hallway before she could come up with a plausible reason for wanting his shirt. *Now what do I do?*

Meanwhile, Mike was anxious to file his story. He apologized for leaving Meg, and rushed off. Meg leaned back against the wall. The Dixie cup was nowhere to be seen, probably lost in the scuffle. She had missed her chance to get a specimen for Luther. *You can bet that Joey Santori won't be allowed anywhere near the press for at least the next few games, and then the Red Sox will be on a two week road trip.*

Meg slid down the wall and sat on the ground. *I went to all this trouble for nothing. Maybe I should just tell Tim what I suspect. Maybe he can figure out a way to get a sample from Joey Santori.*

Meg looked at the spot where Santori and the reporter had wrestled. It was still clean. *Too bad there wasn't any blood shed.* She was immediately ashamed of herself for that thought. She continued to stare at the ground and something caught her eye. Something red was wedged behind a trashcan next to the wall on the other side of the hall. Meg stood up and walked over to the trashcan. She leaned behind it and plucked out a baseball hat. A Red Sox baseball hat. *Could it be?* She turned it over in her hand and saw the name "Santori" stitched underneath the rim. It must have fallen off during the scuffle and somehow got kicked behind the trashcan. Meg stared hard at the hat for a few more seconds, absently fingering the brim. It was still damp from Joey's sweat. She stuffed the hat in her purse. Tomorrow she would take it to Dr. Kennedy.

Twenty-three

The plane had to circle several times because of heavy air traffic before the tower cleared it for landing. They should have landed at 10:30 A.M. and it was already after eleven. Tim peered gloomily out the window at the Atlantic Ocean and Boston rising up on its coast. He pressed his head back against his seat. He was tired of encountering obstacles. He just wanted to get back into the real world and get back to work. The family in Pennsylvania turned out to be another "X" on his now useless list, a list that he had relegated to a trashcan somewhere in Pittsburgh. Tim thought about starting over at square one and the mere thought of it overwhelmed him. It had taken over two weeks to get through the eight names and he began to wonder if he'd be searching for his son for the rest of his life.

His suspension would be lifted on Monday, which meant that in less than forty-eight hours he would regain some semblance of the normal life he once knew. While a hot shower and a long nap were appealing, Tim decided to first stop by the hospital and prepare his schedule for next week. He had a lot of catching up to do and he didn't want to give McConnell any reason to prevent him from coming back.

Quickly claiming his bag, Tim grabbed a cab from the airport and had the driver drop him off at the Emergency Room entrance. He hadn't shown his face at the hospital for more than two weeks, so when he walked through the Emergency Room, he was greeted with welcoming smiles from nurses and other hospital personnel.

"We missed you, Dr. Graves," a nurse blurted.

Dr. Slater looked up when he heard Tim's name. He'd known Tim for years and was glad to see his old friend back in the hospital. Tim often got called to the Emergency Room for head trauma cases, and he never hesitated to come in on the cases that other neurosurgeons considered hopeless. He had saved many patients who would have otherwise died. Dr. Slater handed a chart to the

217

nurse, thanked her, and approached Tim with his hand out.

"I hear you're back on Monday. It's been hell here without you. We can't find doctors who will come in at all hours like you do, Tim." The two men shook hands and Slater slapped Tim on the back.

"Thanks, Jim. I can't wait. Right now, though, I need to get to my office and wade through my paperwork. If I start now, I might be through by Monday," he joked.

"We could have used you earlier today. We had a head trauma and your partner didn't want to come in. The resident had to admit the patient."

"Who's on today?"

"Dr. Maitlan."

"Jess is a good man, he just doesn't like head trauma. Don't worry about it, if you need him, he'll come in."

"That's just it. We did need him and we had a hard time finding him. Sounded like he was on his car phone." Dr. Slater shook his head. He was tired of dealing with difficult doctors.

"Sorry I can't help. Rules are rules," he said sarcastically. Tim was still bitter about his suspension, and he could let his guard down a little with Slater. "When you're an ER doctor rules often get in the way of good doctors and good medicine."

"I hear you. We'll call Maitlan again if we need him," Dr. Slater said, turning his attention back to the Emergency Room as a nurse called his name.

Tim headed for the elevator, then decided to take the stairs to his office. He could use some exercise.

Meg had been looking forward to a quiet Saturday. She'd been running herself ragged at work. After finishing her morning errands, she now had the afternoon free to watch the Red Sox game on television. Meg plopped down on the couch, flicked on the TV and dug her spoon into a bowl of ice cream. The Sox were playing the Angels at Fenway and the game was already underway. Ever since she had inadvertently been an eyewitness at Joey Santori's encounter with a member of the press two weeks ago, Meg had become addicted to baseball. Normally, a quiet Saturday afternoon at home would have consisted of an old Cary Grant movie, but now she wanted to watch baseball. She wanted to watch Joey Santori, who, according to the paper, would be pitching today. It was a sell-out crowd, so the game was being televised. She thought about taking the phone off the hook, but didn't want to miss Tim, in case he called. He should be back from Pittsburgh sometime today.

Just as Meg was taking her first bite of ice cream, she saw a hard hit line drive sail right into Joey Santori's head. He collapsed in a heap and lay on the pitcher's mound, unmoving. The announcer exclaimed in horror that Joey Santori had been hit in the head by a line drive and appeared to be unconscious.

Thirty thousand people gasped and then were silent.

Trainers and coaches ran to the mound, surrounding Joey. A few of the Sox players rushed to the mound, as well, keeping their distance while the team doctor examined him. Meg stared at the television screen, her ice cream forgotten. One of the coaches motioned for a stretcher. Joey was carefully lifted onto it and carried off the field to the waiting ambulance. As the ambulance pulled away from the ballpark, sirens blaring, the crowd came to life. The drone of their conversations voiced the concern of everyone. *What will happen to Joey Santori? Was he even alive?* The announcers had no more information than the fans, all they could do was speculate. Meg knew she couldn't sit idly by and wait for an answer. Jumping up from the couch she ran to her bedroom. Slipping her feet into sandals as she ran for the door, she paused by the phone. She wanted to get to the hospital, but first she had to call Luther Kennedy.

Tim's office looked the same as when he had left it weeks ago, except for the mountainous stack of mail in his "in box." There were letters from doctors looking for residencies, tons of brochures from drug companies, and dozens of other correspondence, all requiring his attention. Tim clicked on his dictaphone. *Might as well get going.* He was pleased to find that Judith had slit the envelopes for him and had separated them into "must do now," "should do now," "do whenever" piles. An hour later, when he had made a dent in the mail and had dictated twenty letters, Tim thought about Meg. They had played telephone tag while he was in Pennsylvania. In one short conversation she mentioned an idea that she was pursuing, but she didn't elaborate. As soon as he finished up in the office, he would call and see if they could get together for dinner.

He continued to work through his mail and came across an envelope marked "Personal and Confidential." The return address read "Luther Kennedy, M.D." As he opened the envelope he could feel his heart begin to pound. He read the short note: "Dear Tim, Marcus Leon's hair sample is a match. You are his biological father. I'll call you next week when I get back from Washington."

Tim ran his fingers through his hair as he reread the letter. He couldn't believe it. The likelihood of a person with similar DNA to his was one in three billion. That was close enough for Tim.

Tim stood. The rest of his paperwork could wait. He wanted to get home, call Meg, and share the news with her. He was just about to lock the door when his office phone rang. Preoccupied, he reflexively went back to his desk and picked up the phone.

"This is Dr. Graves."

"Dr. Graves, I'm so glad I caught you. This is Julie Giddings, the charge nurse in the ER. Dr. Slater wants to speak with you right . . . " There was a muffled sound and Slater came on the line.

"Tim, you won't believe what's happening here. An ambulance just brought in Joey Santori." Dr. Slater's voice was hushed but anxious.

Tim thought quickly. "From the Sox?" He was wondering why Slater was calling him.

"Yeah, and his father is down here. You know who he is, don't you?"

Everyone in Boston knew about Lefty Santori and his organized crime connections.

"Yes," Tim replied. "What's the problem?"

"I paged Maitlan, but he hasn't responded. We need somebody right away. He wants to speak to the best neurosurgeon in the hospital. It's getting rough down here. There's a tough guy, Paulie somebody threatening everyone. It's crazy, Tim."

Tim was exasperated with Slater. "I meant what's the problem with the patient. Why is Joey Santori in the ER?"

"Sorry. He got hit in the head with the ball while he was pitching today. He's zonked out down here."

"Have you gotten a CAT scan?"

"No. There's no time for that. He has a blown left pupil and his pulse rate is fifty, BP 200."

Tim didn't need to hear anymore. "He's got Cushing's reflex." Tim knew that meant that Joey Santori was in serious trouble with brain stem compression and needed surgery right away. Slater was right, there was no time to do a CAT scan. "I'll be right down," Tim yelled as he hung up the phone. He immediately picked it up again and dialed the operating room. Janet Flaherty answered on the first ring. Tim was livid when she told him that he couldn't operate. "You don't have privileges, Dr. Graves. Your suspension doesn't end until Monday. Dr. McConnell specifically told me that you couldn't book any cases until Monday."

Tim fought to remain calm. Pissing off Flaherty wasn't going to do anybody any good. Tim had known Janet for years and knew that she was a nurse who went by the book. He also knew her bark was worse than her bite—and she was an avid Red Sox fan.

"Joey Santori is in the ER with a head injury. If he doesn't have a craniotomy within the next half hour, he'll die. Dr. Slater can't locate Dr. Maitlan, so he called me."

There was silence while Janet Flaherty weighed the pros and cons, good medicine versus the political fallout. The answer was simple.

"I'll get the trauma room open right away. There's an anesthesiologist who just finished a case. We'll be ready for you in five minutes."

"Thanks." He hung up the phone and dashed out the door. He took the stairs two at a time and reached the Emergency Room in less than a minute. Breaking through the crowd gathered around the treatment room door, he made his way into the room and saw Joey Santori on the gurney. A resident had just finished placing a subclavian line and intravenous fluid was running. Tim quickly assessed the patient and confirmed Slater's findings, announcing that Joey was going directly to the operating room. Only then did he glance around the small room and recognize Lefty Santori from pictures he had seen in the *Globe*.

He was about the same height as Tim, but slimmer, with gray hair. Probably in his early fifties. He wore a collarless silk shirt with a gold chain around his neck. The shirt was purple and he had on well-tailored dark slacks. Purple socks and Gucci loafers completed the picture. Lefty was talking to one of the nurses and Tim approached him.

"I'm Tim Graves, head of neurosurgery. I'm sorry, but your son belongs in the operating room immediately." Tim held out his hand. Lefty shook it and said, "Doc, it's in your hands. That nurse's closest friend is the cousin of one of my associates. She says you're the best, even though you're having some political problems in the hospital. I don't give a crap about that—unless they get in the way of you operating on my son. Just give me the word and I'll make your problems go away."

"I don't think that will be necessary, Mr. Santori. Where is Mrs. Santori?" He preferred to talk to both parents before operating. With this type of injury there was no guarantee of a favorable outcome.

"She's out in the car, but don't worry, I'll paint her the right picture. I just don't want her to see her boy like this. I'm counting on you, Doc. Don't disappoint me."

If Tim didn't know better, he could be talking to a New York stockbroker. Mr. Santori appeared calm, intelligent, and in control. He turned to the short man standing near him, then quickly turned back to Tim.

"Excuse me, I need to speak to Paulie for a moment." He leaned over and whispered something in the short man's ear. Paulie responded with a nod and quickly left the Emergency Room.

Tim returned to Joey's gurney and nodded to the ER nurse and the respiratory therapist. "We're ready," they acknowledged with a return nod. Tim began to push Joey to the operating room. Dr. Slater went with them, then ran ahead to call for the elevator for the ride to the fourth floor.

Janet Flaherty was as good as her word. The operating room was ready and it had been only fifteen minutes since Tim had called her. She had the air drill in the room and ready. The scrub technician was gowned and gloved and was busy sorting instruments on the back table. The anesthesiologist helped position Joey on the table while he took over control of the endotracheal tube. Tim was working fast. He positioned Joey so that the left side of his head was facing up and began shaving off his hair. When half his head looked like a cue gall, Tim left the room to scrub. The junior resident arrived and began prepping the head with an antiseptic. The anesthesiologist administered drugs to lower Joey's blood pressure and shrink his brain.

The chief resident was scrubbing at the sink next to Tim.

"I'm glad you're back, Dr. Graves," he said as he kicked the water on. "Is he coning?"

"He's in bad shape and is coning." Tim hated the word, since it meant the brain was so swollen that the brain stem was being compressed. "Coning" was just another noun in medical parlance that was made into a verb to speed up communication. Anatomically and physiologically speaking, it didn't tell the whole story, but this was not the time to dwell on nuances. Besides, he liked Peter, who was the resident working with him during that fateful case which had led to his suspension.

Tim turned off the water with his knee and said, "I think we have time to decompress the brain and come out with something."

Returning to the operating room, gowned and gloved, Tim draped the left side of Joey's head. Noting the obvious bruise on the forehead he was confident that he was going to find an epidural hematoma. Tim turned to the anesthesiologist. "How's it going?"

"Okay, but his vital signs have been all over the map. I gave him some mannitol to shrink things, so you better get a move on before we get a rebound."

Tim nodded and took the knife and made a vertical incision in front of the left ear. He quickly cut through the scalp layers to the bone. Using the air drill, he drilled a hole down to the dura. He was dismayed to see that the dura was not bulging. He gradually teased the dura open and was shocked to find that the brain was slacked away. There was no blood. He had taken Joey Santori to the operating room and done a craniotomy, only to find nothing. And he had done no tests to prove his presumed diagnosis. *I take a high profile case to the operating room, improperly prepared, while I'm still on suspension. I might as well submit my resignation now.*

Meg had been unable to contact Luther Kennedy. *Do I stay*

here or go to the hospital? She wished she had heard from Tim. She dialed his number but got his recording. She left a message for him to call her and hung up. "Hell," she muttered. "I'll call a cab and go to the hospital."

She only had to wait a few minutes on the sidewalk outside her house in Cambridge before a cab came along.

"Take me to University Hospital . . . fast," she told the driver as she laid a twenty-dollar bill on the front seat. She had the driver drop her off at the Emergency Room entrance. She paid the fare and left the twenty dollars on the seat. Meg rushed through the Emergency Room entrance and came face to face with a crowd of reporters, camera crews, nurses and doctors. People were milling around and talking in hushed voices. She recognized one of the reporters from the *Globe* and made her way over to him.

"What's going on, George?" she asked. George Longley had been a sports reporter with the *Globe* for twenty-five years. He was a master at finding the story behind the story with his probing questions. He had gone to law school, but failed the bar exam too many times to count, so he settled for being a top-notch reporter.

"Hey, Meg. I was covering the game and when I saw Joey go down and stay down, I headed over here." He leaned closer to Meg and whispered, "Don't look now, but Lefty Santori is sitting over in the corner."

"Where is Joey Santori?" She risked a glance in the direction of the mob boss. She couldn't believe her eyes; he was the man who got the sandwich at the delicatessen just before Girardi was shot. How close she'd been to the truth that day, without knowing it.

George looked down at his notes and said, "A Dr. Graves was here and talked to Lefty. Then he rushed Joey to the operating room. No word so far."

"Dr. Graves!" Tim was back from Pennsylvania? And performing surgery? She had to get the DNA results from Luther. If Tim had taken Joey Santori to the operating room, he needed to know if he was operating on his son.

Meg ran to the nearest pay phone and slammed the door shut. She fumbled with her address book, trying to locate

224

Luther's number. He had given her both his home and office numbers, but she got his machine at both places. She dialed her own answering machine, but she had no messages.

It was four-thirty. There would still be graduate students working in Luther's lab. Maybe somebody could help her. She ran outside and jogged the whole way to the biochemistry building. She took the stairs two at a time and raced into the laboratory. Two students wearing clear goggles were working together at a rack full of test tubes.

"I'm Meg Logan with the *Globe*. Can you help me?" she blurted.

One of the students took off his goggles and laid the test tube rack on the counter. He smiled at her and said, "We'll try. What seems to be the problem?"

"Dr. Kennedy was given a specimen several weeks ago and was going to call the results to Dr. Graves' office. Do you happen to know anything about it?"

The other student spoke up, "Yeah, I ran that test myself. We sent the results to Dr. Graves' office last week. It appeared the sample matched the control DNA . . . "

Oh, my God. I was right. She hurriedly thanked the student and turned to leave. She had to get back to the hospital as quickly as possible. It took a minute for her mind to register that the student continued to talk.

"What did you say?"

"I was just saying that this is the first time we've extracted DNA from a hair follicle. We're kinda excited about that."

"Hair follicle. I thought Dr. Kennedy was using sweat from the brim of the baseball hat."

"Oh, that one. That one was interesting, too. We recovered enough cells from the sweat band to do a DNA analysis." He walked closer to Meg so he wouldn't have to raise his voice to be heard over the noise of the centrifuge.

"Do you have the results of that test?" Meg remained calm but she wanted to scream at him to hurry.

"You know, I don't have any idea. Dr. Kennedy ran that one himself. He might have finished it before he went out of town." He walked toward Luther's office and rummaged through a stack of papers on his desk. "Nope, nothing here."

Meg's hopes plummeted, and she was about to leave when the student called out, "I remember now. He said he had finished the sample analysis and the chromotography results would be ready this afternoon. He'll read them when he gets back."

"Is there any way someone could read them today? It's extremely important." Meg was at her wit's end. She had to get those results.

The student went back into the lab and searched Dr. Kennedy's work area, finally coming up with the answer. "You're in luck. The sample and control are developed. It looks like a close match. It's as close as the other one." He turned to look at Meg but she was already out the door.

"It must be important," he said to his fellow student. "I wonder who the control is?"

"Dr. Graves, I'm sorry to interrupt, but there's a reporter from the *Globe* who needs to talk to you. She says it's urgent. Her name is Meg something."

Tim tore off his gloves and thanked Flaherty for the message. When he spotted Meg waiting in the corridor he grabbed her by the waist and pulled her into the doctors' lounge. He gave her a quick hug and then collapsed into a chair.

"Well, I've gotten myself into another mess. I took Joey Santori directly to the operating room and didn't find anything. He's going to die. McConnell's going to have my hide, not that it matters."

Meg's lips quivered as she said, "The DNA match was positive. He's your son."

Tim looked at her quizzically and said, "I know. I read Kennedy's report today. He sent it to my office last week. I guess those hair follicles I stole told the story."

"No, I'm not talking about Marcus Leon. I'm talking about Joey Santori."

"What are you talking about?"

"I collected DNA from Joey Santori's sweat band and it matches yours. I'll explain it all later, but right now you need to find a way to save him. He's your son."

Tim looked stunned. But before he could contemplate the implications, something flashed across his face. "Of course!" He

226

ran back to the operating room just as Joey was being transferred to a gurney.

"Hold it. Put him back on the table with his right side up."

As soon as he was positioned Tim began to shave the hair on the right side of his head.

"Give him more mannitol and steroids and cool him down. Get his temperature to twenty-eight degrees. Hyperventilate the hell out of him and give him lidocaine and magnesium. I don't want him to fibrillate."

"What's going on?" Peter finally asked. This was the Dr. Graves he had come to know and respect, but he couldn't figure out what was happening.

"He has an aneurysm and there's no time to do an angiogram."

Meg had decided to wait in the doctors' lounge. She paced back and forth, wondering if she had done the right thing. She could only pray that Luther hadn't made a mistake. *Wow. This is frontier science. Neurosurgery based on cells from a baseball cap. What a great story. And I have the exclusive.* She huddled in a chair in the corner and wept quietly.

While Joey's body temperature was being lowered with ice packs and a cooling blanket, Tim had the nurse sterilize his aneurysm instruments. He would need the microscope for this very delicate operation. He would have to keep his emotions in check. He could not be distracted with thoughts of the patient on the table before him being his only living child. As he raised a bone flap he knew that time was running out. He could only pray that he was not too late.

"Peter, hand me the dura scissors."

"Well, this time the dura is bulging," Peter remarked in a whisper.

"What's the temperature now, Eddie?" Tim looked over the screen at the anesthesiologist, who was, fortunately, one of the best in the department.

"Twenty-eight degrees and the heart is steady."

"Thanks. Is there blood in the room?" Tim hesitated to ask such a basic question, but he knew that his good results were because he was compulsive. The best anesthesiologists weren't threatened when he checked and double checked.

"Yep."

Tim aspirated the blood under the dura and satisfied himself that the epidural artery wasn't torn. He gradually retracted the frontal lobe and found what he was looking for. There was a hematoma in the area of the anterior cerebral artery.

"That's a bitch, boss."

Tim appreciated Peter's implied respect in referring to him as "boss," but his description of the aneurysm wasn't a confidence builder.

"It's a piece of cake, Peter. Let's go for it."

Tim spent the next three hours dissecting the artery in front of the aneurysm, being careful not to get into the hematoma. He breathed a heavy sigh of relief when he felt he had control and the aneurysm hadn't ruptured. He stood back and stretched to prepare himself for the hard part. He was pleased that the hematoma was small and had not damaged the frontal lobe, at least not grossly. There might be cellular damage, but there was nothing he could do about that now.

"Eddie, I'm ready to open this clot."

"No problem, boss," he replied, miming the resident. Eddie was paying attention.

Tim began to aspirate the hematoma with his sucker. There was no sudden gush of blood when he finally identified the aneurysm. There was fresh clot in it. Eddie had kept the blood pressure low. Tim knew that Eddie deserved as much credit as he did, but Eddie didn't suffer from poor self-esteem. He'd thank him later. Tim placed two Cushing clips across the neck of the aneurysm.

"Nice going, boss. I couldn't have done it better myself," Peter quipped, to break the tension in the room.

"Gee, thanks, Peter. That is high praise," Tim laughed. "Let's put the bone back since his brain doesn't look all that swollen. We'll keep him cool for three days and continue to shrink the brain."

"Gotcha," Peter acknowledged, since he would be the one taking care of the patient. He also knew he'd better do it right.

It was midnight when Joey was brought to the recovery room

and placed on a ventilator. Tim was exhausted. He hadn't realized how out of shape he was. Thankfully, it was not a complicated aneurysm and there were no technical problems during the surgery. He left the recovery room and went to the doctors' lounge. He found Meg asleep, curled up in a chair. He gently shook her shoulder.

"Thank you, Meg. If Joey comes out of this, it's because of you," Tim breathed in her ear.

"He did have an aneurysm? It went well?" she said, ignoring his words of gratitude. She knew if Joey Santori survived, it would be due to the skill of the man standing before her.

"The operation was technically perfect, but we have to wait and see how much brain damage there is. Come on, let's go tell Lefty Santori that his son survived the surgery." Meg got to her feet, running her fingers through her hair, as Tim went inside to get a clean white coat from his locker.

In the Emergency Room, they found Lefty Santori asleep on the wooden bench, but his two bodyguards were wide awake. The one closest to Lefty nudged him awake. "The doc's here, boss." Santori was awake in a second.

"What's going on?" He nodded curtly to Meg, who stayed in the background.

"Where's Mrs. Santori?" Tim countered.

"I sent her home with Paulie. Tell me about my son."

"Well, it was more serious than I thought. Joey ruptured a blood vessel in his brain. It's called an aneurysm. It's a weakness in the blood vessel that he's had all his life. He probably inherited it," Tim explained, knowing that this was going to generate a lot of questions. Nevertheless, he felt obligated to tell Santori the truth.

"I don't remember that in my family. Wait a minute. My dad's brother died suddenly of a some kind of brain hemorrhage when he was in his twenties. Could that have been an aneurysm?"

"Absolutely," Tim said, nodding his head with relief.

Santori was more concerned with Joey's condition now.

"The operation was a success, but it will be several days before we know if there is any permanent damage. We'll keep him sedated for three days and then wake him. Then we'll know."

"Doc, I mean this sincerely. If it turns out right you have my undying loyalty."

"Thank you, Mr. Santori." Tim didn't want to think about what would happen if Joey didn't do well. Meg could sense Tim's thoughts and shuddered when she thought about Leroy Washington.

"When can I see him?"

"In the morning. It'll take time to settle him down and he'll be asleep anyway. Why don't you go home and tell Mrs. Santori."

"Okay, I'll do that. And doc, one of my colleagues will be outside Joey's door at all times. For security. You just tell them where Joey is."

After Lefty Santori had departed in the company of one of his thugs, Tim turned to Meg, "We found him, just in time, too. How can I thank you?"

Meg smiled weakly. "I'm glad he's okay. But . . ."

Tim looked at her with concern. "What's wrong?"

"Just don't do anything stupid, okay? I mean, maybe it's best for the truth to not come out in this case."

The hospital was buzzing Monday morning. Tim Graves, without benefit of X-ray studies, made the correct diagnosis of a cerebral aneurysm on celebrity baseball player Joey Santori, and successfully operated on it. Everywhere he went he was greeted with, "Way to go, Tim," "Glad to see you back," or, "Santori's a lucky guy." Many of these were the same people who reveled in his medical staff problems and ultimate suspension, but Tim was ready to forgive and forget, if they were.

Monday afternoon Tim was still basking in the glow of well-wishers when he was interrupted by a phone call from the medical staff secretary. It seems there was a problem with restoring his privileges. Moments later he received a call from McConnell.

"What the fuck gave you the right to break the rules? I got the full story from Flaherty. She says you bullied her into opening up a room and that you refused to wait for the on-call neurosurgeon to respond. I'm taking this before the Executive Committee. You might as well bend over and kiss your ass goodbye."

Before Tim could respond McConnell had hung up. *Well, well, well. The articulate Yalie has got a bug up his ass.* He finished seeing patients in his office and headed directly to the surgical ICU. The nurse had called earlier to let him know both of Joey's parents were there and wanted to see him. The Santoris were sitting in the waiting room with Paulie. Tim decided to steer clear of him.

After profuse thank-you's from Mrs. Santori, Tim filled them in on Joey's progress.

"Tomorrow we'll discontinue the sedation and wake Joey up. We'll know more by tomorrow afternoon. Why don't we meet here at this time tomorrow? In the meantime, you can page me if you have any questions."

Judith was getting ready to leave for the day when Tim returned. She told him that J.C. was waiting for him in his office. He hadn't seen J.C. in a while and he was anxious to talk to him.

"How ya doing?" J.C. greeted him.

"Great. It's good to be back. How are you, and Helen?"

"Fine. Listen, we need to talk. McConnell is on the warpath and has called another emergency meeting of the Executive Committee for Wednesday. I need to know exactly what happened so I can shoot the bastard down."

"Not much to tell. Joey Santori came in with a ruptured aneurysm and Slater couldn't find Maitlan. I happened to be in my office and he called me. I took him to surgery and clipped a right anterior cerebral artery aneurysm. He had obvious signs of brain stem compression and there was no time for any studies. End of story."

"The way I hear it, you opened the wrong side," J.C. said softly. "I also heard you left the operating room and then came running back and did a right craniotomy. What's that all about?"

"I was misled by a blown left pupil and decided that the lesion must be on the right side." Tim had decided to tell no one, not even J.C., the real reason he had suspected an aneurysm. He couldn't afford any leaks where the Santoris were concerned.

J.C. stood up, shaking his head. "This is going to be a hard sell, but if Joey does well, even McConnell won't be able to stem the tide in your favor." J.C. scrolled his hand from right to left and said, "DR. FIRED FOR SAVING SON OF LOCAL MOB BOSS." He laughed. "All those Red Sox fans would boycott us and the Mass General would be in clover." Still laughing, he left Tim's office.

Tuesday afternoon Joey showed signs of intact neurological

function after the sedation wore off and his body temperature returned to normal. The Santori family was there, en masse, and Tim gave them the good news. Then he asked to speak to Lefty in private. Paulie came along.

"I'm having trouble with the political forces around here for sticking my neck out and performing Joey's surgery. The chief of staff is out to get me. He's called an emergency meeting for tomorrow. I'm telling you this in case things don't go my way. If that happens, another doctor will be assigned to Joey's case until he's ready to be discharged. I just want you to know that Joey will be in good hands no matter what happens."

"Maybe I could have a little talk with this chief of staff guy," Lefty suggested.

"Bullshit, boss. Let me handle this. Doc here saved Joey's life and we owe him." Paulie was obviously fiercely loyal to Lefty and his family. The expression in his eyes as he spoke caused Tim to shudder.

"I'll reason with him first, Paulie. Give him a chance to have a change of heart. If not, then we'll see." Lefty shrugged. "What's this guy's name?'

Tim hesitated, but just for a moment. He took a certain amount of pleasure in giving McConnell's name to Lefty. What harm could it do to have a grateful family express concern to the chief of staff if they thought their doctor was going to be replaced? Besides, McConnell deserved to be on the receiving end for a change.

Wednesday morning Tim received word from the medical staff secretary that he had been restored to full privileges. Not only had the emergency meeting been cancelled, but McConnell had resigned his position as chief of staff and had asked for an extended leave of absence from the hospital. Tim refrained from speculating with the other members of the medical staff.

Joey Santori recovered rapidly in the ensuing weeks with virtually no neurological deficits. Luther Kennedy had called Tim and congratulated him on the fine job he had done. He also confirmed with the utmost discretion that the DNA test he had run on Joey's blood, provided by Tim, was conclusive. Tim's daily visits with Joey allowed him to get to know his son—an intelligent, thoughtful and highly principled young man. Tim was torn.

A part of him wanted to tell Joey that he was his biological father. But then he would see Joey's eyes light up whenever Lefty came to visit. They obviously shared a special bond, far beyond any blood ties.

On the afternoon of Joey's discharge, Maria Santori had scheduled an appointment to meet with Tim in his office. Through the long weeks of Joey's recovery, Lefty had done all the talking. That Maria had requested this visit was very unusual. Tim sat at his desk, waiting nervously for Maria to arrive. When Judith buzzed him to say Maria was there, Tim nearly jumped out of his skin.

"Show her in."

"Okay. While you're with Mrs. Santori I'll go down to X-ray and get those films you asked for. I should be back in ten minutes or so."

Judith knocked softly on the door and opened it to allow Maria Santori to enter. She was short, but well groomed and attractive. Joey had inherited her Italian features, so his resemblance to Tim was less striking than that of Sean Pitt.

"Please sit down, Maria. Have you seen Joey today?"

"He looks wonderful, thanks to you." Maria came around to the side of the desk where Tim was standing and hugged him. "I've wanted to do that for a long time, but you know Tony."

Tim blushed and waved Maria to a chair before sitting down himself. "You know, I'm very pleased with Joey's progress. He'll have full use of his left arm and be able to pitch again, I'm almost certain."

Maria smiled, but she hadn't come here to talk about baseball. "Twenty-one years ago Dr. Taylor made me pregnant with sperm from a fine young doctor, one who worked here at this hospital. Dr. Taylor told me the donor was handsome, a great athlete, and left-handed. He said my son would be a great baseball player. When I read about you in the *Globe* recently, I suspected you were the one. Then when I saw you write your notes on Joey's chart, I could see that you are left-handed."

Tim was flabbergasted. Maria had taken the punch right out of his worries. He recovered some of his composure and asked her, "What do you think I—sorry—we should do?"

Maria chose her words carefully. "Obviously, Tony doesn't

know anything about this. For everyone's sake, it must stay like this. Joey worships his father and likewise for Tony. But more than that . . . if Tony ever found out, all hell would break loose."

Tim thought for a moment before replying.

"Tony will never hear of this from me. You have my word." This was a bitter pill for Tim to swallow, but it was the only way. Hopefully, Joey would return to the Red Sox and Tim could satisfy himself by being the pitcher's number one fan—and doctor.

Maria stood up and walked around to stand next to Tim. She leaned down and kissed him on the cheek. Smiling shyly at him, she said, "I knew you would understand and want to do the right thing. Someday I may tell Joey, but Tony must never know. In many ways, my Tony is not a nice man."

Judith got off the elevator with an armful of X-ray films. As she awkwardly swung around the corner she bumped into a man who was just leaving her office.

"Sorry. May I help you?"

"Uh, no, thanks. Sorry. Wrong office," Paulie muttered as he hurried down the hall.

Epilogue

July 23, 1986—*Boston Globe*

GLOBE LOSES ONE OF ITS OWN:

Reporter Meg Logan and her companion, Dr. Timothy Graves, a neurosurgeon at University Hospital, plunged to their deaths when their car failed to make the sharp turn on Highway One early this morning. Witnesses state that the car Dr. Graves was driving appeared to lose its brakes. Ms. Logan had recently distinguished herself when the *Globe* published her in-depth story on the life and career of Dr. Graves. Dr. J.C. Parker, Dr. Graves' college roommate and closest friend, could not be reached for comment. Dr. Parker was not at home and had not reported for rounds at the hospital yesterday, as was his usual . . .

July 24, 1986—*Boston Globe*

VERMONT:

A fiery inferno claimed the lives of Dr. Malcolm Taylor, world-renowned fertility specialist, and his long-time secretary, Meredith Gunderson. The fire allegedly broke out around midnight in the home of Dr. Taylor. Dr. Taylor had recently relocated to this rural area to continue his research. Both his home and his clinic were burned to the ground within an hour. Preliminary investigation of the scene points to faulty wiring, but arson has not been ruled out. Colleagues of Dr. Taylor state that a lifetime of work has been lost, as Dr. Taylor had taken all of his files and computer disks with him.

September 29, 1986—*Boston Globe*

SANTORI STRIKES AGAIN:
Joey Santori pitched the Red Sox to victory again last night. Joey pitched a shut-out following a remarkable recovery from brain surgery for an aneurysm. His illness was on the heels of the murder of his grandfather, father-in-law of crime boss Tony "Lefty" Santori. Following the murder of her father and near-loss of her son, Maria Santori has reportedly been confined to a sanitarium after suffering a nervous breakdown. According to a family spokesperson she remains in seclusion. . . .